Twice a Target

by

Susan Vaughan

Task Force Eagle, Book Four

Twice a Target

Cover Art by *Lisa Dawn MacDonald*

The Wild Rose Press, Inc.
PO Box 708
Adams Basin, NY 14410-0708
Visit us at www.thewildrosepress.com

Publishing History
First Edition, 2025
Trade Paperback ISBN 978-1-5092-5860-4
Digital ISBN 978-1-5092-5861-1
Previously Published 2013 by Gullwood Press

Task Force Eagle, Book Four
Published in the United States of America

Dedication

For my friends and critique partners Diane Drew, Lois
Winston, and for Karen Davenport, sadly missed.

Prologue

March 10
Mexico

BY AFTERNOON, THE notorious drug kingpin known as El Águila would be history.

If everything went as planned.

DEA Agent Holt Donovan slipped on sunglasses against the Baja California sun. The light breeze blowing in off the water helped about as much as a folded paper fan. He reached back to adjust the automatic pistol hidden beneath the loose tail of his sport shirt. Sweat glued the holster to his heated skin. Ducking beneath a shade umbrella, he peered at the hotel's side exit. Nobody yet.

Not a bad setting for a stakeout. The towers of the Hotel Corona Royal rose as regal and white as a wedding cake. Beyond the snowy sands of the Playa Royal, the rolling Pacific waters gleamed azure under the relentless sun.

He and other agents of the U.S. Drug Enforcement Agency, U.S. Customs and Border Patrol, and the Mexican Federal Police had spent months tracking the cartel kingpin's movements, hoping to set up a trap. No luck until now. They spent the past week at the resort scoping out his routine and planning strategy. No pictures existed of the secretive man. The agents were operating only on a sketchy description from hotel employees. But frightened workers didn't necessarily impart the complete truth.

Once every ten days or so, the man registered as Juan Perez and a small entourage left the penthouse for the maze of Tijuana streets and other parts unknown. Juan Perez—that was an alias if Holt had ever heard one, the Spanish equivalent of John Smith.

Today they would get no farther than the parking lot.

While he waited for his quarry to descend from the penthouse, he tipped down his Broncos cap and scanned the crowd at the wedding reception on the patio. Might as well enjoy the view.

Dressed in Spanish lace, the fresh-cheeked bride smiled. The groom, in the traditional silver-braided Mexican tuxedo, stood attentively at her side. Perfect. Holt hoped what would go down would disturb none of the celebrants. Families deserved peace for such occasions.

He sure as hell recalled a humdinger in his family. Maddy leaving his younger brother red-faced at the altar had trampled the whole family like a cattle stampede. Rob was married to someone else now. Maybe he'd let it go, but Holt wouldn't forget—or forgive. His involvement in the mess didn't bear examining.

A detour to Colorado before he had to return to his regular post in the Boston DEA offices would suit him fine. He had yet to see his nephew, less than a month old. Once they had El Águila plucked and stowed, Holt had some time coming. Leaving Rob to run the Valley-D chafed at him, but that was the decision they'd made years ago when their dad left them the family ranch.

The hotel's double doors opened, and two burly men

stepped outside. Like him, they wore cotton shirts, loose over their khaki trousers to conceal weapons. One was a hawk-faced man Holt had seen in the elevator. The other sported a bushy mustache. Bodyguards.

The remainder of the group exited. In the center of the group walked a stocky, older man wearing a white open-collared shirt and dark trousers.

El Águila. The Eagle.

Holt thumbed the speed dial on his secure cell phone. "The bird is on the wing," he said into his headset.

"How many in the flock?" came the response.

"Six. Our bird and five chicks. Four muscle and one lieutenant."

"We'll have 'em on camera as soon as they move to the parking lot. The Federales have picked up the driver. Our bird has no getaway car. We're set."

"Roger." Success depended on patience and strategy, waiting until their prey entered the trap before dropping the net. Could be a problem if some of the newer agents didn't understand that timing meant as much as action. If not more.

Like any flock, the group moved and stopped as one.

"Hold on. They've pulled up twenty feet away." He sat on the lounge chair beneath the umbrella. To appear in casual conversation, he continued to mutter an inaudible—he hoped—description of the action into the receiver.

At his boss's side, the lieutenant, young and tall in a flashy red shirt, spoke quietly. Perez nodded. Then the lieutenant issued a brief order to Hawkface. The bodyguard dashed off to the wedding tent. A moment later he returned with a paper plate stacked with wedding delicacies.

With apparent reluctance, Perez sampled a cake. In his fifties or sixties, he wore his hair slicked back, as did many Latino men, but its unnaturally black color betrayed his vanity. His sharkskin gray complexion and cavern-deep eyes gave him an appearance both repulsive and fascinating.

"He just sampled the wedding goodies. Here they go." Holt waited until they'd passed well ahead of him. "I'm moving in behind."

A flagstone path wound through bougainvillea, flowering trees and hibiscus toward the sprawling parking area and beyond that a three-story parking garage. The little flock would soon enter the open area.

Keeping behind the shrubbery, Holt followed his quarry. He drew his pistol and flicked off the safety.

Behind him, mariachi music cranked up. The celebrants would dance and dine until the sun dropped into the Pacific and the moon rose to take its place.

Hawkface and Mustache, bringing up the rear, glanced around, but didn't make him.

Ten more steps brought them to the edge of the net. Holt could hear the agitated voices, enough words to catch Perez's irritation at the driver's tardiness. Now they would move out into the open, and agents would surround them.

"*¡Alto!* Federal Police. Drop your weapons and surrender!"

Holt's gut clenched and his heart rate shot up. Shit! Some Federale jumped the gun. Instead of inside a circle of agents, the gangsters stood at the brink of the net.

At the brink of escape.

Then all hell broke loose. Two of the bodyguards hunkered down behind hibiscus bushes. They drew handguns and fired volleys at their unseen enemy.

From all sides, agents returned fire. Bullets slammed into the ground. Shots ricocheted off the flagstones around the shooters. One of the gunmen went down.

Holt ran forward.

Hawkface, Mustache, and Redshirt began to edge their leader away from the danger.

"*¡Alto!* You cannot get away," Holt called in his American-accented Spanish. "Agents surround you." He ducked behind a tree as skinny as a flagpole and about as much protection. The others should be moving in to flank them and cut off their escape.

At his warning, the bodyguards wavered. Redshirt drew a pistol and pushed his boss behind him. The others raised their weapons in his direction.

Holt knelt to form a smaller target. Put himself in the zone. Calm. Focused. Where the hell were the Federales and the American agents?

Gunfire boomed from the perimeter of the parking area.

El Águila stood his ground. He stared at Holt, challenge in his eerie gaze. But not fear. The malignant intelligence in his sunken eyes scrutinized him as if he could see through the scrawny tree. Damned clear why the criminal was named for a bird of prey.

At Redshirt's signal, El Águila's protectors fired.

Splinters erupted above Holt's head. The hibiscus blossom beside him exploded red petals. He dropped to his belly and squeezed off four rounds.

Hawkface dropped his pistol and clutched at his arm. The younger lieutenant fell like a heel-looped calf.

Holt fired another round into the ground before them. "Drop your weapons."

El Águila roared like a wounded puma and knelt beside his downed man. Still firing, the winged goon dragged him away. Mustache heaved the young man over his shoulder. The four of them melted into the bushes.

The rattle of shrubbery announced the cavalry.

About damn time. "Through there," Holt yelled to the approaching agents. "Don't let them get away."

****

March 24

San Diego

Holt tapped computer keys as he completed yet one more report on the Operation Bird Net fiasco. He'd had the man in his sights. Could have taken him down, but stopped because higher-ups wanted the scum alive. Fuck. That might've been his only chance at El Águila.

In the confusion, somehow the gangster's party escaped. To show for their trouble, the task force had one clear photograph of the missing men. The two captured bodyguards and the driver weren't talking.

For two weeks they combed Tijuana and environs for any sign of their fugitives. No sign of the kingpin and the three men who'd escaped with him. No doctor or hospital reported gunshot wounds, but that was no surprise. Such a powerful underworld figure would have resources.

"Yo, Donovan," Another DEA agent across the room said. "There's a phone call for you. From Colorado."

"Must be my brother." Holt punched the Save button.

"Guy says his name's Luke Rafferty."

"Rafferty?" Unease crawled over Holt's skin. If the

6

deputy sheriff tracked him down in California, it wasn't with good news.

He reached for the phone.

Chapter One

April
Colorado

HOLT STARED AT the mountain vista he'd missed like a lost limb. April's snow-edged meadows rose into the verdant shades of Ponderosa pines and budding aspens. To the distant southeast, the lowering sun painted a magenta wash on the slopes of Pikes Peak. He swore in this valley he could hear the heartbeat of the mountains.

He should be enjoying the spring with Rob. Grief squeezed his heart. A man wasn't supposed to lose his younger brother. And sure as hell not the way he'd planned to return and take up the reins of the ranch. With his mug of coffee in hand, he turned away and sank onto a chair at the kitchen table.

"I'd stay if I could, you know I would." Esperanza O'Grady folded the dishtowel on its rack over the sink and flicked off the country music radio station she favored. She cocked her head and smoothed back raven hair edged with silver. The housekeeper's Ute heritage shone in her burnished visage. "Two days a week is all I can give you from now on."

"That's okay, Espie. Two days is all I can afford after this. You've done more than anybody else, and I appreciate it."

Espie had worked part-time on this ranch since he was a kid. Her tenure began before his and Rob's mother left and continued after Rob married. Gradually, her cleaning business expanded with her family. Cleaning wasn't what he needed the most, even if he could afford full time.

"I'll lose my other customers if I put them off any longer. You won't need me forever, and I need to keep the fridge stocked. Danny and Sean would devour the shelves." She slipped on her jacket, and then lifted her leather tote to her shoulder.

"I've left you a casserole for tonight and a chicken dish in the freezer. See that you eat proper, now. You need your strength." She wagged a finger at him.

"You're not kidding." He levered to his feet, removing his broad-brimmed black Western hat and holding it over his heart. "My hat's off to single parents everywhere."

"Single is the key word. What you need is a wife."

The word made him shudder. "A wife would only complicate a situation already as convoluted as a Rocky Mountain pass."

He needed help big-time, and fast, but not the kind she meant. He slapped his hat on the table and crossed to the door. "Before you can say it, not a mother either. Last person on earth I'd call."

At the bitterness he never could quite conceal, Espie reached up to pat his cheek. "Time you let that go. Bonnie wasn't cut out for ranch life. Not every woman's tough enough. Many can't take the isolation."

At least Maddy had bailed out on his brother *before* the wedding. She couldn't take it either. Lit out for the big time. Violet eyes and a filly's long legs flickered in his mind. He shook away the vision, but the memory stung like a picked scab.

"No wife. No mother. I have a good hand to help me on the Valley-D. The rest I'll figure out as we go."

"A good hand." She gave a snort as she eased out the door. "If that old coyote works half as much as he flaps his jaw, I reckon he'll do. Don't you tell him I said so neither."

Holt watched from the porch as she left in her pickup. He rubbed a hand over his gritty eyes. Running the Valley-D on the scant sleep he'd had the last few weeks was taking its toll. Most of the cows and the bred heifers had calved, so the damn midnight vigils were close to being finished.

The ones outside, anyway.

"That ornery female gone yet?" Bronc Baker, spare and weathered as an old fence post, sauntered toward the house.

"Ornery? Bronc, I thought you liked Espie. Besides, we couldn't have made it these last few weeks without her."

"Shee-it, I know that." Bronc removed his tan rolled-brim hat from his grizzled head and whacked it against his grimy jeans. A dust cloud rose from both hat and pants leg. "But the woman talks all the time. A man can't pry in a word with a crowbar. Bronc this and Bronc that. Asks about the calves, have we got heifers or bulls and will we have a good hay crop and—"

"Whoa, I get the picture." Holt's mouth twitched, but he held back a laugh. Between them, those two jabbered so much, a conversation could kick up a dust devil.

The older man settled his hat on his head. "Um, I did

10

mention to her we might need her boys to help with the brandin'."

"Good idea. Nothing better than calf roping for teenaged boys." Calf roping had kept Rob and him out of trouble for many years. The memory tightened his chest.

"Anyways, I come to tell you things look peaceful in the calving pen. Moms and babies is doin' okay. Lower pen's quiet too. No signs of more labor right away."

"So it looks like I get the night off. I can use it."

Bronc nodded. "And you'll get to the field truck tomorrow? You're a better mechanic than me."

"Or Rob, I reckon. The tractor needs some work too." Holt scratched his head. His brother's ranch management was an oxymoron. "Back east, they thought all we did was ride around on horseback and herd cattle."

The ranch hand barked a laugh. "City folks don't know a rancher's got to be a mechanic, a vet, and a farmer."

"Don't forget shoestring businessman."

Holt offered to share Espie's casserole. Bronc excused himself, saying he had stew on the stove in the mobile home that served as a bunkhouse.

The peaks beyond the valley drew a lingering look before grief pulled Holt's gaze toward the aspen-topped knoll behind the house. A neat brown scar in the greening grass, Rob's grave was the newest one beside their father and two sets of grandparents.

Past regrets and present burdens heaped on his shoulders, he plodded into the house.

He dug into his dinner like a wolf on fresh kill. Five o'clock. His daily chores on the land were done, but his

Susan Vaughan

nightly ones were about to begin. Maybe fate would grant him a peaceful evening.

The first plate was finished and a second heaped before he took time to savor the spicy beef, tortillas, and cheese. He was rinsing his plate when he heard the engine. He expected no one, and the hairs on his nape lifted in warning. Lately every new arrival, every phone call heralded more trouble.

A glance out the window in the kitchen door revealed the back view of a long drink of female. Mile-long legs in tight jeans and running shoes, sweetly curved butt, and short blond hair. She was waving good-bye to the deputy sheriff's white SUV as it chugged down the gravel drive.

What the hell? He snatched open the door and stalked outside.

When the woman turned around, the sight of her face sucker-punched him in the solar plexus.

"Hi, Holt. Guess you never expected to see me here again." Madelyn McCoy propped her hands on her hips and gave him a crooked smile.

Sweat popped out on his brow. Had he somehow conjured up Maddy? Same sassy mouth, violet eyes the exact shade of the pansies Espie planted every May in the window boxes.

"McCoy, you're the last person I *want* to see. What the hell are you doing here?" He stopped before his temper got the best of him. The mere sight of her pushed all his hot buttons.

She'd lit out eight years ago a twenty-year-old girl, pretty and tempting as a mountain spring, but the female who stood hip-sprung before him was all woman—and twice as sexy.

And twice as deceitful. He'd bet the next newborn calf on it. The sooner she left the better.

Maddy held out open hands in a peace declaration. "Look, I know with you I'm *persona non grata*." Her shoulders slumped, and her sass slid to sorrow. "Faith Rafferty emailed me…about Rob. I had to come to pay my respects."

Faith and Maddy used to be close. So that's how she knew. His throat clutched, and he gritted his teeth. He didn't want to share his loss with the woman who'd broken Rob's heart.

Facing Holt showed a measure of unexpected courage. As children, they'd all been friends, Rob and Maddy and him—kids running wild during the summers. Even if she didn't love Rob enough to marry him and stay on the Valley-D, she'd once cared for him. Holt had to admit that, at least to himself.

Much as the sight of her troubled him, he'd accept her condolences.

He stared at the dust settling on the driveway. She had no transportation. "Why did Luke Rafferty drive you here? You in some kind of trouble?"

A shadow flickered across her eyes. Or it could be his imagination. His DEA work dealing with lowlifes made him as suspicious as a calf at branding time.

"Just car trouble," she said lightly, picking up the metal case at her feet. A fancy camera case, if he wasn't mistaken. "My SUV broke down in Rangewood. Luke happened to see me at the diner."

Close up, he saw exhaustion in her eyes. "Reckon I could drive you back later."

"How did it happen, Holt? The accident. All Faith said was a car accident." She marched up the porch steps toward him like an invading Amazon.

Damn, he had to tell the story again. His gut twisted with the prospect. He ran his tongue around his teeth and focused on the distant peak, still rosy with sunlight. "The crash happened about a month ago. Rob and his wife were headed down to Cripple Creek for a night out. They took the shortcut from north of Rangewood that leads southeast to the state road. Went off the road on a mountain curve and rolled into a ravine."

Tears welled in her eyes. "Oh, Holt, how horrible. Did they…were they—"

"Rob and Sara died quick, I reckon." He couldn't let himself think about their pain and fear. "That old truck barely had seat belts, let alone air bags."

There was more to the story. A lot more. Including the crash was no fucking accident. He had no proof yet, but he knew. Dammit, he would find the bastard who'd murdered his family. He couldn't tell Maddy any of that, and she didn't need to know. He cleared his throat before he turned back to her.

Her voice caught on a sob. "I'm so sorry. What a terrible loss."

He swallowed his pride. "I appreciate that. You didn't have to come all this way though, from Timbuktu or wherever you were."

"Malibu." A wobbly smile lifted the corners of her mouth. "I figured if I telephoned you'd hang up on me. I had to come in person…to see the grave."

"Fine. You know where the family plot is." He sketched a wave in that direction.

"You don't give an inch, do you?" Maddy shook her head, the movement lifting her short blonde hair like a buckskin fringe on a sleeve. "I'd appreciate the use of your bathroom before I go sit by Rob awhile."

Holt's first instinct was not to let her in the house, but he couldn't act the ogre about it. Besides, she was shivering in her denim jacket. He stepped back and held the door as she sashayed in.

Chapter Two

MADDY'S STOMACH MUSCLES relaxed with relief at Holt's capitulation, though he'd win no prize for hospitality. When he'd confronted her outside, she feared he might send her packing, on foot. His overwhelming male presence had her shaking in her trainers, but he apparently bought her bravado. Striding past him, she caught familiar scents that brought back the past—cow, hay, horse, leather, and male sweat from a hard day on a working ranch.

He looked at her as if she were a bobcat that might leap at any moment. Time had settled on him well. His shoulders had filled out, widened with a muscular heft that tested the seams of his blue chambray shirt. He wore his light brown hair longer than she remembered, but its frivolous tendency to curl didn't detract from his authoritative air.

At sixteen, a tangle with a wild mustang had given him a boxer's flattened nose. That and the harsh planes and angles of his strong-boned face kept him from being classically handsome. His face was compelling in its severity. And his blue eyes, the dark blue of a mountain lake, still had the power to mesmerize her.

Chagrin at her attraction to Rob's brother pleated her brow. *Here I go again.*

She set her case down inside the kitchen door. Where a wood-burning cook stove used to reign sat a

Shaker-style china cabinet. A matching cherry table turned the space into a dining area. In the functional part of the kitchen, all new appliances had replaced the old. "The house has changed."

He shrugged, his features schooled into the expressionless mask he must use when in DEA mode interrogating bad guys. He leaned against the kitchen counter. "Sara put up some new curtains, bought a damn dishwasher." His eyes narrowed to chips of dark ice.

"Rob's wife."

"I'm surprised you know her name."

Her cheeks heated. "Rob wrote to me once in a while." She took a step toward him.

The way his mouth dropped open, she might have whacked him with her camera bag. "He *wrote* to you? Letters?"

She raised her chin. "What do you think, notes rolled up in little tubes and delivered by carrier pigeon? Yes, letters at first. Then e-mails. Once a year, sometimes twice. Not so often since he married. You may think I'm Public Enemy Number One, but Rob is—*was* more forgiving." Her mouth tightened at the slip-up in tense.

"You know his temper. When he finally got through his love-mushed brain the meaning of your Dear-John note, he tried to tear the altar apart. It was all I could do to get him out of the church." He tunneled his big fingers through his hair, leaving tracks in the waves, as if of bitter memories.

This conversation was twisting her stomach, as though spiders had woven a thousand webs. "I've regretted how I left every day of the last eight years, but I had to end it. I'm sure Rob blew up. That was Rob, but he never stayed angry. Unlike some people—" She

17

glared at him pointedly. "—your brother didn't hold a grudge."

"If it eases your conscience, you go ahead and believe Rob forgave you. I know better."

She sighed and rubbed the bridge of her nose. Holt's grief was still bloody raw, so she'd let his attack on her pass. "Rob is dead, and our sniping at each other won't help either one of us. Or him. I don't want to argue about this with you. I'm too tired."

"Oh, yeah, crossing time zone after time zone will get you. The jet set life must be rugged." He rolled his eyes and crossed his arms, drawing her gaze to the bunched muscles of his forearms below the rolled-up sleeves.

"Some jet set. I bummed a ride from Nepal in a cargo plane. I crashed at a friend's house before I got Faith's email. Then I drove here." *And slept in my truck.* Her belly churned with emotions better left unexamined.

His mouth thinned, and he shoved his hands in his back pockets. "Tell me one thing, McCoy. Why did you wait until the last minute to run? If you didn't want to marry him, why didn't you tell him *before* the damn wedding day?"

Maddy couldn't utter the words.

Rob's and her connection had grown from shared childhood fun and dreams into what she thought was love but stood only as a house of cards. She had doubts but didn't want to hurt Rob. Then what happened between her and Holt after the rehearsal dinner collapsed the fragile structure. Then she'd hurt and humiliated Rob.

"Holt, you know why. Do you really want to dredge up that mud after all this time? Now if you don't mind."

She scooted out of the room.

Behind her, he said, "I expect you remember where the bathroom is."

The hallway to the left of the kitchen led past three doors to the bathroom at the end. The first door, to Rob's childhood bedroom, was closed. With his only brother dead, perhaps Holt couldn't bear the memories every time he walked this way.

Tears welled, and she allowed them to fall this time. She leaned her forehead against the door frame and remembered. Mostly the memories were good.

Every summer since she was ten until eight years ago, visits to Gramma and Grandad's Circle-S and this neighboring ranch had nurtured roots for a girl whose airline pilot father planted none. When they were kids, Rob was her best friend, as reliable a presence in her transient world as he was carefree and adventuresome. Together, they worked the animals and swam the streams and climbed the hills.

"I don't know if you ever really forgave me, Rob," she whispered to the closed door, "but I hope you did. And I hope Sara made you happy."

The second door stood ajar, revealing jeans slung over a chair and clean laundry piled on the iron-framed double bed. So Holt occupied his old room, though the feminine décor must seem alien to him.

Baskets of dried flowers, teal and rose throw pillows and a dainty rocking chair in a teal print transformed into a trendy guest room what had been the typical boy's milieu of rodeo posters, football paraphernalia, and bunk beds.

The wife again. Sara.

Older by four years, by eons to kids, Holt had

watched over her and Rob, guiding them to the shallower parts of the creek and helping them practice roping on the smallest calves. Sometimes he dared along with them. They explored the abandoned silver mine on Ghost Mountain, a distant, eerie foothill on the Valley-D. Bringing in the mustang that broke Holt's nose was another of those times. Protective and responsible, that was Holt. The threesome dissolved during his tenure at college. When he went on to law school and she and Rob entered UC, everything changed.

After she jilted Rob, she left Colorado, and her photography career took her everywhere in the world except back to the only real home she'd known. She wouldn't change the last several years but more wandering had no appeal.

Maddy dragged herself away from the contrast between chamois shirts and lace-edged pillow shams. The last door, to the master bedroom, remained closed, but the bathroom door stood open.

Grief and exhaustion swam in her head, and she sat on the toilet lid. Last night she spent reliving memories and regrets. Dawn found her still restlessly tossing in her sleeping bag. She'd slept in tents on rocky ground, in mud huts and in campers as well as in good hotels, but the trip from the coast proved her first experience at round-the-clock driving. She'd have to shore up her bank account somehow to pay the mechanic.

For now, she was in a real bathroom. She might as well take advantage. She stood and dumped her denim jacket on the tile floor. After taking care of business, she rolled up the sleeves of the green print shirt she'd bought in Kabul and cleaned up in the sink. She'd kill for a shower but then she'd have to explain her circumstances to Holt.

She opened the cabinet between the sink and tub for a fresh towel. Masculine toiletries cluttered one shelf. She should've brought her camera bag in with her since it contained a toiletry kit. But Holt's disquieting presence had unfocused her brain.

Applying Holt's lotion—unscented, of course—she peered deeper into the shelf and spotted a bottle of perfume that was missed when someone cleared out Sara's things. Amazing. It was her favorite with alight citrus floral scent. She whispered an apology to the dead woman as she spritzed it on.

With tentative fingers, she picked up his hairbrush. Not that her short do required much brushing. The fluffy, layered style was easy to manage—necessary on the road.

Running the brush over her hair, she heard an odd noise like a cat's meow. From the kitchen? She hadn't seen a cat. Low, soothing responses followed the squalling. Holt's rumbling baritone sounded oddly reassuring.

Finished, she opened the bathroom door. The escalating cry no longer seemed feline. The wailing sounded like a—

She dashed back to the kitchen.

—baby.

Standing in the center of the large room, Holt held an infant in disposable diapers and a blue polka-dot undershirt. A baby screaming its head off as if Torquemada and all his Inquisition zealots were torturing it. The crimson-faced infant, no more than a couple of months old, waved its tiny fists in fury. Or in pain.

Her heart raced, and prickles like ants crawled over her skin.

Holt, married? With a child?

She hadn't anticipated that.

Then where was his wife? What was going on?

He cradled the child in his brawny arms as if it were a precious gem. He crooned to it. He jiggled it. He rocked it.

Against her will, warmth slid into her at the gentle way her gruff host handled the infant. She remained implanted in the kitchen doorway. "Holt?"

He raised solemn eyes from the screech factory in his arms. "I hoped he'd sleep longer. Meet Robert Trask Donovan, Jr., human air raid siren."

Robert Trask Donovan, Jr.

The name trickled into her consciousness, like water into the desert floor. The sense of it percolated through her slow brain for a moment before the dimensions of the tragedy found their level. Her heart stuttered. "Rob's son? He and Sara left a *son*?"

Nodding, he paced the length of the kitchen. "That drive to Cripple Creek was to be their first dinner out since Bobby here was born."

"How old is he?" She could barely speak over the thickness in her throat.

"Bobby's two months old. Just yesterday."

"Two months? Then he was only—" A month old when his parents were killed. Tears burned again as she approached the disconsolate child. "Maybe you should change him."

"Done."

"Could he be hungry?"

"Among your many accomplishments, you're a

baby expert?" He cocked a bushy eyebrow to express his skepticism. "He ate about an hour ago before Espie put him down."

Two months old? She searched her memory for what tidbits she'd picked up in her travels. "He's on formula?"

He nodded, pacing the room with the fussing infant. "Sara was nursing him. Obviously, I don't have the equipment. He hasn't adjusted to the formula. Gives him gas pains. Doc says that's one reason he cries so much. That and missing his mom."

She folded her hands in beneath her chin. "But...but there has to be something we—*you* can do."

"I'm doing it, McCoy. Walking him and holding him. He'll run down after a while." He paused in his circuit of the room and halted before her. "I suppose *you* could do better."

Emotions swirled inside Maddy. She'd held plenty of babies. Haitian babies, Afghan babies, Ghanaian babies. Getting to know the families was part of setting up photo shoots. But the moms had always been there to take them back if they cried.

Holding babies, cuddling them, and cooing nonsense to them—that was the extent of her knowledge. She probably knew less about child care than Holt.

He'd had the last month to learn. On-the-job training.

But this bawling, round-faced cherub with a head of light fluff like duck's down entranced her. "I can't do any worse than you, Dr. Spock."

Fierce concentration on his features, Holt passed his nephew to her. "Here, hold him in one arm. Then you can rub his belly. Sometimes that helps."

In the transfer, his shoulder and arm pressed against hers. She felt every muscle imprinted on her skin and couldn't resist the pull of his blue eyes. The other hand grazed her breast as he released his hold on his nephew. She chalked up her leaping pulse to fear of dropping the squirming child.

As soon as little Bobby was settled in her arms, Holt stepped back as though from a kicking mule.

Propping the baby's head, she jiggled him and cooed at him. She concentrated on soothing him and forced herself to ignore the much larger male across the room.

The screaming stopped. The wailing and gnashing of gums ceased. Only gentle gurgles emitted from the tiny bow-shaped mouth. Tear-spangled, spiky lashes framed rounded kitten-blue eyes. He stared at the strange woman who held him.

Both adults sighed at the resulting peace.

"You have custody of your nephew?" She stood in place, rocking the apparently contented child. Baby scents of powder and milk and innocence. Too sweet for words.

Something gooey melted inside her and she tried to harden it. She couldn't get involved with this household. Her heart couldn't afford renewed attraction to this man.

"Temporary custody for now. I'll adopt him as soon as I can and raise him as my son." Pride and determination roughened his deep voice. "What did you do? Hypnotize him?"

She shrugged her dismissal of that notion. "Maybe it's because I'm new. Will you take him back east when you return to work?"

He lifted a tired gaze to her from Bobby, who had discovered his fist and was sucking on it noisily. "I *am* at work. Here. I'm staying to run the Valley-D. My resignation from the DEA became final two weeks ago."

The announcement punched her in the chest, but she kept a sigh from leaking out. Holt was no longer a federal agent. He lived *here*. "Oh."

He scowled. "You said 'back east.' So Rob told you where I was, about my work?"

Maddy shrugged, affecting nonchalance. "Probably. And Faith kept me posted on all the old friends from this valley. So you're giving up law enforcement?"

She swayed rhythmically with the baby as Holt explained. "I spent the last year and a half in San Diego as part of a task force chasing a Mexican drug lord. We didn't get him, so the DEA would either return me to that detail or send me somewhere else. Whichever, it's not the life for a single parent. Rotten hours, dangerous, moving a lot."

She knew firsthand what that life was like for kids. Her nomadic life was one reason she remained unattached.

He spread his arms in demonstration. "Plus I have the ranch. Bronc's a good hand, but he can't run the place alone. I can't pay anyone else, and I *won't* sell."

The jangling of the telephone precluded her having to fabricate a response or more questions. Two long-legged strides took Holt across the kitchen to the wall phone.

Holt in permanent residence at the Valley-D was a development she hadn't counted on. She'd had no home anywhere in this high valley since her grandparents sold their ranch several years ago. The Rafferty family ran the Circle-S as a guest ranch.

Between shoots—and paychecks—she'd been

25

weighing her options. Her assignments haunted her dreams—swollen-bellied children, refugee families, bulldozed hovels, and teenaged suicide bombers. This valley had always called to her. If she limited her gigs, she could put down roots and find some stability and peace.

Living even part time in Rangewood or anywhere in the valley might not've been awkward if Rob were alive. He'd have shrugged off her return like rainwater on his hat. He'd forgiven her. She was pretty sure.

Maybe she would have made friends with his wife. And little Bobby.

But Holt was not Rob. The man whose motto was Family Loyalty would resent her return like a personal assault. He nearly cut her legs off just for this visit.

Her admiration for his integrity and responsibility was mushrooming because of his leaving his career for his nephew and the ranch. She couldn't stay here for long. She would sit by Rob's grave awhile before phoning one of the Raffertys for a ride. She wouldn't accept Holt's offer of a ride, couldn't let him see where she was staying. That was for sure.

She snuggled the infant, whose eyelids were drooping, and laid her cheek on his soft, warm head. Inhaling his clean, powdery scent, she eased into the rocking chair by the hutch and tried not to let her attention wander to Holt.

Chapter Three

HOLT LEANED AGAINST the counter and tried to concentrate on the voice at his ear and not the woman across the room. "Yes, he's fine."

"Now that little Bobby's two months old, he's going to need his immunizations," said Phyllis Patterson.

"Yes'm. I have an appointment this week." He shifted on his tired feet. His eyes remained riveted on Maddy.

She had short, breezy hair instead of the long silken mane he remembered. He wouldn't let himself like it. Or her. He didn't want to think about the softness of the breast he'd brushed against either. That flimsy shirt the color of spring aspen leaves provided little barrier.

Shit. What was he, some pervert, to think about sex when all they were doing was transferring an innocent baby?

Getting her out of here pronto would suit him just fine. He didn't need her interference in his already disrupted life. Neither did Bobby. The woman was trouble. A pampered female like his mother. And like Rob's wife. Seemed like that was true. Judging from the fancying of the house. Maddy drove an SUV, probably some overpriced foreign job. Served her right if it broke down.

All looks and no substance. Like the woman.

Phyllis chattered away, her advice the same old ride

up the mountain, like the cog railway that chugged day in and day out up Pikes Peak. Except her voice held a nervous edge that had Holt wondering what else the woman wanted.

He punctuated her monologue with an occasional "Yes'm." He tried to keep on good terms with the Pattersons, but at a distance. They were the baby's grandparents, but Bobby was a Donovan.

Phyllis's mention of Esperanza broke through the haze of his ruminations. "What are you getting at? What do you mean?"

"Oh dear, this is so upsetting." She cleared her throat before continuing. She'd learned at the hairdresser that Espie was returning to her regular customers. "How are you going to run the ranch and care for Bobby without full-time help?"

He gritted his teeth. "We'll manage."

Maddy regarded him with curiosity from across the room where she sat and rocked the sleeping infant. Something in his tone must have alarmed her.

"You cannot take that dear little one with you into the barn or out on the range. Think of the *dangers*. Think of the *dirt*. Think of the *germs*." Shrillness broadcast Phyllis's emotion.

He'd figured out how he could keep Bobby with him. He could carry the baby in the cloth sling-carrier or in the car seat. It ought to work. He would make it work. It *had* to work.

"We'll be just fine, Phyllis." He slid his jaw sideways to loosen the muscles.

"Without reliable child care, the judge may not consider you a fit guardian, let alone a parent. It's bad enough you know so little about raising a baby."

"I'm learning fast. New mothers know nothing about babies either. Most do okay." His patience with the interfering old biddy was sifting away fast.

When he heard the words *attorney* and *custody*, it was all he could do not to slam down the phone.

Maddy gaped at him, puzzlement on her delicate features. The baby drifted off. In the circle of her slender arms, he looked angelic and peaceful, not like a critter with the lung capacity of a full-grown steer. His head of blond fluff resembled hers too much for comfort.

Seeing how at ease she was with his nephew sprouted an idea in Holt's mind. An idea he didn't relish. He'd sooner house a rattler. Madelyn McCoy had tempted him once. He wouldn't allow her a second time.

"After we've filed a challenge to your custody, Judge Gilbert will appoint an advocate to investigate your situation," continued the voice in his ear. "When he sees your lack of responsibility toward my grandson, I don't think Edgar and I will have any trouble." She snapped a goodbye.

If she hadn't hung up at that moment, Holt would've barked out words he would've later regretted.

The only way out of this box canyon meant more regret, but he had no choice. The Pattersons were challenging his custody. Espie could stay only two days a week, and most of the time involved cleaning and laundry. The only possible hires for nanny were teenage girls who'd dropped out of school. Not worth consideration. Not for Bobby. Holt's only rescue was the last person he should trust.

The last person he should trust himself with.

Maddy was the impulsive one, but impulse was all he had. No time to find other options. He stared at the toes of his worn cowhide boots. He mentally kicked himself with them for what he was about to do. Temporary, only temporary.

He shifted his jaw. "You thirsty? I got iced tea and coffee, maybe a beer or two."

"Why, Holt Donovan, I didn't know you had it in you to play model host." She grinned, the same impudent expression he'd seen many times when they were kids. Only now the expression didn't strike him as childish.

He scowled. "Just trying to be civilized. Or did all your foreign travels make you forget Western hospitality?"

"Iced tea would be wonderful. Please." She eyed him with skepticism, but kept rocking the sleeping infant.

He used the tea preparation time to work out how to proceed. Edge around the subject. Or maybe just ask her flat out. He took his time finding a glass, dumping in ice cubes, and pouring the tea. "Already has sugar in it. Espie knows how I like it."

"You always had that woman wrapped around your finger."

Feeling like the awkward teen he used to be, he extended the glass. "I think Bobby's asleep enough to go back in his crib. You want me to take him?"

She looked as reluctant as he must at the idea they pass the baby again. "No, just show me where, and I'll do it." She scooted to the edge of the rocker and rose smoothly to her feet.

"It's Rob's old room." He followed and stood in the doorway while she deposited Rob's son in the crib and laid a light blanket over him. "Put him on his back. Doc said—"

"Yes, I know. It cuts down on the danger of SIDS." She rolled her eyes as she breezed past him back to the kitchen. A light flowery scent rose to muddle his senses. "Your nephew is fine, Donovan. I didn't break him."

He wiped his clammy hands on the seat of his jeans. While she sipped her tea and wandered around the room, he yanked a beer from the fridge and pulled a long swallow. "Looking good, Maddy. The footloose life agrees with you."

She shrugged. "The way my family migrated around the damn world, it's all I know."

"Your wheels going to need much work?"

"I don't know yet. Tomorrow's Monday. The guy at the garage said he wouldn't know much until late afternoon. He'll probably have to order a part."

"So you're sticking around for a few days. You're in no hurry to get someplace like the Riviera or the Big Apple." Damn, how lame did that sound?

"I'm in no rush. I'm…between assignments. Thought I'd hang out in Rangewood. Take pictures. Enjoy the scenery."

Rangewood was no tourist town. No decent place to stay this side of Manitou Springs. "Staying at the Valley Motel with the cowboys and feed salesmen, are you?"

Frowning, she put down her glass and folded her arms. "This small talk isn't like you. What are you getting at, Holt?"

He drew a breath. "How'd you like to stay here a while?"

Maddy's pulse quickened. She stopped dead at the cherry table. Had she heard him correctly? A laugh bubbled from her throat. "I must be more tired than I thought, or maybe that beer dulled your brain. I could've

31

sworn you just invited me to stay at the Valley-D."

"I did."

She cocked her head. "Now why would you do that? A few minutes ago, you couldn't wait to see the last of me."

Crimson daubed his lean cheekbones. As if aware of the effect, he stalked to the door and gazed out at the lowering sun. Definitely not at her. He jammed his hands in his pockets, pulling the denim taut against his backside.

Still a world-class butt too. Maddy joined him at the door.

He nodded toward the hill behind the ranch house. "It'll be dark soon, and you haven't been to the cemetery yet. You would only have to come back tomorrow. You have no car. We can fetch your stuff."

He wanted her to stay, was making excuses for her to stay. But why? He hadn't forgiven her for jilting his brother. Nor himself for his part in that fiasco. That was as obvious as a flash bulb.

She didn't get it. What was he after? No way could she stay at the Valley-D. She could sleep in the SUV another night. Maybe her funds would be deposited tomorrow. Or the next day. Shit. "I'll call Luke or Will for a ride. Tomorrow I'll rent a car."

"Rent a car? In Rangewood? You have to be kidding." He turned to face her, and his sandy eyebrows beetled. He retreated a step in apparent dismay that she stood within arm's reach.

Inordinately pleased that her proximity could disconcert the man, Maddy smiled sweetly and edged a pace nearer. If she crossed her arms in the same power stance, they'd bump. It would be like hitting a wall.

A very hard, very masculine wall.

A safe wall. Or a dangerous wall?

She curbed her impulse. News flash—Maddy McCoy not acting on impulse. What was he up to? "Being nice to me for old time's sake? Another dose of Western hospitality?"

"Go ahead and bunk at the motel. The drunks probably don't make too much noise." He sidled away and leaned back against the cabinets, folded his arms.

No kidding. Into the wee hours last night, shouting from the bar across the street from the garage had penetrated the walls of her Rover. "An early alarm."

"See? No five-star resort like you're used to."

"Little do you know. Photography assignments pay a living, but not that much. Most of what I own is in one blue duffel and a couple of titanium cases like that one by the door. The rest is in storage. On the last trip to Kashmir, I slept in a tent. With bugs you wouldn't believe."

He uttered a skeptical grunt. "I have a spare room you can stay in. With its own bath. No bunk beds."

"I don't buy it, Holt." The anxiety, the shiftiness in his eyes began while he was on the phone. "All this thoughtfulness has something to do with your phone call."

"Now why would you think that?"

"Get real. You don't want me here anymore than I want to be here." That was a lie. The Valley-D had once been her second home. Holt and Rob's dad had welcomed her like his own. Their mother too, when she was still here.

For now she had no home except her duffel bag. Since her parents traveled so much, their Huntington

Beach condo didn't count. A pitiful state of affairs for a grown woman.

She couldn't stay, whatever his reason for asking. They wouldn't get along. He'd needle her about her non-existent fancy lifestyle and about the past. Opening her heart to his Code-of-the-West integrity and protectiveness would bring the dulled ache of her feelings for him into floodlit exposure. Staying would prickle them both with guilt. Staying would confuse her choices. Staying would be too dangerous for her heart.

Teetering on a figurative corral fence, Maddy stared through the window in the upper half of the kitchen door. Cirrus clouds tinted apricot by the setting sun arched a perfect background for the violet-shaded crags around them. Purple mountains' majesty, in spades. Her fingers itched to capture the images.

Why was he asking, was the question. She couldn't quite adjust her mind's lens to clarity. She grabbed the doorknob. "Thanks for the offer, but me staying here is a bad idea all around. I'll just walk up to the family plot before the light goes."

The door half open, she paused. She didn't understand why, but she didn't want to go to Rob's grave alone. Maybe she needed Holt's stiff disapproval as a buffer against more painful emotions. "Do you want to come with me?"

His cheek muscles tightened, and his jaw rotated the way it did when he chewed over a thought. "I don't like to leave Bobby in the house alone."

Eyeing him with speculation, she buttoned her jacket. Images of the past minutes clicked in her head as the picture came into clear focus. Holt was in a tight spot. A rancher alone with an infant. Pressure of some kind in that phone call.

Her eyes widened and she stared open mouthed at him. "You need help with the baby. That's why you want me to stay."

Color again smeared Holt's cheekbones. Like a small boy with his hand caught in the cookie jar, he looked appealing. Too appealing. She didn't want this softening attraction that pounced on her when she least expected it.

As if on cue, a pitiful howl erupted from the nursery.

He lifted one shoulder in defeat. "It's a long story. I'll get him and walk outside with you." He strode toward the siren wail like a dedicated fireman to a blaze.

"Holt." Her voice halted him at the door. "I can stay, but only for a few days. Until my truck is ready."

He jerked a sharp nod before disappearing into the darkened nursery.

Already she regretted her rash decision, made by simply opening her mouth and not by conscious deliberation. But Bobby needed her, and well, how could she resist that poor little tow-headed orphan? Helping Rob's son was something she could do for her old friend—the *only* thing she could do.

And what about Holt?

Eight years ago, his rugged appeal and the chemistry sparking between them had cinched her decision not to marry Rob. Despite Holt's need of her assistance, he distrusted her. How long could she tolerate her attraction and his resentment?

She'd remain only as long as she had to.

Chapter Four

BOBBY'S SIREN WAIL penetrated Holt's consciousness like a nail in his skull.

He opened one eye. The lighted digital clock beside his bed read two o'clock. *Right on time, little guy.* "Coming," he mumbled.

One foot on the floor. The other. He raked fingers through his hair, then pushed to his feet. Starting for the door, he snapped alert as though slapped.

Maddy McCoy.

He'd finished some paperwork in the office, then slipped off to bed early. But escape didn't work worth a damn. The image of Maddy's sassy face and the memory of her scent kept him torturing his sheets for hours before he finally slept.

Shit, she was in the master bedroom. He couldn't troop through the house in his skivvies. Blinking in the darkened bedroom, he stumbled back and forth like a drugged steer as he searched for his jeans. Didn't he leave them on the chair? Or on the floor? No. He put away the clean ones and tossed the manure-smeared ones into the washing machine. Where they remained.

Bobby cranked it up a notch. He could rival that opera singer, Luciano something.

Hell with it. Holt hit the door and burst into the hall.

And collided with a slim figure in filmy white.

He stumbled to a halt and braced himself as his arms

went around her to stop her fall. She emitted a small yelp like a cartoon *eek*. Under his hands, her slender body in the silken covering was a miracle of curves and soft, toned female flesh. His body tightened and his pulse raced off to distant planets. The hallway suddenly didn't have enough air.

He immediately set her away a step. Then he stepped back another. "Sorry. Bobby." The baby's cry subsided to hiccups and whimpers. No emergency, to his relief.

"Thought that was my job," she said. "Two o'clock bottle. Diaper change. Like that."

"You're here to spell me when I'm doing ranch work."

"A rancher needs sleep." She returned his scowl, although humor tugged at the corner of her lips. "Why do you want me here if you won't leave Bobby to me?"

He opened his mouth, closed it again with a snap.

Bobby cranked it up again. Only taking a breather. His wail rivaled an air raid siren.

"If you'll get out of my way," she said, tossing her hair and smoothing her nightshirt so it highlighted her breasts, "I'll see to the baby." The grin popped out, accompanied by a slow perusal down Holt's body. "Nice…legs."

He blinked, shot a glance downward. Damn, betrayed by his tented boxers. His Adam's apple jumped as he swallowed hard. He jerked to the side along the wall, as if someone had pressed a knife to his side. "Bobby's all yours."

"Great!" She turned and swung her hips as she flounced toward the baby's room.

****

Closing the door behind her, Maddy stepped to the crib and gathered the squalling infant in her arms, damp diaper and all. "There, there, Bobby. Auntie Maddy's got you."

She kissed his downy head, sweet with baby sweat from his efforts at rousing help. Eyes closed, she rocked him in her arms and let his warm weight soothe her. Her pulse downshifted, with an occasional blip of vibration.

Who had escaped whom out there? She had no business tempting Holt. He'd gone on the defensive, barely verbal and practically growling. She'd best remember not to tease the mountain lion again unless she was prepared to be mauled. Not the best image, but it would serve to make her stop and think next time. Would there be a next time? Did she want a next time? Her heart raced like that of a frightened rabbit.

****

The next morning, Holt drove to Rangewood. Guiding the pickup over the long gravel driveway and the highway gave him time to ponder how drastically life had changed.

Though he'd made it to town only a couple of weeks ago, it seemed like years since he'd gotten away from the ranch. Calving and little Bobby tied him to the Valley-D but good. He loved the work nearly as much as he loved his nephew, but running the ranch shouldn't turn the place into a prison.

Having help there would free him to come and go as ranch chores let him. Then why did he feel so antsy?

Maddy McCoy. With her flowery scent and her long legs. She was one reason he beat it out of there early today before the offices and stores in Rangewood opened.

To have the woman who'd left his brother at the altar caring for Rob's child scraped barbed wire across his nerve endings. A little voice reminded him he was partly to blame for that but he shushed it. To have her in his house, eating at his table, sprawled over her laptop in the living room burrowed under his skin like a tick. To have her sleeping across the hall in the master bedroom was idiocy.

He should have switched rooms with her. Better yet, he should move out to the bunkhouse with Bronc.

Except he'd be too far from Bobby.

Not that he needed to be there for the kid during the night. Maddy had been on the spot when the little screech engine cranked up. His blood heated with the memory of their midnight encounter.

He'd slammed back into his room pronto, but that didn't eliminate from his brain the image of Maddy in her short silky nightshirt and maybe nothing else. He had to fight his way back to sleep in that prissy iron bed. From now on he'd leave to her the privilege of night duty.

Beat the hell out of him why he was so obsessed with her.

She was as feisty and bold as ever, but changed in other ways. Confusing ways. In the old days, the princess, as her granddad had called her, wanted for nothing. If she asked for a pinto pony or a new saddle or God knew what, the next day one appeared as if conjured by a genie.

After she flew off to pursue her photography career, the headline jobs landed in her lap. She flitted to more countries than Holt could name. Yet she arrived in Rangewood practically empty-handed. All she claimed to have was her fancy camera case, a laptop, and a big duffel bag. When he drove her to town to pick up her things, she directed him past the motel to the garage where her ride sat out back, waiting for the mechanic's verdict. An older model, more truck than utility vehicle. She said she'd checked out of the motel because Faith's friend in town rented rooms and she planned to go there later. A lie, he suspected, confirmed by what he saw in the back of the SUV. She tried to block him, but open and stuffed into a corner was a sleeping bag.

Something was eating at her, some secret. She was as wary of him as a green colt, so her agreeing to stay awhile came a mite too quick to make sense. But he had his own mystery to handle without pursuing that one, so he'd let it go. For now.

The highway snaked through the high valleys past gates that led to neighboring ranches. Not much traffic this morning, except for the black pickup behind him. He'd seen no one in any direction when he left the Valley-D. Then out of nowhere the black truck appeared. He didn't recognize it as belonging to anyone he knew, couldn't see the driver clearly. Too far back to read the license plate.

He jabbed fingers through his hair, knocking off his hat. Hell, too many years watching his back had him imagining a tail. Probably some kid tooling around in a hot rod jerry-rigged of spare parts. That's why he couldn't recognize the make.

By the time he hit Rangewood's Pike Street, the black truck had disappeared. Along with that, Holt relegated Maddy to the back of his mind.

Other than a few residential avenues, Pike was the only paved street in the quiet, friendly town. He pulled up to the curb and turned off the engine. As he exited the truck, the last person he wanted to see sauntered down the sidewalk toward him.

"Well, Holt, not too often you tear yourself away from that ranch to come into Rangewood." Edgar Patterson, Bobby's grandfather, stuck out his hand.

Reluctantly, Holt shook it. "Edgar."

"Ranch that size takes full-time work to make it pay." With a meticulously manicured hand, Edgar smoothed his graying hair, its long strands coaxed to conceal growing baldness. His tan business suit matched his sharp amber gaze.

The dig hit its mark, but Holt had spent too many years dealing poker-faced with street slime to let on to the banker. "You'll get your loan payments on time. Don't worry."

"Oh, I'm not worried. Not a bit. The wife's concerned you can't do right by our grandson. Financially, I mean."

It was all Holt could do not to grab the older man by his chicken neck and shake him. "Bobby's well taken care of."

"By the way, where is the little guy?" Patterson peered in the truck window. He fixed a probing gaze on Holt, a hawk sighting vulnerability in his prey. "Left him at home? Espie must be there today."

Holt didn't intend to be the hawk's hapless rabbit. He smiled. Now was the time to drop his news. "No, a…friend is staying with me for a while to care for the baby."

Patterson gave an indignant huff. "Not that old reprobate Bronc Baker?"

"Bronc lives on the Valley-D, but no. It's Madelyn

McCoy. She used to spend summers on the Circle-S with her grandparents. Grew up with Rob and me."

"McCoy?" Edgar's eyes narrowed with speculation. "She the one who jilted Rob?"

Holt shifted his feet. "That was a long time ago. We were all close. She's good with Bobby." Patterson might buy that description, but did he?

"Staying there? Living in the house?"

"Down the hall from the baby's room." Better not to mention she was in the master bedroom. "Like a nanny."

"A nanny." Patterson seemed to turn the idea over in his mind. "The McCoy girl?" He uttered a terse farewell and hustled toward the bank.

For sure the man was on his way to phone his wife about the latest development. Whatever they cooked up together after that wouldn't be good for him. Or Bobby.

He turned to the office he'd parked beside—Turner and Hawke, Attorneys at Law. Last night Holt had phoned Chris Hawke, a cousin of Espie's, about handling the custody case. Patterson probably figured out what Holt was doing there too.

Hell of a thing. The Pattersons' challenge of Bobby's guardianship was going to cost him money he needed for the baby and money he needed for the ranch. He—or Chris—had to find some way to avert the custody suit.

Inside the building, Chris Hawke greeted him in his office, a book-lined space with diplomas and certificates on the walls. The two of them had played football together for Rock County High and started law school in tandem.

"It was supposed to be Donovan and Hawke on a shingle in Denver, remember?" Holt said.

"Funny how things work out different." Chris shook his hand and waved him to a chair. "If your dad had lived, do you think we'd have made it as a team?"

"Hard to say." Losing their dad to a massive heart attack Holt's second year in law school had torn his and Rob's world apart, but they'd rebuilt. He could do it again. "At the time, I thought Rangewood was a hell of a bore, but after chasing drug dealers and other dregs in big cities, it seems like heaven. What about you? Why did you set up shop with Agatha Turner?"

"Seems minority hiring was full up in the big city. Not one law firm wanted a newly graduated Native American attorney." Chris's laugh was ironic but not bitter as he smoothed his thong-tied ponytail over his shirt collar.

"Boot-licking in a big firm doesn't sound like you." Holt nodded toward the Anasazi-bead amulet that hung to the middle of the other man's Western dress shirt. "Cut your hair and wear a tie? I can't feature it."

"Yup. Not my style. First time some suit gave me a hard time, I might've decked him and been outta there fast. Agatha's a tough old bird, but she trusts me. Lets me help out my people if they need it."

"Good catching up, and we should do more of it," Holt said, "but now I need your help."

"The Pattersons," Hawke said, opening the folder on his desk. "This is going to be hard on you. I hope we can make it easy on your little nephew."

Holt's gut clenched. "Do Bobby's grandparents have a viable case?"

"Maybe. Maybe not."

"Lawyer-ese for what, Chris? Give it to me straight. I'll do whatever it takes to keep Bobby. He's a Donovan and he'll be raised on the Donovan ranch."

"The Pattersons are alleging you're an unfit guardian for an infant on the grounds you can't provide adequate care."

Holt saw a sliver of light. "Adequate meaning money or nurturing, like love and attention and feeding?"

"Could be both, depending on what their attorney pushes. Vague for now. They have Ingrid Kline of Tobias and Kline in Colorado Springs. A reputable firm, have done a lot of custody cases. I've never seen Kline in action but hear she's clever."

"Things could be worse." Holt considered his options, but had only one, and a temporary one at that. "Bobby has a nanny. Trial basis for now. Then we'll see."

Chris Hawke smiled and made a note. "Tell me about the nanny."

A half hour later Holt practically ran from the law offices, his stress level shooting up like a thermometer in July. He'd been thanking God Maddy agreed to stay until he heard Chris's assessment of the situation. The court would be looking for stability, not temporary measures. Maddy would leave. Then what the hell would he do?

"I'm right behind you." Chris Hawke closed the door behind him and jogged to join him. A head shorter and of stockier build, he stepped out to match Holt's long stride. "I'll go with you to the sheriff's. They should have more on Rob's accident by now."

"Thanks." Checking in with the sheriff was his other errand, tying up the loose ends of his brother's death. He'd told Chris last night about his doubts on what exactly caused the crash. He appreciated his friend's company and support. He backed the truck out and headed south to the county seat of Fort Adams.

When they arrived at the building housing the sheriff's department, the dispatcher was talking on the telephone at the reception desk, a rectangular enclosure containing the radio equipment and filing cabinets. She waved them toward the offices. "Sheriff ain't busy. You boys can go on back."

Chapter Five

THEY FOLLOWED THE rumble of male voices past a departing deputy and two secretaries to Sheriff Jarvis Foley's office.

"Hey, Donovan. Come on in and pull up a chair." A jovial, barrel-chested man with a gray-streaked handlebar mustache, Foley reclined in his executive swivel chair with his booted feet crossed on the desktop.

His chief deputy, Luke Rafferty, sat in a wooden chair. Odors of musty files and stale coffee permeated the office.

"Thanks, Sheriff." After shaking the older man's gnarled hand, Holt took an empty chair.

Behind him, Chris slid inside quietly. He stood to Holt's left, one elbow propped on a bookcase.

"I see you brought your Legal Eagle." Scowling, Rafferty turned his chair to face Chris. His tawny hair and cool green eyes gave the impression of a cougar about to pounce.

"Never hurts to have counsel." Chris's level, dark stare matched the other man's. "You of all people should know that."

Holt blinked at the palpable animosity arcing between the men. Rafferty had left the Denver police force under hazy circumstances, but most folks in Rock County knew better than to mention it to him. Apparently Holt had missed bad blood between Chris and Luke.

"How's it goin' out there at the Valley-D? You managing all right with just you and Bronc?" the sheriff asked.

"We're getting by." Holt was here to get to Rob's case, but he forced himself to endure the courtesies.

"And Rob's kid? Bobby, is it? How are you taking care of a baby and birthing calves too?" Rafferty put in.

"Maddy's staying a while."

The deputy barked a cynical laugh. "I thought you'd boot Maddy McCoy up the road after she paid her respects. When I dropped her off, it felt like putting a fox in a wolf den."

"Who?" The sheriff wound a finger around one end of his mustache.

Before Holt could explain, Rafferty plowed in. "Eight years ago, Madelyn McCoy was engaged to Holt's brother. When she left poor Rob stepping on his tongue at the altar—and I mean that literally—Holt just about swore a vendetta on the female."

"Ironic," Chris said, "to have her return to care for Rob's child."

"Maybe, but we've all grown up some since then. I'm grateful to have her." Holt winced inwardly. *Having* her was out of the question.

He returned his attention to Foley, who raised one frosted eyebrow of mild interest in the live soap opera. "You got any news for me, Sheriff?"

"Ballistics report came in yesterday. I was going to give you a call." Foley pushed a folder across the desk.

"What took so long?" Holt opened the folder.

"They're real backed up in Colorado Springs. A request from a spit-sized county like Rock don't get priority."

After a moment's perusal, Holt clenched his jaw. He recognized the .50 caliber. "Only a high-powered sniper rifle would use an exploding bullet. We can't call the crash an accident any longer." He passed the folder to Chris.

"Maybe *you* can't, but I'm still not sure. Some hunter shootin' off too fast."

The sheriff was being cautious about treading on local toes, Holt reckoned. Especially those of hunters. Clamping down on out-of-state hunters could raise the ire of county businesses that catered to them.

Holt's outward shell of calm was chipping off. "Come off it, Jarvis. Someone sat in that stand of trees opposite the precipice and waited to blow out Rob's tires. Someone deliberately killed my brother and his wife. That was no accident. It was murder."

"Would a hunter have used this caliber?" Chris tossed the file onto the desk.

The sheriff gave a noncommittal wag of his head. "No one around here has a high-tech rifle like that." He laughed. "Who knows what some of these rich tourists have?"

"Some guy could've seen a bear and been waiting for him to return. Maybe he sighted the critter at the same time Rob came by," Rafferty said.

Holt's patience with these damn-fool suggestions shrank to a nub. He fired out of his seat. "Unlikely. And it's not hunting season."

"Exactly why someone might keep it to himself." Foley held up a hand to stay Holt's impending explosion. "I'm not sayin' it *couldn't* be murder. It's my duty to bring the perpetrator to justice whether it's an accident or murder. I want to be sure is all."

"You taking it slow on purpose, Sheriff? Biding time until your retirement next fall?"

Defensiveness flickered across Foley's lined features before indulgence replaced it. "Now, Holt, you know better'n that. All cases will have serious attention until my last day. Besides, I'm not too sure about retirement. What would I do with my time?"

Rafferty's brooding attention veered from Chris to Holt. "Right after the crash, we checked the whereabouts of practically everyone in town. Me and the other deputies interviewed the guests at the Circle-S and the wranglers on every spread around. Only ones we didn't get were a few drifters who'd moved on."

"We came up empty," Foley said. "All the logical suspects had alibis." His boots slammed to the floor. He straightened in his chair, the politician's easy smile transformed to a determined glare. "Now that we have this report, we'll go over everything all over again."

"Damn right. You missed something." Holt stopped stalking and gripped the back of the wooden chair. His gut churned. "Because someone who knew what he was doing—the killer—arrived ahead of my brother's old pickup on that winding mountain shortcut. He waited in hiding, maybe for hours. He blew out the truck's tires at just the right angle and time to send them over the cliff to their death."

Chris Hawke fingered his amulet with a thoughtful expression on his face. "Suppose it was murder. What possible motive could someone have to kill Rob Donovan? Or Sara?"

"Exactly why I think it must have been an accident," the sheriff said. "Everyone liked Rob. You couldn't find a nicer guy. Why he'd do anything for you, give you the shirt off his back. And Sara was a sweet kid, a new mother. Who would harm either one of them? Who would want them dead?"

No one could care as much about solving this case as Holt did. With most of the county's cases involving drunk drivers, domestic disputes, and kids sowing wild oats, the sheriff's department didn't have much experience with homicides. "Exactly what I propose to find out, Sheriff, if you won't. Or can't."

"Too bad the Legal Eagle here can't help you find the killer's tracks." Rafferty's smile was as thin as splintered wood. "Thought you people were great hunters and trackers."

Chris moved to stand beside his client. "My ancestors, yeah, Rafferty. Just like yours used to be straight-shooters."

The deputy tensed, ready to escalate the confrontation. A cough from the sheriff broke the strain. Rafferty subsided.

Chris strolled out of the office as if nothing had happened.

"Be careful, Holt." Sheriff Foley sat and put up his feet. "The DEA has no jurisdiction in this case."

"All I'm going to do is talk to people." Since he'd resigned, Holt had no status with the DEA. He wouldn't disabuse the sheriff of his mistake. For the time being, his reputation as a government agent would serve his purpose. "Anything I learn I'll share with your office."

After Holt dropped Chris Hawke off at his law office in Rangewood, he stopped at the feed store for calf vitamins.

A man was loading grain sacks into the back of a jacked-up black pickup that might have been the one behind him earlier. If Rob's killer was still around, he might worry about Holt involving himself in the case. He parked beside the truck and eased out.

"Hey, Holt, you've been a stranger. Good to see you, man." It was Will Rafferty, Luke's brother and the manager of the Circle-S. He was as tall as Holt and a few years older. His powerful build reminded Holt of the man's steer wrestling days. A compassionate expression on his face, he slipped off his work gloves and stuck out a beefy hand.

Holt took it. "Good to see you, Will. Guess I've stuck to home since the funeral."

"How's that little nephew of yours?" Will leaned one elbow against the truck and slapped the grain dust from his gloves on the tailgate. "You managing okay? You must be now you have a house guest."

Holt forced back a groan. Didn't take long for Faith to tell her brother Maddy'd moved in. "Just fine now that Maddy's there." It had been only one day, so he wasn't lying.

Humor glimmered in the former bulldogger's eyes. He lowered one eyelid in a conspiratorial wink. "I reckon you're a lucky man as long as you two don't battle it out like the Hatfields and McCoys. Or maybe you've made up. How about it?"

"We grew up together. We're old friends. That's all." Old friends and old enemies and old...nothing, under a white-diaper flag of truce. So far.

Holt noticed for the first time the Circle-S brand logo on the side of the truck. Distinctive. If it was the same one from earlier, Will had spent an awful long time at the feed store. Had to have been some other black truck.

"If you folks want a break from diapers and formula, come on over. My sister wants time to get reacquainted with Maddy."

"How is Faith, anyway? She came to the funeral, but I didn't talk to her much." He pictured the brown-haired woman, once a champion barrel racer, now confined to a wheelchair after a horse fell on her, crushing her spine.

The other man shrugged. "She's mostly okay, but she hardly leaves the ranch. She does manage to organize the children's activities for the guests. We're all just grateful she's alive. She's using a walker a bit now. So that's progress."

"That accident was a terrible tragedy," Holt said.

For a few more minutes, they discussed their calf crops and the weather. Will slammed the tailgate, prepared to drive away. "I meant what I said, Holt, about coming over to the Circle-S anytime. Bring Maddy."

"Sure thing. You might as well know. I'm not entirely satisfied with Sheriff Foley's handling of my brother's case. I'd like to come talk to you about that day and about Rob."

"About Rob?" Will glanced away as he keyed the ignition. When his gaze again met Holt's, his expression was guarded. "I'll tell you whatever I can, but I don't know much."

Holt watched the truck vanish down the highway. Unease edged into suspicion. Will Rafferty would be the first rancher he'd question.

****

He punched in the number he'd been given. The phone rang once, twice, three times before someone picked up. He gave the coded Spanish words.

His employer's accented voice, when it came nerve-wracking moments later, rasped in his ear. "What news do you have for me?"

"He has a woman now. Been there about three days."

"That could be promising. Do not wait too long."

"Can't rush things. You said he wasn't to know for now. Making it look accidental requires planning and time." He knew his fuckin' job. He didn't like dealing long distance this way. The guy had a hell of a nerve.

"If you cannot accomplish a simple task, I will find someone who can. I want no more mistakes."

Adrenaline revved his pulse. He licked his lips. He knew what they'd done to the guy he'd replaced. Gutted like a brook trout wasn't the way he wanted to buy it. He wouldn't fail. "You won't need someone else, *señor*. I'll earn my money."

"See that you do so—and soon."

****

"Who? Whazzit?" Maddy's eyes wouldn't open, but she could see.

Rob stood outside the truck. Smooth-cheeked and slim in his charcoal wedding suit, he was the twenty-year-old boy she'd left at the altar standing beside his dad. He said nothing, a mournful expression on his usually cheerful face.

Her neck hurt. Sleeping in the back of her truck had contorted her to unnatural angles. She opened her mouth, but the air disappeared, forcing her to gasp like a fish on a line. Sweat beaded her brow, and her heart raced. After endless minutes, she managed to breathe, but terror engulfed her.

No, no! Go away! She clawed at the door handle, but her hand kept slipping away.

She screamed soundlessly. A siren rent the mist. Rob disintegrated into the darkness. Again the siren's shriek dragged her from her inertia. She fumbled again, but the door handle had morphed into a table lamp. She turned the button on its base.

The glare shocked her senses and illuminated reality. No car. She was in a king-size bed. Blinking against the grogginess that threatened to drag her back under, she sat up. A nightmare. Only a nightmare. Her clattering heartbeat slowed, and she sucked in air. Anguish wrenched a sob from deep in her soul. She dragged shaking fingers through her hair.

Finally the noise pierced her consciousness. No siren. Her alarm.

Bobby. Two in the morning. Bottle time. She pushed the button and forced herself to sit up. When she swung her feet to the carpet, her heel struck the book that had lulled her to sleep.

Baby's First Months. She'd found it in the bedside table her first night. Whoever had carted away Sara's and Rob's personal belongings and clothing had missed this valuable resource. It was her bible, her treasure, her mine of knowledge on baby care. With what she gleaned from its pages, she was impressing Holt with her expertise.

Then Bobby the foghorn cranked up an ear-splitting wail that was no dream.

"Coming, sweetie," she whispered. Her bare legs chilly beneath the sleep shirt, she padded to the door. Since the first night Holt had allowed her the privilege of feeding time and answering nocturnal sirens.

He avoided her as much as he could during the rest of the day too. Though Holt spent time with the baby, it wasn't in her presence. He trundled him out to the graveside or the barn, or he urged Maddy to saddle a horse and take off.

She needed to talk to Holt, to explain about Rob— at least in part—if he'd let her. Holt had once been her friend, and she was living in his house, caring for Rob's child. The absence of peace between them was too awkward, too agonizing. If she could manage her thoughts and feelings, she had to make him understand her desertion wasn't as hasty as it seemed. That he shouldered some of the blame didn't ease her guilt or make her proud, but it was a fact.

She arrived at the nursery door as Holt emerged with his sobbing nephew. The sight of the big man holding the tiny child melted her midsection. Barefoot, Holt wore faded jeans, aged to a softness that molded to horseman's strong thighs and lean hips. His chambray shirt hung untucked and unbuttoned. The sight drew her gaze more than did the furious infant.

Chapter Six

"ABOUT TIME YOU heard him." Holt jiggled his nephew. His thunderous gaze swept her scanty attire.

How dare he snipe at her for being two seconds late! She glared at him. "Bobby just started crying." But she discerned not disapproval but dismay, maybe at unwanted heat. Tough if he didn't approve. Tough if it turned him on. Tough that it turned her on. But pulling on more clothes would have delayed her even longer.

"We have to stop meeting like this," she quipped.

"I was already up." His jaw worked as he seemed to retrench. "Some folks say it spoils a baby to pick him up every time he cries. But he's so little." His expression relaxed as he turned his gaze to Bobby, who continued to fret.

"You can't spoil a young infant. Crying's the only way he has to communicate, and he needs the assurance that someone cares." Smiling, she silently blessed *Baby's First Months*—and Sara. "Besides, he's not so little. This pumpkin must weigh close to thirteen pounds. A bruiser, like the other Donovan men."

"Fourteen, according to Doc Warner today." Holt's grim mouth curved in a radiant smile that softened his harsh features. Love and pride in his nephew shone in that smile. His dedication to raising his nephew and maintaining the ranch made her wish he didn't resent her so much.

Her pulse skittered at his effect on her, and she took a step backward. She had to shake this attraction to Holt. She had nowhere to go yet that didn't involve a sleeping bag, and Holt needed— No, *Bobby* needed her.

She forced her gaze to the baby. "He's getting your shirt all wet. Give him here, and I'll change him."

Holt glanced at the stain spreading on his blue shirt. As if Bobby were a rain-slicked football, he handed off the soggy child. "I'll grab a dry shirt and get the bottle ready." Peeling off the offending garment, he stalked to his bedroom.

Enjoying the play of muscles in the departing male back, Maddy sighed. It didn't hurt to look. Stepping over the boundary Holt—and she, if she were truthful—had set could ignite the tinder of their chemistry into a wildfire. As it almost had eight years ago.

Bobby gulped a sob and blinked glistening eyes at Maddy. "A-aaga." He continued to squawk, but the screeching ceased.

"Guess he doesn't worry about me dropping you anymore. Come on, pumpkin. Auntie Maddy'll get you cleaned up and dry."

When she finished, she pulled on jeans beneath her sleep shirt before carrying Bobby, calmer but still sniffling, to the kitchen. Having his sleepy weight in her arms soothed her jangled nerves.

Clad in a tee shirt tucked into his jeans, Holt lounged against the counter. He watched the microwave as if it might float away without his stare to anchor it. "Be ready a minute."

"The microwave, just one way this house has changed," she said, noting alterations as she walked and rocked the baby. Gone was the boot-worn linoleum, replaced by the polished boards beneath it. A digital-control range with a smooth electric cook top instead of gas burners. Bright yellow curtains hung in the windows, and in the living room balloon-valanced burgundy draperies and a matching carpet. "Very classy. Rob's wife kept herself busy."

"I hardly know the old place. Rob took out an equity loan so Sara could fix up the house to her liking," he said without turning to face her. "There's more."

"The baby's room. Your old room. The master bedroom."

"Some of it's okay. Place needed a face-lift."

Because she noted disapproval edging his voice, she had to probe. "Sara wasn't from around here. Colorado Springs, right?"

He nodded. "The Pattersons moved here five years ago. Edgar Patterson's manager of the Valley Bank in Rangewood. Sara was a city girl. Like you. Rob wanted to please her."

He'd look at anything but her, would he? He spoke to her only when he had to and only about the baby. She longed to talk to him now about Rob. But how to begin? A glance at the dining table gave her an opener. On yellow sheets from a legal tablet she saw lists of names and a roughly sketched map of the area.

Not cattle records. He did that work on the computer in the office off the living room. What was he doing in the middle of the night?

Holt handed her the bottle and sat at the end of the table. When she settled the baby with the bottle, he said, "Chows down like a hungry calf. You'd think the way he's growing he'd adjust to the stuff by now."

She refused to keep to their single topic. "Holt, what

are you working on here?" She nodded toward the papers.

Elbows on the table, he propped his forehead on the heels of his hands. His expression, when he raised his eyes, was bleak. "I might as well tell you before you hear it from somewhere else, like the Raffertys." His brow-pleating glower expressed his reluctance to trust her with his secret.

"Dear God, what is it? The Pattersons haven't done something to take Bobby away this soon, have they?"

"It's not that." He shoved his fingers through his hair. "But I did get bad news from Chris Hawke today."

"Your attorney? Chris Hawke used to be pretty wild, tearing up the roads on his motorcycle. Didn't he spend the night in jail for pummeling a boy who insulted his sister?"

"That's Chris's old-fashioned sense of justice. These days he attacks legally."

"Then he must be a fierce defender for his friends."

One corner of Holt's mouth quirked in acknowledgment. "He said the custody case went to Judge Gilbert."

"That's bad?"

"Couldn't be worse. According to Chris, Gilbert's so conservative he thinks the only decent family consists of two parents—mom and dad, no single parents, no same-sex couples, God forbid—and two-point-five kids."

Maddy grinned. "Do you think Bobby qualifies as about a point-five?"

"Maybe Espie'd donate her two boys to make up the rest."

His deadpan expression stopped her for a moment.

Then the gleam in his startling blue eyes clued her that the man who never smiled had made a joke. She almost added a quip about Holt and her being the parents in this little equation. *Don't go there.* "But you were starting to tell me something else."

His jaw worked with the words before he could spit them out. "It's Rob and Sara. The crash. It was no accident."

"What do you mean?" Her stomach turned over, as if full of congealed, soured milk.

"Some bastard deliberately shot out the front tires on his pickup. That's what sent them over the cliff." Banked fury glowed in his eyes. "It was murder."

Maddy sat in stunned silence as he spelled out the whole story. How someone had lain in wait. The high-powered, high-tech rifle with exploding bullets. The sheriff's reluctance to call it murder. How Holt was conducting a private investigation.

Bobby finished the bottle, and Maddy turned him over her shoulder to pat his back. The perfunctory duty diffused her focus, but didn't ease her distress at what she'd heard. Tears burned, but she blinked them back. "Why would someone kill Rob and Sara? Murder. It makes no sense."

"Lack of a motive is the biggest roadblock. I've talked to some of the townspeople already. The only motive I can imagine is Rob's temper."

"Quick to explode and quick to fizzle."

"I thought he might have had a run-in with some cowboy who held a grudge." He sagged in the chair. "But I've found nothing so far. Thought I'd visit the Circle-S. Have a talk with Will. Or one of the hands there might know something."

Murder. The idea made the loss new again. She reeled with the horror of it and fisted her hands behind Bobby's back. He whimpered at the pressure, and she forced herself to relax. "I've done a little investigative reporting. I have a pretty good sense of people. I could go with you."

He made no comment on her offer. Some things he seemed to need time to accept. "Will's busy with the first guests of the season. Maybe later this week. There's some other ranches to visit first." He pointed to his map. "I've gone over the scene of the crime and made lists of everyone Rob knew and everyone around who uses that road regularly."

"Could it be someone you know?"

"No telling. It occurred to me the killer might have shot the wrong person."

An idea straightened her shoulders. "What if someone else has a truck like Rob's? What if that was the reason? Someone else could still be in danger."

The baby produced a loud belch.

"Good boy." Maddy cuddled him and rocked. "Now maybe he'll go back to sleep."

"I don't think the sheriff's thought of it being the wrong vehicle." Holt scribbled the word *truck*. He circled it. "Thanks. It's worth checking out."

Her eyes stung again and her chest ached. Feeling the drowsing little one in her lap only served to heighten the tragedy. She had to help if Holt would let her. "Do you have photographs of the accident scene?"

"Sheriff does. Won't give them to me. Says it's police business, not DEA. I should keep out of the case. Butt out, in other words."

"Do the photos show where the shooter was in

relation to the truck? Or what view the shooter had?"

He looked up from his notes. "They don't show much. Reckon I've been so overwrought about the whole damn affair I haven't been much of a detective. What are you getting at?"

"I'm not sure exactly. I could take more pictures if you like. Of course I have no equipment other than my cameras and my laptop."

"You're talking about digital pictures?"

She nodded. "I generally use digital. My Nikon has twenty-four mega pixels. That would give us sharp enough resolution. I can format the images on my laptop but I have no printing equipment. We'd need cutting edge, not a drugstore printer."

"I know a place in the county seat, a lab that might do the printing."

There, a conversation between old friends working together. Warmth wrapped comforting arms around her. Then the topic of the conversation folded the shutter on her pleasure. Photographing the place where Rob and Sara were killed.

"Okay. Let me put Bobby in his crib." She padded to the nursery. The infant didn't wake as she laid him on his back. "Don't worry, pumpkin. You're safe and loved." She whispered it as a prayer and wiped her eyes.

When she returned to sit at the table, she felt Holt's scrutinizing gaze as a physical touch. His eyes, hooded and brooding, held her. Intense alertness and edgy violence in every taut muscle.

"Some son of a bitch took the last members of our family from me and Bobby. I aim to make him pay. I appreciate any help you want to give." He shot to his feet and turned away from her. "Bobby could have been with them. He could have ended up at the bottom of that steep slope."

His gruff words branded her brain. Grisly images of what such a crash could do to a tender little body razored pain through her. "Holt, don't play what if. It gets you nowhere. I should know. Rob and Sara are…gone, but their son is alive."

"Do you sit by his grave every day for Bobby's sake? Or to ease your conscience?"

The comment made her wince. She had to say it now, while he wasn't looking at her. "I did love Rob. I—"

"Not enough, I reckon."

"He was my best friend. I wasn't *in* love with him and I couldn't marry him. I handled things the worst possible way, I admit. I panicked and ran. I never intended to hurt him."

"You know what they say about good intentions."

His harsh tone rasped like a file over her raw nerves. She forced herself to continue. "As the wedding came closer and closer, I knew what we had wasn't magical, romantic, or the thrilling rush it should be. I worried it wasn't a lifetime thing."

"He loved you that way." His wide shoulders rigid, he kept his back to her.

She wouldn't argue the point. "I don't know, but he got over me. Wasn't he happy with Sara?"

He pivoted to face her, his jaw set. "Have you seen any pictures of Sara?"

What? She couldn't divine what he was getting at. She nodded slowly. "The wedding portrait. What does that have to do with anything?"

His long legs ate up the short distance to the living

room and back. He slapped the framed photograph on the table before her. "Take a good look."

Sara Patterson Donovan was several years younger than Rob. The photographer had posed them standing facing each other, her cheek to his chin. Straight blond hair draped her slim shoulders and fanned down her back.

What she saw slapped her hard. She pushed away from the table and stood. "No!"

"Oh, yeah, baby." Holt grabbed her shoulders and forced her to face the picture. "Sara looks—*looked* a lot like you. As soon as the Pattersons moved to Rangewood, Rob went after her."

"No, no..." She couldn't bear it. There must be some other explanation. "You can't be right. Rob just liked blondes." She tried to pull away, but the photograph, more than Holt's firm grasp, held her in place.

With her back flush against his hard torso, his rumble of skepticism vibrated along her spine. His puff of breath warmed the top of her head. "She was a city girl like you. Used to a soft life. Used to luxury."

Through her thin shirt, his body heat seeped into her flesh. Her shallow breaths absorbed his scent, a mingling of soap and sun-warmed skin and leather. His hardness pressed against her spine, coaxing warmth in her belly. Taken aback, she fought the sensual charge. She closed her eyes against him and the smiling newlyweds in the portrait.

He tightened his grip on her shoulders, and his mouth brushed her hair. Holt sucked in a breath, and with a growl turned away.

"Rob gave Sara everything she wanted." He said it

with such bitterness, he might be describing Maddy. "Went into debt. Even talked me into cosigning. I thought it was for repairs to the barn. I didn't find out what he'd done until I came home. He added eight feet to the house to create that humongous bedroom and bathroom you're in, but ran out of money before they could put in a hot tub. All those luxuries for her, and he neglected the ranch for fear she'd leave. Like you."

Her throat tightened. When would he ever let up on her? "Like me? Or like your mother?"

He flinched as if a dozen flashbulbs had exploded in his face.

She instantly regretted her cruel words, but she couldn't back down now. "I refuse to take the blame because Rob wanted to make his wife comfortable."

A muscle leaped in his jaw. He bit out his next words through lips white with rage. "He nearly buried the ranch in debt for fear she'd leave for greener pastures—like you did."

A heavy knot clamped Maddy's chest so she could barely breathe. No, he couldn't heap all the blame on her head alone. She wouldn't let him. "We both know why I had to leave when I did. We need to talk about it so we can move on. So *you* can move on. You're fooling yourself if you think I was running away from *Rob*."

"Maybe. What I know is you *did* run away." With that, he marched into his room. The quiet click of the door latch tolled a louder knell than a slam.

Left unsaid was what he was thinking—*and you would run away again.*

Was he right? Would she? But no answer came into focus.

Chapter Seven

TWO DAYS LATER, Holt grabbed a morning mug of coffee and one of Espie's sweet rolls on his way to the door. He made it outside before Maddy appeared in the kitchen. Work helped him avoid her most of every day, but dammit he still needed to clear his brain after every encounter.

And before. Today he'd have to leave Bronc watching over the sickly calves and mending the corral fence. He and Maddy were heading out to visit some local ranchers. No social calls. This was investigation to find out who had harbored a grudge against Rob, who might've wanted him dead.

By eight o'clock, he'd had a real breakfast and they were on the road with Bobby in his car seat behind Maddy. "First ranch is a ways south of Rangewood. Greg Harper was high-school quarterback when I was a freshman. Married Irene Ingraham in my class. They took over the Double-X when his parents moved to Sonoma. Greg should be waiting for me. Us." He'd phoned yesterday to ask if they could stop by.

Ensconced in the pickup's passenger seat, Maddy nodded, then chattered away about the greening hillsides and distant views of cattle grazing.

"You always so chirpy about ordinary stuff?" He didn't mean to sound so gruff but hell, the woman got to him.

She cocked her head and eyed him for a moment. Instead of blasting him for being so sour, she smiled. A sort of wistful smile that made him feel like shit on a boot heel for sniping at her. "I don't usually get to experience what you call ordinary stuff. Instead of peaceful hillsides, I see bombed out villages or bunkers bristling with big guns. Instead of huge herds of fat steers grazing in lush pastures, I see a few scrawny cattle with skeletal ribs being herded by ragged children through parched scrub. Instead of—"

"Enough. I get the picture."

"The picture?" She chuckled, a trill like a spring brook. "Holt Donovan, was that a joke?"

Hell, no, but he'd never admit it. "There's the Double-X up ahead."

Thank God she let the subject drop and peered ahead, at the big sign announcing the home of prize-winning Herefords, and beyond, at the stone-fronted ranch house with the wrap-around porch.

He, on the other hand, needed to concentrate on something other than Maddy.

Why had he gone on the attack again? Not as bad as the other day when he'd pounced like a cougar on a stray calf. All because Rob couldn't let go. Every time Holt had come home, he watched his brother obsess about turning another woman into Madelyn McCoy. But how much of that was her fault? Hell, she hadn't known how Rob felt. Hadn't known how absorbed he'd been in the ideal Maddy, all in his head, not the flesh-and-blood Maddy beside Holt in the truck.

Holt had witnessed the disbelief in her eyes when he told her about Sara. Maddy'd gone jet-setting and taking her pictures all over the damned world and left them—

not them, Rob—and any regrets behind. Maybe jet-setting wasn't the right term but it amounted to the same thing. She left.

But his temper didn't explain his behavior. What did was his fascination with her. With her maternal care for the baby. With her boldness and quick energy. And with her sexy body. Hell, he kept picturing her in that skimpy nightshirt. And out of it.

When he'd held her, her slender form tight against him, his body detonated with fireworks he hadn't experienced in years. The flowery fragrance of her corn-silk hair clouded his brain and shot all his blood south.

She wasn't immune to him either. Her breath caught and she curled into him. He needed to ditch all emotion where she was concerned and focus on Bobby and finding his parents' murderer. He'd asked Maddy to join him today because she provided a trained pair of eyes and ears. Nothing more. Today's visits would be all business.

If he had to grit his teeth to ignore her softness and womanly scent beside him to make it work, he'd do it or break a tooth trying.

"Howdy, Donovan. It's been way too long." Greg Harper greeted him with a big smile in his sun-creased face and an outstretched hand. These days, the former football star's belly was bigger than his shoulders.

They shook hands and clapped each other on the back while Maddy extricated the baby from his car seat. Bobby waved his arms and babbled with glee at being freed and out with the grownups.

The rancher's wife skipped down the porch steps and gave Holt a hug. Her freckled face beneath a mane of auburn hair was unlined. No longer a slim high-school girl, but sturdy and strong as befit ranch life.

"Irene, you haven't changed a bit." He held her away from him. "Still as pretty as when you were leading cheers. You still barrel racing?"

"Not me," the woman replied. "But you should see our daughter Ginny's blue ribbons."

Holt itched to get to the point but forced himself to make small talk, introducing Maddy and the baby. "Maddy's a family...friend. She's staying awhile to help out with little Bobby. Like a nanny, sort of."

Shit, that sounded lame. He could see amusement in Maddy's wry expression. He figured Irene knew about Maddy and Rob but she said nothing.

The Harpers cooed over Bobby, and Irene dabbed at her eyes. "Such a tragedy for this poor little one," she said. "Thank God you're here for him."

Nice segue into where Holt wanted to go. He readied his opening as the Harpers invited him and Maddy into the house for lemonade and Irene's homemade gingersnaps. But once they were all settled in the kitchen around the trestle table, he felt awkward about his purpose in the midst of such hospitality. The Harpers didn't make it easier, waiting quietly with their frosty glasses.

"Mighty good cookies, Irene." Maddy bounced Bobby on her knee. "We, um, Holt didn't expect you'd go to such trouble. Right, Holt?" Her gaze worked like a cattle prod to spur him to action.

"Right. Thanks, Irene." He jammed his hat on his knee and set down his glass. "You folks are right. Rob's and Sara's deaths are a tragedy. But not an accident."

Greg's glass stopped halfway to his mouth. "What are you saying? I thought it was a blown tire from a stray bullet."

Holt sketched out what he knew about the crash, explained he was supplementing the sheriff's overstretched office, and eased into his purpose for visiting. He stressed he was talking to all the ranchers so the Harpers didn't take his questions as accusations.

While he talked, half of his awareness was on Maddy as she rocked Bobby in her lap. A set of colorful plastic keys held the baby's gaze. Having her present seemed to soften the purpose of the visit so these folks didn't feel threatened.

"Murder," Irene murmured, her eyes wide, when he finished.

"Do you know of anybody who had a grudge against my brother or his wife? Maybe one of your hands had a run-in with Rob?" Holt gripped his hat so tightly against his knee he crushed the crown. He smoothed it and pulled a notepad and a pen from his shirt pocket.

"A grudge? For goodness sakes, no. Two young people in love, with a baby?" She shook her head in vigorous denial such an evil deed was possible.

Greg's expression was more circumspect. "I don't know of anything specific, but now and again I heard talk of Rob's short fuse causing rifts."

"Like what exactly?"

As if feeling the tension in his uncle, Bobby began to fuss. Irene took the squirming infant, and the change immediately quieted him. He cooed at the new person holding him.

"Was it about the ranch?" Maddy asked softly. "Or more about his wife?"

"Rob was very protective of Sara," Greg said, his words measured. "He hovered. Kept the reins tight whenever they went out. Didn't like it when other guys talked to her. Like that. I can see where his over-protectiveness could've riled a few."

Holt glanced at Maddy with new eyes. He'd asked her along as another set of eyes and ears but didn't count on such insight. Having a partner in this mess felt good. But it was business, only business. Maybe if he reminded himself often enough, he might actually believe it.

Irene huffed. "Over-protectiveness? Not exactly. More like jealousy and control. Sara was a meek little thing. She didn't seem to mind Rob's hovering, but maybe she would have down the road. I liked him, but he needed to learn that wives are partners, not pets."

****

Shivering in the dawn chill, Holt traipsed to the barn. Fog spirits hovered above the pond, but the rising sun would soon banish them. Mares' tails over the mountains predicted showers. With May's advent, April's wet snows on these high valleys yielded to rain.

He heard Bronc's drawl before he saw him. "You put the lie to all those stories about taciturn cowboys. You ever shut up?"

The old wrangler poked his head above the second stall, where he was saddling Quickstep, the roan gelding. "Horses like it. Calms 'em down. I tell 'em about where we're goin'. Up to the northwest fence line, if that's okay with the boss." Accustomed to Holt's teasing, he offered a toothy grin.

"Sounds like a plan."

"You have any luck the other day talking to the neighbors?"

"Not much. Only verification of what I already knew. Rob had a temper that might've riled somebody.

71

Who that somebody was is still a mystery. All three ranch owners promised to ask their cowboys if any of them had a run-in with him."

He didn't hold out much hope. Sure hadn't heard a word in the two days since the marathon drive. Who would admit a dispute and heap suspicion on his own head? The only possibility as he saw it was if a cowboy knew of another's argument with Rob.

Rob's jealousy and protectiveness were news but no shock. No wonder, given his history of obsession with Maddy. How Sara had responded bore looking into further, even if she'd seemed passive. Could the new mother have rebelled, maybe with another guy? He hoped to hell not and put the notion out of his head in favor of physical chores.

"I can muck out the horse stalls and tend the other critters," he said.

Finished saddling up, Bronc let the other three horses into the back corral. "These stalls can wait, but the cattle won't. I'll help with the calves afore I mount up." A sly look quirked his mouth. "Espie shooed Maddy outside to ride fence with me. She was good company. You want me to fetch her to help you out?"

"Not what that pampered female signed on to do. She's tending to Bobby today." Grateful for chores that kept his mind and body busy, Holt strode outside to the sheltered pen where the sickly calves and new moms were isolated.

What was he going to do about Maddy? He ought to send her packing, but he couldn't. Bobby needed her. And she was proving to be an asset in his search for the murderer. Why couldn't he just treat her like hired help?

Shit, he knew damned well why. He wanted her

more than he'd ever wanted a woman before. He was as bad as Rob. What stopped him from taking her to his bed was the knowledge she'd take off at any time. He wanted no woman he couldn't rely on. Enough. He splashed water from the faucet on his face.

"You workin' up a sweat already, boy?" Bronc chuckled as he tugged one of the calves toward him.

"Just getting warmed up." So much for keeping his brain occupied with chores. "Two of these Hereford babies look more alert." They had to watch the newborns closely. Diarrhea could kill a calf in a matter of hours.

"Yup, their backsides are clean. The meds are beatin' the scours." Bronc sent them with their moms to the common pen.

Afterward, the hired man led his mount out of the barn. As he trotted away, Holt heard him discussing the sunrise with the horse.

On a sigh, he ordered himself to ease up on Maddy. He had to give her credit for pitching in. Besides riding with Bronc, Maddy helped with tagging the calves. Maybe she wasn't as pampered as he expected or as he claimed to one and all. He just had to keep his distance. His participation in her betrayal of Rob didn't exonerate her one whit. Having her here only reminded him of that night. He wouldn't trust her or let himself depend on her. If an impulse brought her here, another would take her away.

And the mysteries about Maddy bothered him.

Like how come a big-time photographer could afford to hang out indefinitely in the mountains of Colorado? She remarked in an offhand way the other day that she'd talked to her agent. That made sense, but she was hiding something. Made him want to protect her, dammit.

For a man who'd left official inquiries behind with the DEA, he was up to his hat band in two unofficial ones. Sorting out Maddy's mysteries was creeping up a close second to solving Rob's murder. Tough part in the meantime was dousing his hots for her.

He worked his jaw to loosen the cramping muscle there. Then he started on the next chore of making sure the penned-up animals had plenty of hay and water before he headed inside to clean the stalls.

****

"Here you go, Bobby. It's all right, love." Maddy stopped his squalling with the bottle. She sighed with the return of peace and strolled to the nursery window with the infant in her arms. Bobby guzzled his meal noisily, his chubby fingers curled into fists.

Caring for him gave her joy, and she amused herself by snapping pictures with her Nikon—frames of him, of Bronc mending fence, of the wobbly calves, of the surrounding mountains, of the lonely family graves, everything. What she wouldn't give for a darkroom.

The days passed easily enough, but it was false security.

When Bobby finished the bottle, she walked to the kitchen with him at her shoulder. She patted his back to coax a burp from his tummy. "Attaboy. You like that stuff now, don't you, pumpkin?"

She cuddled him, absorbing his sweet scent, then bundled him into a blue footed romper and a quilted red jacket with a matching cap. Her denim jacket over her favorite Guatemalan shirt and she was ready. Carrying Bobby in his infant seat, she strolled out to the barn.

"I'll bet the stalls need cleaning. Do you think the

horses need fresh hay? Maybe some oats?"

His fist in his mouth, Bobby replied, "B-b-brt." He waved his chubby hands as if cheering her on.

Once inside, the massive barn intoxicated her. In the low light of the bare overhead bulbs, the old wood of the stalls and posts gleamed like a sorrel cow pony's coat. The crisp, cold air wrinkled her nose. Tangy scents of horses, grain, and leather threaded the air.

On the roof, old shingles sagged like molting feathers, but inside new boards stood out among the old. New slats on the stalls. A new beam. In his eagerness to pretty up the house, Rob had let more important things go, so Holt had to pay for the neglect. That explained the lack of funds to hire a real nanny.

"Eau de manure. No one has touched those stalls this morning." She set the infant seat securely on two bales. Hay crunched beneath her boots as she tucked a yellow blanket around Bobby's feet. "You like me talking to you this way, don't you, pumpkin? Unless Espie's here, you're the only one I have to discuss things with. Your uncle Holt sure avoids my company like I'm contagious."

Bobby's bright blue eyes followed her smallest movement with apparent fascination. "Ga-ah," he said in rebuke of his uncle.

She couldn't stay much longer, but she couldn't leave without transportation. And Bobby needed her. She gazed out the barn door at the distant solid presence of Pikes Peak, its bare crest the only gray eminence she could consult. "I wish you could tell me what to do."

Like tell Holt about her real reasons for staying so long. Keeping her secrets made sense at first, but ten days later, disclosure seemed awkward and deceptive.

And Holt had too much to deal with. Helping him solve Rob's murder was the least she could do until her next contract forced her to leave.

Leave Holt. And Bobby.

A stony ache gripped her. What about her tenuous relationship with Holt? For days he'd avoided her even more than before. Their awkward midnight encounter had scared him off. Her too. If she and Holt gave in to the heat sizzling between them, he would feel like a traitor and hate himself. He'd hate her more. Then she'd have no choice but to leave.

After donning work gloves, she snatched the manure fork from its hook and jabbed up the first load of urine and manure-soaked wood chips and hay. "Bobby, would you like to hear about the last time I rode a horse?"

She glanced back in time to see a toothless yawn.

Smiling, she carried on with both the chore and the story. "It was on Easter Island. I know you've probably never heard of it, but it's wa-a-ay out in the ocean. A fascinating place with enormous statues I can't begin to describe without a camera." She delivered another malodorous scoop to the wheelbarrow. One stall down. She wheeled the barrow to the next. "A documentary company was doing a video about how the ancient islanders might have moved their huge statues around the island."

"I'll bet they didn't move them on horseback."

Chapter Eight

ONE ELBOW PROPPED against the rough boards, Holt leaned against the wall beside Bobby. He grinned as Maddy whirled around.

She immediately diverted her gaze from him. With what looked like forced nonchalance, she returned to her chore. "Easter Island horses are famous, but no. My ride was a way to take stills before they started filming. Some of those statues are remote. Three of us spent five days trekking and camping."

"Roughing it?" No more being stuck like a burr on a saddle blanket about her luxury-filled life. Well, most of the time. Admiration for her putting up with deprivations for her work was nibbling away at his skepticism.

"Depends on your point of view." She gazed at dust motes in the air. "High cliffs overlooking the Pacific. Wide, windswept rolling hills. The only way to understand the power of those incredible statues is to be there. I think my pictures come closer than words to conveying their beauty."

Or yours as you talk about them. He levered away from the wall to help out. As she described setting up camp in the shadows of the stone statues, her eyes shone. Man, she loved the photography, the adventure of it all.

Maybe it wasn't the jet-set life he'd imagined— though the call of the road would keep her on the move.

She was a nomad.

He'd stood in the shadows watching her before he spoke up. Watching her vigor as she slung manure. Wondering if he could ask her about all those incongruities that puzzled him. He couldn't grill her. He needed her to stay. Bobby needed her. Push her too hard, and she'd run for sure. He didn't like the hollow feeling that idea caused.

He wheeled the barrow out and dumped it, then brought in clean shavings from the storage shed. Cedar scent mingled with other barn odors as the two of them shoveled chips and forked hay onto the stall floors. He added oats to the feed, then stowed the shovels.

Procrastinating, for damn sure. Stud poker was his favorite game. A man should have most of his cards face up on the table, not close to the vest like in draw. He had to lay one card down. Saying his piece upped the ante between them, but it was the right thing to do.

"Look, Maddy. About the other night." He shoved his hands in his jean pockets. "I came on awful strong. I was too hard on you. And—"

"It's okay. I understand. You were right about Rob's obsession. The perfume convinced me."

"Perfume?"

"Sara's perfume. I found it in the hall bathroom that first day and dabbed on a little."

"The Pattersons cleaned out the master bath, and I did that one before I stowed my stuff. Reckon I missed the perfume. What about it?"

"Rob first bought it for me. He insisted I wear it whenever we went out. He must have bought it for Sara." Her mouth thinned as her lips compressed. Emotion glimmered in her eyes. "That scent might also be the

78

reason Bobby quieted in my arms. Mom's familiar smell."

At the notion Rob had asked his wife to wear a former girlfriend's scent, Holt's insides twisted. *Don't even think about it.* He wanted nothing more to scar the image of his little brother. Better to change the topic.

"You've been to some exotic and exciting places. The Valley-D must seem as quiet as the underside of a rock." He ignored the twist in his gut as he waited for her answer.

"Quiet is underrated, if you ask me. You can find adventure anywhere, if you know how to look." She replaced the big fork on its hook, then knelt beside the dozy baby. "Hearing this one's laughter at a curious calf is exciting enough for me."

He grunted his doubt as he ambled to her side. "Still, mighty tame for someone who's seen Easter Island or hiked the Andes."

She stood and turned to face him, arms propped on her hips, a grin curving her lips. "Why Holt Donovan, you read one of my articles."

"Rob had the magazine around. I was curious." He swallowed. Hard. Picked up her scent. If that was the perfume Rob had bought both women, the fragrance ought to remind him to keep his distance. Instead the smell of lavender drew him closer.

"Curious?"

"Wanted to see where that camera took you. That's all."

The grin eased to a softer, dreamy smile. "I've trekked in big utilities, on foot with llamas, and on donkeys and horseback. I've visited ancient Chachapoya ruins on the Huabayacu River in Peru and villages of the

Tharu people in southern Nepal, but nowhere was more spectacular than these Colorado peaks and mountain valleys. The trips I cherish most are the horse camping weekends we did when we were kids. Like the time you and Rob and I spent the night on Ghost Mountain."

He gazed at the rafters. And away from Maddy. "We raced our ponies the length of the meadow there by Ghost Creek."

"And you two shot rabbits for our supper."

"*Our* supper?" Her comment brought his gaze back to her. A mistake. She was close enough for him to see flecks of gold in the violet of her irises. "You refused to eat the 'poor little bunnies.' "

Her lower lip formed a tasty-looking pout. "They were so adorable. And Espie had packed us a perfectly good supper."

"Ham sandwiches. And piglets aren't adorable?"

"It's not the same thing. I didn't see them hopping around in the meadow." She smiled at her own absurdity.

He ought to back up, not stand so close, but the warmth in her eyes rooted him to the barn floor. "That why you tried to shove me down that old mine shaft the next morning?"

"Shove you?" Maddy poked his chest. "No way, José. You insisted on protecting us by going ahead and playing intrepid scout."

Her nails were serviceably short, but the indignant index finger prodding him provoked a lower-body reaction. Not a good idea. He wrapped a hand around the offending digit. Her skin was soft and warm, and instead of yanking her hand away from his dented pecs, he held on. "Maddy."

Her hand relaxed as she flattened it against his belly.

In response his heart thumped like a bass drum. "You wearing that perfume?"

"Not since I realized what Rob did. This is just shampoo and soap." She bowed her head and drew a deep breath before raising her gaze to his. "Look, you apologized about the other night. We covered my travels and old times, but what we need to talk about is the elephant in the room."

He felt like she'd doused him with ice water. "What do you mean?" As if he didn't know. Hell, it was time. Years past time.

"If I'm to stick around for a while to care for Bobby, I need peace between us about that *other* night."

He swallowed. "All right. What do you want me to say?"

"I don't need another apology, if that's what you think. I just want you to admit you were right there with me. We *both* betrayed Rob the eve of the wedding." Her jaw was set, and her eyes gleamed with determination.

Holt stepped back. He cast an eye at Bobby, who was drifting to sleep. No help there.

The memory swamped him, as it did nearly every time he looked at Maddy. Shit, or thought about Maddy.

Rob and Maddy's wedding rehearsal dinner had been at Duke's Lake Resort. The beer and congratulatory toasts had flowed freely, and both Rob and he were awash. After Rob took a swing at one of the waiters, Holt slung him over his shoulder. With Maddy's help, he lugged him outside and left him to sleep it off in the truck bed.

Holt and Maddy meandered down to the summer house on the lake shore. They talked and danced to the distant strains of the DJ's tunes. All summer he'd been aware of her—those long, long legs and the taut body. All too apparent she wasn't his little buddy any more. But he'd ignored his hormones and fought the attraction because she was Rob's fiancée. His brother's wife-to-be.

Until that night. He held her in his arms and swayed to the music. She wore some filmy, tiny-strapped sundress that shimmied against her body. The dress and she drove him nuts. The beer and the music and her scent—the scent Rob had chosen—had drowned his willpower.

He scrubbed his jaw with his knuckles. "I was just talking while we danced. I wasn't coming on to you. It was you. You were the one who kissed me."

"If that's what you prefer to remember, no wonder you don't admit to your share in the evening." She took a hip-sprung stance and glared at him.

"So you figure I kissed you first? Care for a demonstration?" He stepped closer again and yanked her against him. He was playing with fire, but he no longer cared. She'd riled his temper and his libido. The fire raged inside him, too hot to control.

"Neither of us kissed first. The kiss just…happened. We were dancing one minute and kissing the next." Her slender arms wound around his waist as though they belonged there. He'd felt that same sensation back then.

"With my brother, your fiancé, sleeping it off not thirty yards away." He nearly growled.

She heaved a sigh that pressed her soft breasts against him. How could she miss his arousal? "You idiot, we kissed, yes. A hell of a kiss. It was the final straw for me. After that I knew I couldn't go through with the wedding. I'd been fretting about it for weeks, postponing a decision, putting off telling Rob my misgivings. I was caught up in all the wedding festivities and ignored my instincts.

"But, Holt, after all, it was *only a kiss*. Nothing else happened. We didn't have sex. I didn't have so much to drink that I don't remember. What I truly regret is running away the way I did. Leaving a note. So inadequate. So immature."

Hell. The truth of what had gone down that night finally pulled him up to the surface after years of drowning in recriminations. He'd been blaming her to avoid his own part in it. She'd still been a kid, while he'd been a man. He sailed his hands down her slim back. She was warm and curvier than that kid. And his craving for her raced way past that long-ago encounter, closer to desperate.

"Maddy, you're right. The kiss was both our faults. But it wasn't as innocent as you imply. Hell, if that gang of rowdy kids hadn't come along, I'd have wanted to do a whole lot more than kissing." Like now, for instance.

Her gaze landed on his mouth, softened. Violet irises darkened to plum. "You would?"

She wanted him too.

The fire raging in him billowed. He lowered his head and brushed his lips on hers. Bad idea. The worst. The best.

At the exquisite softness, sweet desire surged through him. He felt her sigh, a small puff of warm breath against his mouth, and when she opened to his tongue, blood thundered in his head. Releasing her hand, he pulled her against his chest and deepened the kiss.

Inexorably, the sensations of her touch rippled through him, explored, enveloped. He hardened with an ache beyond casual. She was the wrong woman, a woman not to be trusted. She wouldn't stay. A heartbreaker. At this moment, he didn't care. He craved this taste of her.

He cupped her breast. The bright orange flowers sewn on the cotton had pulled his gaze to where her nipples might be, but now he wanted the layers of shirt and bra gone.

Her breath came warm and sweet against his mouth, and not a sigh and not to say no. She whispered his name. "Holt, I—"

"Oh! I *beg* your *pardon.*"

Holt and Maddy leaped apart as if kicked by a horse.

In the doorway stood two women. Someone might have to pry Phyllis Patterson's jaw off the barn floor before she could talk again. The younger, bird-like woman carrying a briefcase pursed her lips in an expression as severe as her black hair.

Since there was nowhere to hide, he snatched Bobby into his arms, letting the dangling blanket cover his unrepentant arousal. The baby woke, but didn't fuss. Ripples of lava still sluiced through Holt's veins as the clouds cleared from his brain. Shit, the judge's custody evaluator. Why was she here an hour earlier than the appointment?

A smiling Maddy strode to the women, her hand out as she introduced herself. "To what do we owe the pleasure of this visit?" she asked without a trace of sarcasm.

Thank God she found her voice first. He wasn't sure he could talk above a strangled gasp. His pulse thundered in his ears so loud he couldn't hear what the women had replied.

"Holt, this is Dr. Olympia Lombard." Maddy herded

the two women closer. "She's the custody evaluator assigned by the judge."

Phyllis patted her tightly permed hair, a smug twist to her mouth. "Since Dr. Lombard didn't know where the ranch was, I volunteered to show her the way for your appointment."

Show her the way in more ways than one. Get her digs and bias set firmly in the woman's mind before she met Holt.

"Mrs. Patterson," Maddy said, "You have my sympathies for losing your daughter. Such a tragedy."

Phyllis pulled out a tissue and dabbed at her eyes. "Thank you. She was our youngest, and Bobby's our youngest grandchild. I want the best for him."

Holt had heard all this before, had seen Phyllis crank up the waterworks at will.

"Naturally," Maddy said, then gave him a look that meant the ball was in his court.

He turned to the evaluator. "I was expecting you," he rasped out, emphasizing the last word. He sure as hell hadn't expected Phyllis. He'd bet his next hay crop the early arrival was her idea. A hell of a surprise, for both parties. "Sorry I wasn't at the house to greet you. *Dr.* Lombard? What kind of doctor?"

"Clinical psychologist, Mr. Donovan." Lombard spoke in a smooth, musical voice that was probably soothing to her patients. Not to him. Her high-collared business suit gave him an inkling she was as conservative as the judge. "I've been asked to evaluate the fitness of both parties for custody of this baby. I assume this is Robert Trask Donovan."

"Junior," Maddy added in a too-cheery chirp.

"I thought I advised you against bringing a

vulnerable infant out to this germ-laden barn. All these dirty animals." Phyllis glared down her narrow nose and pulled her green corduroy coat tighter around her. No animals dirty or clean charged into the barn to attack her with dirt and germs.

"Bobby's perfectly safe out here, Mrs. Patterson." Maddy reached for the baby.

Holt hung on, gave her a small shake of his head. The last minutes had doused his arousal, but he'd still protect Bobby from these intruders. "Four generations of Donovans have been raised in and around this barn. Kids used to bein' around animals and a little dirt don't get sick as much as antiseptic kids. The boy's fine. Perfect."

Lombard scribbled notes on a small leather-bound notepad. "Shall we go in the house, Mr. Donovan? I'd like to ask you questions about yourself, the home environment you offer your nephew, and the...caretaker you've provided for him."

"I'll toddle along and leave you folks to your interview." Phyllis sidled toward the door. "Judging from what I just witnessed, I wonder what *influences* this *poor innocent* might be subject to. This *is* a bachelor household, after all." She waited, eyes narrowed.

Silence fell like a sack of grain.

Holt waited for some rebuttal to rise in his brain. How could he deny what they saw? The pair had walked in on them nearly swallowing each other. In another minute, he'd have had Maddy's shirt off. He hadn't been involved with anyone for some time, but deprivation was no excuse where Bobby's welfare was concerned.

Olympia Lombard, aptly named for one who would deliver judgments from on high, stood pencil poised, dark eyes glittering with expectation and mouth pursed in disapproval.

Maddy slid her arm around Holt and snuggled close to him. She beamed a smile that nearly toppled him like a buzz-sawed tree. "Oh, but it won't be a bachelor household for long. Holt and I are engaged."

Chapter Nine

MADDY HELD HER breath for the explosion she could feel stiffening Holt's body like fizzing dynamite. She braced herself, but no blast came.

The psychologist was smiling. Aha, the reason Holt merely swallowed. Hard. And kissed Maddy's temple. Phyllis Patterson, on the other hand, would implode if her narrow features pinched any tighter.

He continued to stand there mute, his arms tight around the baby. She'd get more help from a stone statue.

In lieu of a cattle prod, she dug her thumb into his side. "Well, let's go into the house. We don't want to waste the good doctor's time, do we, *honey*?"

He sucked in a breath. "Sure, good idea. We can do the interview inside."

Maddy grabbed the infant seat and led the way. She'd have to nail Holt later on why he hadn't mentioned this appointment. Her heart galloped. What would the evaluator report to the judge? And Phyllis, what would she think? She didn't leave as she'd indicated, not after Maddy's impulsive announcement. She trooped inside the kitchen with them.

Holt secured the baby in his seat, and Maddy fetched his key ring toy, which Bobby promptly jammed in his mouth.

"If you don't mind, Mr. Donovan," Dr. Lombard said, surveying the kitchen with a sharp eye. "I'd like to see the house first. The baby's room and yours, and the living room."

"I'll stay here with Bobby," Maddy said. She needed a breather.

She brewed coffee, decaf because no one needed the jolt of caffeine. Then she sat and played peek-a-boo with Bobby while Holt conducted the tour. She couldn't discern the words from the deep rumbling of his voice, now modulated, no longer strangled with shock. Interspersed were murmurs and questions in the psychologist's smooth voice. And disdainful *humphs* from Phyllis Patterson. Probably doing the white-glove test on the furniture and window ledges. When they finished with the downstairs, Dr. Lombard pointed to the drop-down door for the attic. The attic? What did she think might be hidden up there—a gambling casino? Drugs? Terrorists?

When Holt brought the women back to the kitchen, Maddy set out a plate of Espie's sugar cookies and poured coffee. She crossed her fingers the sweet goodness of the cookies would soothe the visitors. Dr. Lombard and Phyllis sat on one side of the rectangular table across from Holt and Maddy. At the end, Bobby looked on from his padded seat, interest bright in his blue eyes.

Dr. Lombard set aside the legal pad on which she'd made notes during the house tour. From her briefcase she took a printed questionnaire. She started with basic information about first Holt and Bobby, and then Maddy. Education, work history, any marriages, legal problems—all very factual. From there the questions ranged from the absurdly personal to the insultingly invasive.

"I see beer in the refrigerator." Dr. Lombard pursed her lips and looked back and forth between the two of them. "How much alcohol is consumed in this household?"

Holt cleared his throat. Clearly tamping down temper. "I've drunk two beers since I bought that six-pack over a week ago. As you can see, Maddy's had none."

The woman ticked off items on her questionnaire. She set down the pen and studied them over her reading glasses. "Ten days is a short time to be together and then engaged."

"We've known each other since childhood." Probably the psychologist already knew that and about her and Rob but maybe she asked to see what they would have to say about the past. "Old friends, you might say." She stretched her mouth into a smile and crossed mental fingers it didn't look too phony.

"Being here in the house—" Holt blinked twice as he apparently saw the implication of what he'd said, even though their belongings were in separate bedrooms "—and sharing old times and taking care of Bobby changed the friendship. To, um, more."

"I see no ring on your finger, Ms. McCoy. Just how real is this engagement?"

"Hmph," Phyllis huffed. "No wedding plans anytime soon, I'll bet."

Maddy linked her hands in her lap. Dammit, her spur-of-the-moment lie wasn't going to save Bobby. "I don't need a ring for our engagement to be real."

Holt looped an arm around Maddy's shoulder, and she gratefully leaned against him, breathing in his familiar smoky male scent. "We haven't had time. The ranch and little Bobby keep both of us da— darn busy."

"Brr-rrrt," Bobby said, as if in confirmation. He rattled his key ring. When the toy clattered to the floor, he squealed, ready to play his favorite game. He dropped a toy; Maddy or Holt retrieved it. Pretty smart for an infant so young. *Good timing, Bobby.* She scooped up the key ring.

Phyllis Patterson swooped over and plucked up the baby, holding him tightly to her. She jiggled him up and down and glared at Maddy.

The germ issue again, the old biddy. Smiling sweetly, she carried the key ring to the sink. "You can't give it back to him yet, Mrs. Patterson, not until I wash it."

When she saw the evaluator write a note on her yellow pad, she chalked up a mental point for their side. Bobby's little face crumpled and turned red. *Uh oh.* In a moment, he'd scream bloody murder. Keeping an eye on him, she quickly washed the key toy, but handing it to him now wouldn't stop the coming storm.

Holt's jaw worked as his gaze sharpened on the building meltdown. He pushed his chair back, ready to rescue Bobby. "Dr. Lombard, what if we were getting married…soon?"

The psychologist leaned forward. "*Are* you getting married?"

Phyllis's mouth pruned. Waiting for his reply, she was oblivious to Bobby's distress. Tears filled his eyes. He stiffened, shaking his little fists in fury as his lungs fired up a piercing wail. Phyllis patted his back and tried to rock him, but he would not be calmed or mollified. His high-pitched cries were enough to spook cattle on the next ranch.

"Well, we haven't set a date." Holt's brows scrunched together, and a vein in his neck throbbed. He reached for Bobby, but Phyllis backed away, shaking her head.

Oh God, he's terrified he'll lose Bobby. She couldn't let that happen. "What if we *were* married?" Maddy raised her voice to be heard over Bobby's howls. "What would that mean for the baby? Would it make Holt's case easier?"

Dr. Lombard's gaze flicked from Bobby, shrieking and straining in the arms of his increasingly distraught grandmother, to Holt, then to Maddy. A pensive expression on her face, she removed her glasses and tapped the earpiece on her papers. She pushed to her feet. "It's not my decision, of course. Judge Gilbert will examine all the facts, including my report. But I believe, yes, a marriage would make a difference."

****

"Engaged? *Engaged? Getting married?* One hell of a crazy idea. You must have…must have been into the damn horse liniment!" Sputtering, Holt dragged Maddy by the elbow onto the porch.

Her eardrums smarted at his accusation. Good thing Bobby was in his crib and out of earshot. She pasted on a smile and waved as the custody evaluator drove away, followed by Phyllis Patterson's sedan. "You didn't rush to deny it."

"How could I? Denial would have made a bad situation worse. What a stupid idea. McCoy, why couldn't you have held your tongue?"

She gave a huff of indignation. The spur-of-the-moment announcement wasn't her finest moment. And she wouldn't analyze why that particular idea popped out of her mouth. Not now anyway. "They caught us red-handed, or should I say red-lipped? I didn't hear *you* offering any brilliant ideas. As far as I could tell, you'd gone as mute as a mime. When you finally found your voice, you added more fiction. And you could've warned me they were coming."

"The reason I came to the barn was to tell you about the appointment. But I got distracted." He massaged his nape and scowled. "Those women arrived an hour early. Phyllis wasn't part of the deal."

"So she weaseled her way in." No wonder Holt was so afraid he'd lose Bobby to the grandparents.

His eyes as cold as bluestone and his expression as hard, he slammed a hand against the porch support. "Fuck! You'd think it was the early nineteen hundreds. Do they expect single people to have chaperones?"

"I'm sure she's witnessed way more than she found here. Seeing my belongings in one room and yours in another seemed to satisfy her sense of propriety, but not Phyllis's. Bobby's her only link to her dead daughter. I suspect she'll do whatever it takes to get custody."

Scowling and raking a hand through his short hair, Holt prowled the length of the porch. "What am I supposed to tell her or the judge when you light out in a week or so?"

Maddy rubbed the bridge of her nose. The longer she stayed, the more she burrowed into Holt and Bobby's life, the harder she'd find it to extricate herself. But she owed them her help. Besides, she'd blurted out the words that fenced her in.

"Like I told you, I'm between gigs. I'm not expected in New York until June first, so I could stay until then. Is that long enough?"

"Four weeks? Maybe. Chris Hawke said these custody things could take months. We could make it look like we're planning a wedding." He leaned against the porch rail and eyed her with suspicion. "You promise not to take off once your SUV's sold? Or some new assignment pops up?"

Maddy should have expected he'd check up on her. After all, he was a trained investigator. "How do you know my vehicle's for sale?"

"I saw it in front of the garage when I drove into Rangewood to load up wood chips at the sawmill. Big For Sale sign plastered on the windshield. A clue even I couldn't miss." The wry sarcasm didn't alter his stone face.

She shifted her feet. "The transmission's shot. It would cost more than the vehicle's worth to fix it. I bought the old girl second, maybe third hand. I'm not much better at maintenance than Rob was, and it sits in storage most of the time. I forgot to mention it."

"Why didn't you just rent when it broke down? Or buy a new SUV?" He stalked across the porch to stand toe to toe with her. His steely blue glare was meant to intimidate.

Her pulse rattled. Why she didn't beat the hell out of her. Had she subconsciously stranded herself so she had to stay in Rock Valley? With Holt? She shoved away the questions. "I had to decide what to do. You know, weigh my options. Not rush into anything. I didn't want to make an—"

"Impulse buy? You? The woman who hot-footed it on her wedding day, who showed up here unannounced, and who blurted out we were engaged? No, that woman wouldn't want to make an impulsive move."

"Back off, Donovan. I'm not some drug dealer you're interrogating." Her SUV had been her only real asset. Not the time to admit that. But she could tell him part of the truth. "I have a temporary cash flow problem."

Something in her tone of voice or her eyes must have reached him because his expression softened. "Low on funds. Or tapped out, like the silver mine on Ghost Mountain?"

His warm tone melted her bravado. "I haven't been paid for the last job, and most of my money's in camera equipment. And investments. How did you guess?"

"When we picked up your stuff that first day, your story about checking out of the Valley Motel was damned lame, and I saw your sleeping bag—"

"In the back of the SUV." Interesting he'd said nothing at the time.

"Then in Fort Adams when I took Bobby to the doctor, I figured you'd buy some feminine junk or at least clothes in one of those cutesy shops on Fort Street." He placed his hands on her shoulders. "When you met me back at the truck, I nearly fell over with shock that all you had was a camera memory card."

"I needed more gigabytes." The strength of his grasp, his masculine scent seeped into her and made her crave his kiss again. How ironic that the attraction she'd fled so long ago was holding her here in steel manacles.

Because Holt didn't press her further, she felt compelled to reassure him.

"Look, I'm all right. My agent assures me I'll get a check soon. Then I'll buy a new vehicle, and I promise not to run out on you."

"Hell, that's damned reassuring."

She drew a deep breath as she tamped down her

temper. "I'll help you with Bobby and finding Rob's killer for as long as I can." She drew a deep breath. "You'll have to trust me."

"Trust you. Not likely. But I'll drop the issue. For now." His eyes said he hadn't dropped it far. "We do have a new problem."

"The engagement. I'm sure we can explain our way out of it when the time comes. Say you changed your mind."

"Big of you to make me the undependable one." Frowning, he cut his glance away, but still his hands cupped her shoulders. His thumbs traced lazy circles on her collarbones. "No, the kiss is the problem. This...chemistry between us. I can't afford the complication."

Chemistry? A hot spurt bubbled up, but she squashed it. Maybe chemistry was all they had. She'd destroyed their friendship when she split on Rob. Any further involvement with Holt now was out of the picture.

He was strong, honorable, and responsible, everything she remembered and more. But Rob's ghost made a formidable barrier to a relationship. Especially with a man who figured she'd run at the first opportunity.

She stretched her spine to her full height, still too short to look him in the eye. If only he would look *her* in the eye. "I don't need that complication either. From now on, keep your hands to yourself."

He pulled back and gaped at those appendages as though they'd held and caressed her on their own.

"Don't kiss me again," Maddy said as firmly as she could muster, "and we won't have a problem."

She pivoted and slammed into the house before he

had a chance to remind her she'd participated as enthusiastically in that kiss as he had.

Had wanted his touch.

Had needed it.

Chapter Ten

MADDY WANTED NOTHING to shatter the fragile peace between her and Holt. They were preparing to go photograph the crash site and visit neighboring ranches on Tuesday, Esperanza O'Grady's regular day of cleaning and cooking.

"*Engaged!*" Espie clapped her hands. "When I heard it in town, I thought I must be dreaming. Or that old busybody Phyllis Patterson must be exaggerating. Must be more goes on between you two when I'm not here than I realized."

"Well, it was kind of sudden," Maddy said. "Impulsive, you might say." She winced at her choice of words.

The other woman winked. "So when's the happy day?"

"Oh, we haven't made definite plans yet." Maddy should have known Phyllis's gossip network would broadcast faster than social media. She could imagine Holt's reaction when he'd have to handle congratulations from friends and neighbors. She paced the kitchen and rubbed the baby's back in a rhythmic circle. "There's too much up in the air about Rob's death. And about Bobby."

"I suppose. I see this engagement as a good omen all around." Espie pocketed her dust cloth in the wrap-around apron she habitually wore. "Bobby'll be fine with me while you and Holt are gone today. I best fix some breakfast. He'll be in from the barn in a few minutes, I expect." She opened the refrigerator and extracted eggs and bacon and set them on the counter beside the loaf of freshly baked bread she'd brought. A soulful harmonica wailed from her small portable radio. She preferred the tried and true to newer gadgets.

A juicy eruption announced Bobby's digestive success. Maddy mopped up milky drool, then nuzzled his warm head, the downy hair tickling her lips. She strapped him into the infant seat. He watched her with solemn eyes, but didn't fuss.

"Can I do anything to help?"

Espie shook her head. "Don't you need to change clothes before you go?" She glanced pointedly at Maddy's light sneakers and Machu Picchu T-shirt.

"I'll be fine. My denim jacket will keep me warm, and I have a sweater." A cotton sweater, and not very warm. She didn't want to tell the perceptive housekeeper she hadn't brought anything heavier. Her other suitcase with her warm clothing had been stolen off the tarmac in Katmandu. For not the first time.

Clucking her disapproval, Espie arranged bacon strips in a skillet. "Gets colder than you'd expect in those woods. You watch the bacon while I fetch some things from the attic." Wiping her hands on her apron, she whisked from the room.

Before Maddy could react, the older woman climbed the pull-down stairs. What could she be looking for?

The bacon was browning nicely, its tempting aroma making Maddy's mouth water. She turned over the strips and broke eggs into a bowl. A few more moments' rustling and scraping upstairs before the bang of the attic door announced Espie's return.

"It took some rummaging, I don't mind telling you." The housekeeper, her crow-black hair flying about her lined face, entered the kitchen bearing a boot box and a sheepskin jacket. "These were Bonnie's. She didn't take to anything about the ranch, not horseback riding nor cattle nor nothin' except the wildness of the mountains. So instead of western boots, Ford bought her these for her birthday."

"Holt's mom?" Maddy eyed the boot box with trepidation. Apprehension crawled up the back of her neck. Just what she needed, something else to remind Holt that she'd bolted like his mother. "I don't know…"

Espie led her to a chair and proceeded to wait on her like a clerk in a shoe store. "You're part of the family now, so don't be foolish. Traipsing around the woods, those flimsy sneakers will be soaked in five minutes."

"I could wear my riding boots."

The Ute woman tsked. "You'd ruin them. And you get sick, what would little Bobby do?" She laced the cordovan-leather hiking boots. "Holt's daddy thought Bonnie might like hiking the park trails."

Despite Maddy's trepidation about Holt's reaction, she yielded. When Espie slipped the boots on her feet, she had to admit they felt wonderful. "They fit. Well, almost, but with a second pair of socks, I'll be fine. Imagine a woman with bigger feet than mine." Her size tens always seemed like flippers to her. She laughed, then peered more closely at the boots. "She didn't use them. They've never been worn."

"Not once," Holt said from the kitchen doorway. "She left the day before Dad planned to give them to her. I didn't know they were still around." He sent a black look Espie's way.

"Your dad had me pack 'em away in the attic. Boots'll rot up there unused." She closed the subject by snapping the lid on the boot box and crossing to the stove.

At the sight of Holt, tall and strong and grim-faced, Maddy's mouth went dry. Her cheeks warmed. Did they look as hot as they felt?

The baby emitted a happy squeal at the sound of his uncle's voice. "Aah-ga!"

Holt hung up his barn coat on a hook by the door.

Maddy stood, determined to smooth matters. "Will it bother you if I wear the boots?"

Espie bustled to the table with two cups of coffee. "You start on this, and I'll have the eggs ready in a flash."

His gaze was opaquely neutral, and determination firmed his jaw. "Somebody should get some use out of them."

Maddy couldn't expect more yielding than that, but no telling whether it was directed at her or at his mother.

He bent to the infant seat and lifted a cooing Bobby into his arms. "How's my little buddy?"

Seated opposite her with the baby snug in the crook of one arm, he sipped his coffee. His open and obvious affection for his nephew softened his expression and squeezed Maddy's heart. "Wear that heavy coat too. You'll need it. Wind has a chill to it."

He was wrestling with powerful emotions, and she had to ask. "Do you ever hear from her?"

"My mother?"

She nodded as she started on the scrambled eggs and toast Espie placed before her. "Does she ever write or telephone?"

"You can't eat proper with that bundle on your lap." Espie scooped Bobby up in her arms. "Oops, someone needs changing." As though escaping, she hustled out of the room with the infant complaining about being rousted from his cozy seat.

Jaw working, Holt stared at congealed egg bits. "Mom wrote us regularly for a few years after she left for Las Vegas. Rob answered some of her letters, but I was too angry."

"Sounds like you have regrets." He wouldn't welcome her reaching out, offering comfort. Instead, she gripped her fork, crumpled her napkin in her lap. "Maybe it's not too late."

He shook his head. "It's been too long. Finally after she remarried, she stopped writing." He pushed away his plate. "She still lives in Vegas."

His bitterness and regrets radiated into her. Without further thought, she grasped his hand. Calluses from physical labor toughened his long, capable fingers and palm, but they couldn't armor the vulnerable man inside. "She might want to see her grandson."

"Maybe. Leave it alone, Maddy." He freed his hand, slid his plate closer, and aimed his fork at her like a weapon. "Now eat up. We ought to get going." He tucked into his eggs and bacon as though starved.

An act of bravado. And if their cease-fire wasn't shattered, it was at least shaken. She stirred the eggs around, but her appetite had disappeared. She needed sustenance and managed to swallow half her eggs before Holt declared it time to go.

****

An hour later, Holt headed his Silverado southeast

toward the site where Rob's old truck had spun out of control over a steep embankment. Behind him, he caught a glimpse of what could be the same black truck as before. He slowed, looking to see if it was that Ford with the Circle-S brand, but he couldn't get the right angle. The vehicle passed behind them as they turned onto the two-lane back road the locals called the Wagon Spur. He shrugged off the prickles of suspicion. It was a small community. He was bound to see the same vehicles from time to time.

Rangewood and the surrounding ranches spread across a series of high mountain valleys and rolling peaks on the edge of the national forest. The Wagon Spur wound along the sides of two mountains and through the forest. Today he couldn't appreciate the greening beauty of the forest or the distant vistas from its hilltops. Awareness of the woman beside him and the grim task ahead kept him in a state of heightened alertness. It was too much to expect they'd find any evidence, but he nurtured a kernel of hope.

"The crash site is just up ahead."

Maddy was loading a new memory card in her camera. "Something bothers me about this ambush. How did the killer know Rob and Sara were going out that evening? How could he know they'd take this road?"

"Hell, the whole town knew. Sara went into Rangewood that day to have lunch with her mother at the Bull's-Eye. I reckon she bragged to everyone she met that her husband was taking her down to Cripple Creek for a night. Those she missed her mother told."

"And Bobby. Where was Bobby that night?"

"At Espie's house." He shuddered. "Thank God."

"Why not at the Pattersons'?"

"You're wondering if they feel resentment at the slight. Maybe, but they had some civic function that night. Chamber of Commerce or Elks." If the grandparents had had possession of Bobby when Sara and Rob were killed, he might not have received even temporary custody. His chest tightened and he shook away the thought.

"What about this route?" Maddy asked, fiddling with her camera.

"A calculated risk the killer took. Unless it's storming, most folks prefer it. He had a seventy-five percent chance anyone leaving Rock Valley would go this way."

"If the killer was actually after Rob and Sara and not someone else in a similar truck."

He'd put together some facts. He looked ahead, paid attention to the curves before he replied. "I haven't come up with a motive, but it wasn't mistaken identity."

"But how do you know?"

"I had a look at the wreckage in back of the sheriff's office. Since I was last home, Rob replaced the rusted-out front fenders with used ones from a junkyard, but he didn't repaint the truck. It had one blue fender and one black one—on a green truck. No mistaking that heap."

They reached their destination, and Holt pulled over to the left verge. He hadn't passed any other vehicles, but he ought to be well out of the roadway.

Along this ridge, the pine-dotted hills rolled on toward the distant gray cone of Pikes Peak. The air, crisp and clean, was redolent with juniper and the sweetness of decayed grasses. At their intrusion, two gray jays exploded from the roadside with squawks. Holt had to stifle a reaction.

"Just look at that sky. It's so blue it hurts your eyes." Maddy clambered out with her smaller camera case slung over her shoulder.

He watched her scan the fir and juniper lining the roadsides, uphill and across to the steep downhill slope that was nearly a cliff. Maybe her photographer's eye would find something everyone else had missed.

Today he couldn't win. Either he focused on the gut-wrenching task of examining this site or on the woman who had him teetering between horny and crazy.

She tugged the fleece jacket closed against the chill and zipped it. Her mouth thinned to a taut line as she blinked back tears. She shook her head, flipping her short hair around her face. "Where did the shooter sit?"

Grief rimmed her eyes, and horror dulled the violet irises. He saw her caring for Rob, though she hadn't loved him. He saw her passion for people and her vulnerability. Something he wasn't ready to name tugged at his chest muscles, and he turned aside.

"Up in this grouping of rocks." He led her up the short slope above where they'd parked.

They poked around in the rocks and scrub brush, but found nothing unusual. The thawing ground held a litter of Ponderosa pine cones, sticks, and dried grasses, but no prints or human debris like cigarette butts. No sign a stalker had hunkered there waiting for a green truck with mismatched fenders.

Propping one foot on a lichen-encrusted rock, she shot several frames of the spot, including close-ups. After changing lenses, she took more of the approaching road—the shooter's view.

Immersion in her professional task made him aware of her on a new plane.

Apparently oblivious to his gaze, she bent and twisted around to frame her shots. He tried to think about how enlargements might reveal some telling evidence to them rather than how delectable her curvy backside looked, even partly covered by the borrowed jacket. Hell. He dragged his gaze back to the camera.

"Should you have a tripod?" he asked. "Or another camera?"

"This Nikon's a versatile enough camera for this kind of work. Besides I stashed my other equipment in storage." She cocked a hip. "You think I don't know my business?"

He threw up his hands. "Just anxious."

"Me too."

Her soft smile started an unwelcome tingling. He looked away—*again*—and paced a tight circle. "So, what now?"

"How about where the truck landed? Do you think there's anything to find down there?" She pointed toward the low side of the roadway.

"Can't hurt." He adjusted his Broncos cap. "When we're done, I want to go on into Fort Adams. Got to lay in the vaccines I need for next weekend's branding."

"I heard Espie's boys are coming to help. Will that be enough hands?"

"Bronc'll rope the calves. The boys'll wrestle them. That leaves me to do the rest." He shook his head at the prospect. That wasn't nearly enough wranglers. He should have at least two more, but he couldn't afford more wages.

"Rob's extravagance on the house hurt the ranch, didn't it?"

He sighed. "You've noticed."

"Hard not to. You've done lots of recent repairs. The barn roof. And I've seen you babying that old field truck to get it running." A sad tilt to her mouth, she gave a quick, apologetic smile before she zipped the camera in her case.

"Yeah, he let upkeep go. Rob was never very practical. The ranch'll be all right, but I have to watch every penny. There's enough to pay those two teenagers."

"But no more hands. Espie said she'll be there. She'll be happy to see to Bobby. I'd like to help." She beamed him a smile, like she was remembering other brandings when they were kids.

Maddy had already woven her way into their lives, his and Bobby's, with her gentle care and energy. Depending on her for any more was a bad idea. He couldn't let himself want to. He shook his head. "No."

She gripped his arm. "I know how to do the vaccinating and ear notching. Come on, you know you can use the extra hands."

The same restlessness that had her volunteering for ranch chores would take her away sooner than Holt wanted to think about. He worked his jaw. "Your responsibility is Bobby, not the ranch. I'll have to make do. It'll just be slow going."

Her cheeks pinked in the freshening breeze. Even without makeup, her creamy skin glowed as if lit from within. "And you don't have to pay me any money."

No, but he'd pay, one way or another, and it would come out of his hide. Or another vulnerable organ. He couldn't contain a wry grin as he replied. "Denying you's as hard as saying no when Bobby reaches out his little hand toward the hot stove."

"Except I won't get burned."

But *he* might.

Chapter Eleven

MADDY WATCHED AS Holt started down the steep slope, edging sideways in the loose scree and pine cones that crunched and clattered as he went. Rough going for anyone.

"You need any help? I can carry your camera case," he called back.

At his protectiveness, she concealed a grin. Didn't he remember the tomboy who used to race her pony alongside him and Rob? It ought to irritate her how he kept underestimating her, but instead it amused her.

She strapped on her case like a backpack. Using his same crabwise maneuver, she scooted along behind him. "No, I'm used to this. My camera stays with me."

Rocks and pebbles skittered downhill, kicked free by their progress.

Halfway down, she stopped and extracted her camera. She pointed at scarred and splintered tree trunks. "Were these broken trees damaged by the crash?"

The inner pith stood out as white as bones against the peat-brown boles. Jagged points speared skyward. On one, a lone cedar waxwing kept sentinel.

He hunched his shoulders. "The truck rolled and bounced over and over. It slammed into the pines and Douglas firs. Snapped them like twigs. It landed on its roof at the foot of the incline. You can see the digs in the soil down there."

In the long, muddy scrapes at the foot of the incline, tiny green shoots poked through the soil where determined roots had taken hold. New life where life had ended.

The futility of their effort stabbed Maddy like one of the splintered branches. Seeing the fury and misery pleating Holt's brow twisted the point. Tears blurring her focus, she snapped pictures of the hillside and trees before stowing the Nikon.

A few minutes later they reached the bottom.

Stones and pebbles skittered down from their recent path of descent. The clatter built to a tumble of stones.

Before she could move, he tackled her from the side. "Get down!" With her wrapped in his arms, he dove for cover behind a jumble of boulders.

Like a growing snowball, each skidding nugget and pebble attracted brothers. Stones the size of bricks caromed downward. Finally a mass of rock and stick-littered earth crashed down the steep slope.

Maddy's heart raced and rattled like one of the stones that banged off their protecting boulder. Whether her reaction stemmed from fear or from lying beneath Holt's big body she couldn't say. "Did we do that?"

"Looks like we started something, for sure."

Started something? A landslide and something as overwhelming.

Long legs on either side of hers and arms caging her, he pressed her to the ground. His sheepskin jacket was pulled up to protect their heads. Scented with rich, dark coffee, his hot breath warmed her cheek. As long as the landslide didn't smash into them, she could lie like this indefinitely. Never mind the rocks digging into her spine.

Only when Holt slid down his jacket collar and cool

air brushed Maddy's face did she realize that quiet had returned. An occasional ricocheting ping announced further settling of the altered mountainside.

"Landslide's over," he murmured, his mouth a millimeter from hers. His puff of breath brushed her lips, set them tingling.

"We're okay," she whispered. Complication or not, she willed him to kiss her again. If he didn't, she would grab him. Except her arms were trapped beneath his.

He hovered above her, his eyes depthless lapis, molten with desire, his parted lips brushing hers. "It's safe now. We can get up."

Deep and thick and roughened, his voice enveloped her like a steam bath. Honeyed excitement sluiced into her. Even through their thick clothing, each place on her body he touched became a pulse point, trembling with want.

Arms. Breasts. Belly. Thighs.

"I know."

On a deep breath, he lunged upward and away from her. Standing, he held out his hand. "You all right?"

All right? More than a little loony to think she could avoid the complication of involvement with Holt. Other than that, all right. He had more will power than she. And yet she trembled in the aftermath. Only adrenaline fleeing her system. That was all. Sure.

She hoisted her scuffed case. "Fine. Just fine. I want a few more shots before we leave."

Grasping her shoulders, he turned her toward the hillside. Clouds of dust wafted from the stretch of rubble. More trees lay bent and broken in its wake. No sign of the gouged earth or the hopeful sprouts that had sprung up in the wounded soil.

He released her and lifted his arms, then swung them down, his hands in tight fists. "Underneath that little mountain was where Rob's truck landed. Might as well forget it. If there was any evidence down here at the foot of that slope, that damned slider has wiped it off the map."

****

The next evening, Holt and Maddy pored for the umpteenth time over the four dozen images parading across her laptop screen.

"I hope you had fun with those last shots at the bottom of the landslide," he grumbled. "Nothing to see in those but rocks." He was being unnecessarily grumpy, but he couldn't seem to help himself. Maddy's presence, fresh-scrubbed with wet hair sleek and golden as honey, disconcerted him. Even the weather conspired against him, flinging curtains of rain across the valley all day long.

Add to that his frustration over finding so little evidence. Nothing he could see in the pictures. In the last week, they'd visited nearly every ranch in the valley, talked to every foreman and owner and found nothing. No motive. No hint of lying. Nada. Only rumors of Rob's jealousy and temper but nothing concrete.

And a niggling suspicion that landslide didn't start by itself. He'd found no tire tracks up on the roadside, but the ground might've been too hard to show a trace. Hell.

"Rocks, yes. Maybe more," Maddy said, a noncommittal expression on her face. "Let's label them and decide which to enlarge and print. Then we'll begin to see something."

"If anything's there to see." He was grumping again.

He shrugged. "Murphy at the Ponderosa Photo Lab in Fort Adams is a friend of mine. He said he'd give your photos priority and do whatever you need with them."

A short time later they'd selected a dozen images.

"I could take the flash drive to the lab tomorrow. Espie'll be here," she suggested.

He ought to agree. She'd be far enough away so maybe he wouldn't itch to run his finger across the smooth slope of her cheek or kiss the vulnerable hollow of her collarbone.

Damn. It had been too long since he'd had a woman. He'd have the hots for any woman under these circumstances. Maybe. Eight years ago, when he'd returned home to see the girl he'd thought of as a bratty kid marry his brother, her fresh beauty and subtle sensuality had jolted him with heat that'd had him sweating.

His attraction to her and their devastating kiss had shamed him, but that was mild compared to this craving for the woman she was now. Her boundless enthusiasm and energy fascinated him. Why would she want him, a stolid drudge? A grouchy, stolid drudge.

He left the table and fished a beer out of the fridge. "In the morning after the animals are fed, I'm heading over to the Circle-S. If you send the photos to the lab by email, you can go there with me if you want to." Hell, it was once her granddaddy's ranch. He gulped a long swig of the frosty liquid.

Maddy's eyes glowed amethyst with pleasure. "Oh, I'd love to see it in operation now they have guests."

"Trail rides and trout fishing and campfires for tenderfeet aren't my way of ranching, but I reckon they help pay the bills. They do run a hundred or so head of cattle too."

She lowered her gaze to the photographs on the screen. "Is there any reason to suspect anyone on the Circle-S?"

"Luke Rafferty may be a deputy sheriff, but he works part time on his family's spread. He acted mighty odd when I was at the sheriff's office last week." He described the face-off between Rafferty and Chris Hawke. "Afterward, Chris clammed up. Wouldn't say a word about why they pawed the ground like a couple of bulls."

An unaccountably relieved expression on her face, Maddy laughed, a melodic sound that heated his blood. "I know Luke, and I have one thought. *Cherchez la femme.*"

"A woman. You think so?"

"We'll see what we can find out tomorrow." Standing, she yawned and stretched. The movement pulled the soft cotton of her tee across the swell of her breasts.

Holt downed another slug of beer.

****

During the night a front swept the rains away, leaving behind puddles to mirror the radiant blue sky.

At mid-morning Holt tore himself away from ranch work to ride to the Circle-S. He wanted to just get there and talk to the Raffertys and their hands, but no, Maddy had to make it a damned outing like they used to when they were kids. Innocent kids.

By the time he joined her in the barn, she'd already saddled both horses—Bandito, his paint gelding, and Chica, the buckskin mare she'd co-opted. If she had a picnic in her saddlebags, it wouldn't surprise him.

114

As they crested the first Ponderosa pine-dotted hill and meandered toward the bank of Ghost Creek, he hung back to study Maddy. She wore Bonnie's sheepskin jacket and a flat-crowned white hat of her own.

He chuckled at the excitement in her every movement. In the high color on her fine cheekbones. In her restless gestures. In the way she could barely sit still in her saddle. Her manner put Holt in mind of a bird ready to take flight.

Not too far off the mark.

With customary tolerance, the gentle buckskin walked at an even pace, but her tulip-shaped ears angled upright and inward with curiosity.

Maddy cocked the hat back on her head for a better view of the scenery. With the reins looped over one hand, she made a frame of her gloved fingers and peered intently at a stand of budding aspens, their trunks gleaming white in the sun. She withdrew her camera from a saddlebag and clicked happily away.

She turned around to the south and stood in the stirrups. Her enthusiasm made her complexion appear even more luminous. "Just look at that, Holt. It's so clear today you can see all the way to Pikes Peak. It's framed perfectly above the tree line. The angles and shadows are so dramatic. This high meadow is such a magical place." *Click.*

Though he'd seen the panorama more times than he could count, he obediently followed her gaze. The bare, rocky crest of the Peak stood head above the fir-covered hills before them. He couldn't help grinning—and agreeing with her. It was a special place. Now if he could only afford to keep it his.

"Do you look at everything like it's a photographic

subject?" He let the sociable Bandito edge closer to Chica as they continued on their way.

Maddy lifted one shoulder carelessly. She aimed her camera at the creek, splashing along with spring run-off. *Click, click.* "It's second nature. Once I look at these on my laptop, I'd like to be able to print some out. That could get expensive." She stowed the Nikon.

"I can't pay you for taking care of Bobby, but I'd lend you money for some prints."

"No way. You're feeding and clothing me. I can wait until my check comes. I gave my agent your mailing address."

"It wouldn't be charity. I'd like pictures of Bobby."

A wide smile was his reward. "That's different. A gig. You've got a deal."

He didn't want her gratitude. She intrigued him too much, and it bugged the hell out of him. "When did you take up photography? I don't remember seeing you with a camera when we were kids."

"You were away at college. In high school, the art teacher put the itch in me. Back then it was film photography. Then in college, I majored in art." Her grin flickered to a sober expression. "Of course, I never did finish college."

Following her and Rob's sophomore year and the aborted wedding, she'd jetted away to greener pastures. "You always raved about these peaks, their shades of green, their shadows, like they were paintings." Or photographs. She was a natural.

Her musical laugh triggered a reaction that made straddling a horse damned uncomfortable.

"I have a good sense of composition and color, even drama I'm told, but I can't draw or paint worth a lick.

That's why the art teacher handed me a camera."

"I saw drama in the article on the Sudanese orphans. And the emotion."

"Too much emotion. It was a very tough assignment." She lowered her hat brim, maybe blocking the memories. "I wish I could have done more for them than take their pictures. I've told you about Easter Island and the Andes. Those were the fun assignments. But mostly I shoot disasters, wars, and refugees. I always feel so helpless in the face of such tragedies."

"Where do you see your career heading next?" Dammit, he shouldn't ask, or care. A knot tightened his jaw. By the time Maddy left he'd need dental work.

"This next assignment in June is a calendar." Anticipation glowed in her oval face. "I'm supposed to photograph Haitian children for an international charity."

"A charity, huh? Sounds like you can help people after all."

Her smile widened, sending sparklers through his blood. "How perceptive of you, Holt. If the pictures help the people I photograph, that keeps me going when I'm worn to the bone from too much travel and too many starving babies."

"And you've wound up here taking care of a baby."

"Bobby's a pleasure." Her smile was genuine.

Maddy's life wasn't frivolous jet-setting. It had substance and noble purpose. But her career still meant world travel. He'd likely never see her again. She was only a temporary solution to his problems. And a temptation he didn't need. He kicked the gelding into a trot.

Maddy followed suit, guiding her mare close behind

him.

Weaving among clumps of aspens and smatterings of pines, they chased the creek's course. Then they crossed the second of the three hills and entered a long valley. Aspens rimmed the creek banks and the other verge, but stubbly greening grass was the only other cover. The sun warmed the morning so both wore their jackets open to the fresh mountain air.

"An old dirt track follows the base of the foothills." Holt pointed west. "Staying with the creek the entire distance will take too long. At the end of the valley, we'll meet the track where it swings toward the Circle-S. We can follow it the rest of the way."

"Okay. Let's take a break and water the horses." Maddy headed for a clearing by the rushing stream.

They dismounted and led the animals closer to the creek bank. The clear water careened over its rocky bed.

She stretched and opened her arms to the scenery. The blue T-shirt lifted enough to give him a glimpse of her smooth, pale stomach.

Tempted to slide his palm over that creamy skin, he forced himself to turn aside to oversee the animals drinking the icy water. "After the branding, I'll move the herd here for the summer. Better feed where it's not such scrubland. Plenty of water."

"Up there, isn't that Ghost Mountain?" she said. "And the old silver mine?"

"Yup." He didn't have to look to know she was right. To the northwest, a jagged, treeless ridge heaved itself above the surrounding pine-spiked hills. Buried in one of Ghost Mountain's convolutions was the played-out silver mine they had invaded as kids. It had sat dormant for a hundred years.

"The stuff of legends, and a damned dangerous hole in the ground. I keep meaning to board the place up to prevent accidents, but I never get to it."

"Ranching is non-stop work."

She sounded so damned cheerful about it that he turned around to see if she was laughing at him. But she was again snapping a photo, this time of the mysterious mountain.

Grinning, she aimed her lens at him. "So, Rancher Donovan, turnabout is fair play. What are your future plans? What will you do with the Valley-D?"

Chapter Twelve

HIS JAW TIGHTENED at the question. "First job is to pay off that damn equity loan. If the herd does well this year and cattle prices are up, I can put a big dent in it. I should've helped Rob out more. It'll be a while before I can build the place back up." He led the gelding away from the creek and ground-tied him beneath a tall aspen at the clearing's edge.

Maddy followed suit, letting her mount's reins dangle. She removed her hat and placed it on the saddle horn. The breeze fluffed her feathery hair. One corn-silk strand blew across her cheek.

He had an urge to brush it back, to feel its sleek texture. He shoved his hands in his jacket pockets.

"Why didn't you stay here and run the spread with Rob?" she asked.

"You don't know?" When she shook her head, he went on. "When Dad died, one of us had to work to pay medical costs. I was the logical one, and the DEA liked my two years of law school."

"I know you always had an interest in the law, in law enforcement. Why the DEA and not the Denver Police?"

Back then, he'd wanted to get away, see more of the country. He could hardly say that to the woman he'd criticized for having jet fuel in her blood. Besides, it was more complicated than that.

"The federal job paid better, and I knew if I lived too

close, I'd second-guess Rob, tell him how to run things. We didn't usually agree on ranch management. Or much else." With Rob gone, it pained him to admit that. It seemed shameful, disloyal, but somehow he expected Maddy to understand.

"I don't doubt you two were at odds. Rob the fun-loving extrovert and Holt the serious problem-solver. You were always bossing us kids around." Humor flicked across her liquid gaze, replaced by compassion. "So, you couldn't be there to take charge, but you sent money now and then?"

"What is this, an interrogation?"

She folded her arms and waited. The set of her full mouth meant business. "I'm an old friend. And I care. And yes, I'm nosy. Well, did you send money?"

Holt stalked in a circle. What the hell did she think he did? He sighed, staring into the distance, across the valley. Beyond the line of trees that hid the dirt track, something moved. Probably mule deer. Hard to tell at a distance as far as three gridiron lengths.

"Dammit, of course I did." He faced her again, faced her probing. Nimble perception lurked in her questions, but he let her herd him anyway. "Every month. The Valley-D was half mine. Rob worked the place, but I helped pay the bills."

"And you came home to help out whenever the DEA gave you leave. I'll bet you never took a real vacation or went anywhere but right back here."

How could she read him so well? "Pretty clever, aren't you, McCoy? Roping me in and dropping on the hackamore."

"You did the best you could, Holt. You had no choice. Don't beat yourself up about not having done more. You can't always be in charge. You can't fix everything. Rob bore much of the responsibility." A shaft of sunlight gilded her hair like gold in an old painting, just as her questions illuminated his assumptions.

"I can see you made a hell of a reporter. How'd you learn questioning techniques?"

She smiled wistfully. "From an old newspaper hound in San Diego named Pete Muñoz. I followed him around on countless stories until he told me I was wasting my photography talent and booted me in the direction of a travel magazine. I've been on the go ever since."

"Not just photographing, but photo-journalism. He taught you well. He did the right thing making you fly on your own. Suits you, the international gig, does it?

"I've had a good ride." She said it with a smile that didn't brighten her eyes.

At a loss, he said, "Maybe you'll get a chance to use that sharp digging at the Circle-S." He handed her Chica's reins. "We ought to get going now."

One minute she sparkled with excitement, and the next shadows dimmed her eyes. The woman was a puzzle. If only he could get her to open up. She'd popped him open like a beer can so his secrets came pouring out, but he couldn't work it the other way around. His interrogation techniques fizzled where this blasted female was concerned.

Holt gathered Bandito's reins and waited for Maddy to mount up. She sat a horse well, comfortable, as skilled as any ranch kid. Which she was, more or less.

She retrieved her hat and eased it on her head. "Guess I'll just have to ignore hat hair." Grinning, she placed her left foot in the stirrup.

With her long legs, she needed no assistance mounting a horse, even a tall one like Chica. The faded denim of her designer jeans stretching across her rounded behind drew his gaze like a lodestone.

Holt dragged his glance away, afraid he'd be tempted to give her a boost, as an excuse to put his hands on her. No matter what he thought of her, his desire for her only grew. Hell, he was getting used to constant arousal. Sex with Maddy would be like the woman herself. Sensual. Exhilarating. Nothing but trouble.

And he couldn't stop wanting her.

A flash of light across the meadow caught his eye. Sunlight reflecting on a mirror?

Or on metal?

He lunged for Maddy before she could swing her right leg over the saddle.

"Get down!"

She gasped with surprise, falling into his arms like a newborn colt, all long limbs and slender body. Her hat tumbled away to the side. "What the hell!"

Something whizzed past them. The aspen branch above exploded into splinters. The crack of a rifle shot echoed across the meadow.

Holt and Maddy dropped to the ground.

Both horses startled. The mare jolted away. Bandito reared and hoofed at the sky. He bolted upstream after Chica.

Another shot slammed into the aspen's trunk. Shattered wood fragments sprayed them like pellets.

Maddy's heart raced. Trembling, she clung to Holt. "Gunshots," she whispered, more to express the reality of it than to state the unnecessary.

Holt kept one arm around her as they crab-crawled toward a scraggly cedar bush. "Stay down. This isn't much protection, but we have no choice. At least he can't see us."

"Who could be shooting at us?" Dried stubble beneath their shelter pricked at her bottom. She huddled in his embrace, taking comfort in his familiar smell and the heat of his hard body. Shifting for comfort, she scooted closer.

"He's over there on the dirt track." Expression as hard as the silver in Ghost Mountain, he peered across the meadow. "And I doubt he mistook us for a deer. Must have a hell of a site on that rifle."

Her discomfort flicked away, and a moment later, an idea ramped up fear to full-blown panic. "It could be Rob's murderer!"

"Similar weapon. Long range and powerful. If it *is* the same guy, it means we're getting too close. Could be there's something in those pictures."

She peeked around the shrub. "If there was only some way to sneak around the meadow and catch him."

He turned to her, his eyebrows raised, almost disappearing beneath his hat brim. "You have a death wish, McCoy? Or maybe your travels to mystical lands have taught you a way to make yourself invisible?"

Before she could respond to his smartass crack, a distant vehicle engine coughed and rumbled. She closed her eyes in brief thanks. "They're leaving."

"Stay down." Holt squeezed her shoulders, although she hadn't made a move to rise. "He may figure he can't get us without revealing himself. Or it may be a trick." Eyes flinty with intensity, he continued to stare across the meadow.

Maddy stared also, but could detect nothing. She'd had enough of death and destruction, but why the hell couldn't they have gotten a look at the shooter?

"One of those bullets may still be in the tree. The state lab can tell us if it's from the same weapon. Our killer may just have made his first big mistake." Holt's smile was as cold as a north wind. "We'll call the sheriff from the Circle-S."

"But the horses—"

"Are right over there." He pointed to about fifty yards away where both were grazing peacefully. "They're too well trained to go far."

Her brain whirred, trying to puzzle out what she and Holt could know, why the killer wanted them dead. Clearly his intention wasn't merely to frighten them. "If we get back early enough, I'll drive to Fort Adams to the photo lab. Maybe the enlarged prints will tell us what we need to know."

Holt gave a noncommittal grunt, his laser focus trained on the distance.

A few moments later, he stood and held out a hand to her. "It's okay. We can get going."

She hesitated, then accepted the hand up. "Are you sure? How do you know?"

"Look out across the meadow."

She followed the direction of his nod. In the same general area of the gunshots' origin, three deer grazed. Two of the graceful creatures munched peacefully on new tender shoots while the third, a young buck, stood watch. He flicked his tail and cast occasional wary glances at his equine cousins on the near side of the meadow.

She exhaled the breath she was holding. Relief sent

adrenaline tremors through her, turning her knees to pudding. She gritted her teeth to keep them from clacking. She'd ducked gunfire before but always she'd had a job to do to distract her. This time it seemed her job had led to the flying bullets.

Holt wrapped his powerful arms around her and held her on her feet. He tucked her head beneath his chin. "Hey, McCoy. I've got you. It's okay. You did great. I guess it's not every day you get shot at. You're entitled to let it get to you."

She couldn't speak, lost in the aftermath and the heady sensations of Holt's embrace. Enveloped in his sheepskin jacket, she wrapped her arms around his middle. Soft fleece and his body heat warmed her hands, icy even in gloves. Adrenaline must cause hypersensitivity, because with her ear against Holt's throat, she could hear the steady beat of his heart, even the rush of blood through his veins. The curves and planes of his hard muscles were hard and solid against her hardening nipples.

Almost imperceptibly, his heart sped up, and a fine tension pervaded his muscles. The arousal prodding Maddy's belly told her he was every bit as aware of her.

She had never before felt so thankful for a man's protection. In her profession, she'd had to be self-sufficient and independent, relying on herself for everything, including safety.

But she was getting too used to Holt's protection and strength. When her time here ended, she'd have no choice but to return to her peripatetic life. Although he seemed to have forgiven her, he didn't love her. Worse, he still distrusted her. For now, she'd inhale his scent and savor the feel of his arms. She'd commit those sensations to memory. Leaving him would leave a hollow the size of Colorado in her chest.

Twice now he'd pulled her from harm's way and sheltered her with his body. He used his rugged strength to save her, yet his handling of her was gentle and considerate, never rough. He was a protector by nature and by training.

A powerful combination. A powerful aphrodisiac.

She turned to touch her lips to the rapid-fire pulse in his neck. His scent—sun-warmed skin and horse and leather—made her giddy. She pulled back and gazed up at him. "Holt?"

Laser-blue flames flickered in his eyes. He stared at her a moment, a muscle in his jaw jumping. "Aw, hell, Maddy."

Holt swept off his hat. Cupping the back of her head with his left hand, he bent and pressed his mouth to hers. His lips were warm and soft, and he kissed her with devastating skill. His tongue stroked her teeth, her inner textures, her essence.

Pleasure rose through her in soft flutters. Heat licked over her body. This was Holt, the man she'd run from for years. She didn't want to run any more. She drank in his taste and his desire. She absorbed him with all the passion she'd bottled up for so long. Each caress of his lips and tongue brought the blood leaping through her veins.

Suddenly her tee was yanked up and one breast cradled in his right hand. Even through her bra, when he caressed a puckered nipple, longing swept through her, and she moaned in need. Excitement tingled through her, suspending her in shimmering sensation.

Gradually he eased his grip on her. He gave her one

more soft kiss, then tugged down her shirt. "We ought to get going. Call the sheriff."

She trembled, not from fear but from wrenching, primitive desire.

"Damn. I was all over you like an animal. Just after you could've been killed." He hooked a finger beneath her chin and turned her face. "I did shave this morning, but I've marked you."

Her heart thumped wildly, and her breath came quick and shallow. His kisses had nearly dissolved her knees and melted her insides to syrup. She wouldn't let him apologize for something they both wanted.

She gave him her best, most confident smile. "Beard burn? Just what we need to convince everyone at the Circle-S that we're engaged. Phyllis has spread the story to every other ranch we visited. They must've heard it here too."

He stared at her blankly for a moment, then scratched his head. Sometimes she drove him nuts. Looked like this was one of those times. Or maybe he just realized *again* he would have to act engaged, even accept congratulations.

He nodded his understanding. "I'll get the horses."

He strode across the field, all loose-limbed confidence and male grace. Maddy had run from her attraction to him once. She ached at the prospect of repeating that. What was she getting herself into?

Mentally shelving the problem until later, she stared at the bullet-wounded aspen. The first jagged hole was almost too high for her to reach on tiptoes.

Her heartbeat clattered anew, and her knees wobbled. "Holt, that bullet was aimed high. As high as…the body of a mounted rider. Like *I* was the intended target."

Returning, he handed over her mare's reins. "If those shots are connected with Rob's murder, they could've meant to scare us off. Aimed high not meaning to hit us. Just coincidence you started to mount at that moment."

She bit her lip, not convinced. "I believe I heard that you lawmen types don't believe in coincidences."

Mouth tight and eyes averted, he made no reply.

Chapter Thirteen

BY THE TIME Holt finished with the county detectives and returned with them from the ambush site to the Circle-S, it was afternoon. The rocky trail beneath Ghost Mountain had contained no tire tracks, but the aspen had yielded bullets to be sent to the ballistics lab.

The combination guest and cattle ranch was a larger spread than Holt's by a thousand more acres and bordered the Pike National Forest, where the Raffertys had grazing rights and access to riding trails for their guests. Outbuildings clustered around the main house like Herefords around a feed trough. A new stable to replace the one that had burned stood next to the barn. In addition, the string of guest cabins attested to the ranch's prosperity.

Witnessing what other ranchers had to do these days to make ends meet, let alone flourish, made his gut queasy. Some of the larger ranchers sold off great parcels of prime acreage for vacation homes and wildlife refuges. Others, like the Raffertys, eked out their living by entertaining city folks who wanted a taste of the real West.

What would he have to give up to make a go of the Valley-D? He was sure no genial host like Will Rafferty. Nor did he have enough acreage to spare for vacation real estate.

"The sheriff will notify you when we have more

information," the chief detective said. He tipped his hat in farewell. After the detectives picked up the other deputy who'd been questioning the ranch employees, they drove away.

Holt strolled toward the ranch house to find Maddy. She'd been more sanguine about that hot embrace than he had. Damn, he'd nearly ripped off her clothes and had her there on the hard ground. And he had the feeling it would have been with her cooperation.

If they had sex, could they keep it uncomplicated, casual? Would a sweaty bout or two between the sheets excise his craving for her? She already had him tied in knots, had him sniffing her scent and listening for her voice in the breeze.

Hell, he didn't need this. He had to concentrate on the ranch and on solving the murder of his family.

With all the excitement, he'd thought he might have to forgo a discussion about Rob with the Raffertys. He spied Will on the porch. Shit no, he had to get it over with.

Like the authorities, he'd found no inconsistencies or shaky alibis for any of the ranchers or cowhands he'd interviewed. Whoever wanted Rob dead must have hired the gun, and this neighboring property was a prime staging area for a paid killer waiting his chance.

The ranch manager greeted Holt from the ranch-house porch. A wide grin crinkled his eyes as he tipped back his high-crowned hat. "You've had a day to put a crimp in your hat. Want some coffee or a *cerveza*?" Will stuck out a hand.

Holt took the firm grip. "A beer would go down just fine about now." In a few minutes, he'd find Maddy and the horses, and they could be on their way.

Will fetched a couple of long-necks, and they sat on padded cedar chairs in the screen-enclosed section of the porch. "They find anything?"

"Not much." Holt knew better than to disclose information. Word got around, no matter how circumspect one intended to be. "Did anyone go out hunting this morning? Or see a vehicle between the creek and Ghost Mountain?" He figured he knew the answer before Will responded.

The other man shook his head. "Most of the guests went out with the wranglers on a trail ride through parkland. That's the other direction. They're still out."

"Anyone not go on that trail ride?"

"Some kids and a few older guests. My sister organized activities for those who wanted them. Two of my regular hands are working on props for next weekend's cowboy action shooting matches. My folks went to Denver for a few days. Aside from me, that's it." He slanted Holt a consoling smile. "I went all through this with the deputy."

"I appreciate that, Will." Holt tipped up his bottle for a calming gulp. "You're real understanding to let me grill you like this without taking offense."

"After what happened to your brother, I don't blame you for trying to find out all you can. I'd do the same thing if anything like that happened to my family." Will plunged a blunt-fingered hand through his thick reddish-brown hair. "You think the two incidents are connected?"

Holt's gut tightened but he schooled his features into a noncommittal mask. "Your guess is as good as mine. I'd sure like to know why someone might have wanted to kill Rob. And why they might want to kill Maddy and me."

Anxiety creased Will's freckled forehead. "You think it was murder and not a hunting accident of some kind?"

"I do. For lots of reasons. And whoever shot at us today meant to kill us."

Will's mouth curved in a wry grin. "So I'm a suspect along with my cowhands and paying guests?"

"I suspect no one and everyone. No offense, Will."

"None taken." He shifted in his chair and crossed his legs, propping one ankle on the opposite knee. "I'll level with you. Rob and I had our differences."

Holt's pulse kicked into a fast trot. In spite of his temper, Rob had charmed everyone he met. Was this just another example, or something more? "What do you mean?"

"When my family bought the Circle-S a few years ago, we knew we'd have to keep adding activities and entertainment so guests had plenty to interest them. We wanted repeat visitors, and visitors who'd tell their friends about us."

Holt tipped back his hat and scratched his forehead in puzzlement. "What does this have to do with Rob?"

"One of the things I wanted to feature was a real silver mine. I offered to buy the entire Ghost Mountain section of the Valley-D from Rob. He turned me down. Twice."

Holt blew out a breath. "That's just business. I won't sell it to you either, but that doesn't mean we can't be friendly neighbors. Is there more to it?"

"Not really. Rob took the offers the wrong way. He thought I was offering charity because he was having trouble making ends meet." He scraped fingers through his hair again. "Hell, I never even knew about his financial troubles until he told me. Ordered me off his place and wouldn't let his wife come visit with Faith after that."

Holt could picture his brother exploding like that. "You're not telling me anything new about my brother. He was the cheerful charmer unless you crossed him. Usually he got over it pretty quick though. My apologies on his behalf."

"Not necessary. I just wanted you to know. I gave up tryin' to tame tornadoes a few years ago, so I wanted to give him time to cool off, stop tossing his horns. If he hadn't got killed, I'd have suggested a compromise. My offer's open."

The former bulldogger's analogy was apt, and the possibility of a compromise piqued Holt's curiosity. Not that he was interested, but he might as well listen. Just to be neighborly. "What sort of compromise?"

Will swallowed some of his beer. He leaned forward, placing his elbows on his knees. Excitement gleamed in his eyes. "A lease for recreational purposes. Rights to take trail rides through the meadows and up Ghost Mountain. Rights to shore up the mine supports so folks could explore, even dig if they wanted to. We could work out a fair price."

Here was one answer to Holt's question of what he'd have to do to save his ranch. But would leasing some land cost the integrity of his family's heritage? "I'll think on it, Will."

"That's all I ask."

Holt followed Will out of the stable. "I'll collect Maddy and head home. Thanks for the beer."

"Sure thing. Maddy's helping Faith with the kids'

activities. On the way to the corral, I'll take you to the new stable." He grinned. "It'll give me a chance to show off the place."

As they walked, Will pointed out the signboard announcing the day's activities. "The trail ride's only one of our offerings. Fly-fishing's real popular. There's more in the summer, but even now we have hiking, archery, riding lessons, roping lessons, and a nightly campfire with yours truly on the guitar. And the Circle-S boasts the best ranch cook in three states. To be successful today a dude ranch has to offer a family vacation. Faith has excellent children's programs geared to age and ability."

Holt couldn't help smiling at the other man's ebullient enthusiasm. "Mighty impressive. You're a walking brochure."

Will laughed and clapped Holt on the back. "Here's the stable. About half the remuda are out carrying the dudes, but you can get a good idea of my stock."

They detoured to the new red-stained building beside the barn. Holt agreed because he'd neglected some questions. They crossed the yard and the dusty ground to the gleaming wooden structure beyond.

From the open doors, it was clear the stable floor was swept clean, and bare new wood gleamed bright as the overhead lights. Dust motes and odors of oats and hay floated in sunbeams slanting through the windowpanes. He entered reluctantly, thinking his envy would only increase after seeing such a dazzling facility.

He was wrong. The new stable was great, but his old barn built by his great-grandfather was fine for the Valley-D. He didn't want or need a fancy building for twenty or thirty animals. "Damn nice facility." He meant it. "Perfect for your operation."

While they checked the occupied stalls, he turned the conversation to the day of Rob's death. "You get much turnover in employees?"

The other man nodded. "We have our year-round hands and wranglers, but in the summer we hire on short-term hands. Mostly itinerants who don't want to stick around long anyway."

"What about in March?" Holt hoisted a shoulder in rueful dismissal. "I expect the sheriff asked you about any strangers working for you about the time Rob was killed."

"He did—twice." Before Holt could apologize for bringing it up again, the other rancher held up a staying hand. "But I don't mind telling you we did have one extra man for a week or so then. Fellow said he had a job in April down in Sonora and needed cash to tide him over. Since I could use an extra hand to finish the stable, I hired him on the spot. Some cowboys resent having to pound nails, but it didn't seem to bother Riggs. He was a bit older. Driver's license said thirty-six."

They stopped in front of a dun-colored horse with a star on its forehead. "Faith needs help mounting up, but she didn't let the accident stop her from riding. This is her favorite. Daybreak's as gentle a mare as you'd find."

"Morgan, is she?" Holt noted the upright ears, the tossing head. "Looks like she expects a treat."

Will fished a hunk of carrot from a hanging pouch. He gave Holt a wide grin. "I'm too soft with these animals."

"Riggs. That's the fellow's name? The one who left?"

"K.C. Riggs. He showed up in a small RV. That was

the first odd thing."

That he might finally be onto something started a twitch in Holt's jaw. None of the other ranchers had sensed anything unusual in their help. Transient hands were typically young cowboys on the circuit, guys who worked wherever they could during the week so they could travel to the next weekend rodeo. "Odd, how?"

"He stayed in his RV, not in the bunkhouse. He was friendly enough with the other hands, but mostly kept to himself. Real private. Almost secretive."

Holt's cop senses clicked to alert. "Did you tell the sheriff this?"

"It didn't come up. He just wanted the name, when he worked here, when he left."

"And that was?"

"The day after Rob was killed." Will's russet brows drew together in thought. "Gave no notice, no warning. He up and left before anyone else here had their boots on—without his pay. I did tell the sheriff that."

Holt's excitement grew. He scooped up a handful of clean woodchips from a nearby wheelbarrow and let them drift between his fingers. " 'First odd thing,' you said. What else was odd about Riggs?"

Will leaned on the stall door. He lifted his hat, dragged a hand through his hair and adjusted the hat again. "What with building the stable and all, I never got around to examining his paperwork until he'd left. A buddy in the Federal Building helped me research his identity. Riggs's Social Security number didn't check out. It belonged to K.C. Riggs all right, but to a K.C. Riggs who died in 1985."

"A phony ID." Holt squeezed his hand closed, crushing the wood chips to dust. "You did tell the sheriff about that." The first real lead, and he should have already known about it.

"I telephoned as soon as I discovered the problem," Will said. "Talked to my brother. Said they'd get right on it. Foley or Luke didn't tell you about that development?"

Holt's throat tightened. "The sheriff has no obligation to tell me how he's conducting the investigation. I have no official status here." *I'm only the dead man's damn brother. 'Sorry for your freaking loss.'* He flung the mangled wood chips back into the wheelbarrow.

The dun mare's nostrils flared, and she tossed her head. Will smoothed a hand down her nose. "Easy, girl. It's okay."

Holt headed toward the other end of the stable, the one leading to the corral. "I didn't mean to upset your horse."

Will caught up to him, waved off the apology. "Luke's supposed to show up this afternoon after his shift. You could ask him about Riggs."

This might be Holt's chance to dig into Luke's issues. He cinched up his resentment toward the sheriff and drew a deep breath. "Maybe. Luke's problems in Denver have anything to do with Chris Hawke?"

Confusion creased Will's forehead. "Can't imagine how they would. Why?"

Holt described the tense exchange between the two men in the sheriff's office, how each man had implied deceit on the part of the other. "What's that all about?"

"You'll have to ask him. I know about as much of what's goes on in my brother's head as I do in a mustang's. Luke's always kept to himself. More so since he came home." As they rounded the barn, Will stopped Holt with a hand on his shoulder. "Luke would have no reason to kill your brother and his wife."

"Like I said, I suspect no one and everyone. I'm just tossing a wide loop to see what it catches."

Chapter Fourteen

AT THE CORRAL, Faith Rafferty lifted a hand from her metal walker and beckoned eagerly. "Hey, Holt. You have to see this." Her sturdy build and coloring marked her as part of the clan, for sure. Her brown hair was tied back in a single braid. She guided Holt's attention to the activity in the corral.

Faith dealt with friends and with the kids, but on her own oblique terms. He reckoned she'd had a hard time adjusting to her physical limitations. The pain in her brown eyes likely didn't stem from strictly physical causes. But the youngest Rafferty sibling greeted him with a warm smile.

Surgery and therapy for extensive muscle and nerve damage must be damned expensive. This family had its troubles, reasons for needing money, but he couldn't see how Rob turning down Will's offer was a motive for murder. Developing Ghost Mountain would be a long-term project, not instant cash.

At this point, he couldn't, wouldn't eliminate anyone or any reason.

"Try again, Maddy," Faith called. "Maybe you can rope that fence post before it gets away."

"Lessons in lassoing are always prime entertainment. Slick's a good teacher," Will murmured to Holt. "Don't drag her away just yet."

"I'm starting to get the hang of this." Maddy

adjusted her gloves and picked up her rope from the dusty ground.

Holt tipped his hat to her. He didn't know what to say. They were supposed to be engaged, but how did you act engaged? Should he grab her butt or bend her over for a lusty kiss? Maybe carry her off over his shoulder? The images stirred his blood, but no way would Maddy thank him for caveman tactics.

Four children ranging in age from about six to twelve were attempting to build loops with thin lengths of kids' roping. A smooth-cheeked young cowboy in a new slant-crowned black hat helped the oldest boy ready his.

"Now build that loop before you swing it, ace," Slick said. "You want it to sing through the air."

The gangly boy weighed the loop in his right hand and held the coil in his left. He bit his lower lip as he stared down the wooden dummy steer. He tossed the rope.

"Good throw, Brian," Will yelled.

The loop snaked out toward the "steer." It settled over the pair of horns and caught. "Whoohoo! I did it!"

Flinging her hat in the air, Maddy gave a cheerleader's leap for the excited youngster. She urged him to bow to his clapping fans, the kids as well as the adults. In a greening pasture beyond, a horse neighed as if in approval.

Brian beamed as if he'd won an Olympic gold medal, and Holt smiled at Maddy's ease with the boy. Her cheeks glowed pink with pleasure.

Leaving the kid to unhook his rope and prepare to toss again, Slick cocked his head at Maddy. He ambled closer.

Judging from the cowboy's lazy-lidded look, Maddy's awkward grip on her loop wasn't his only interest. Hot steel pierced Holt when the suitably named Slick put his arms around her on the pretext of guiding her toss.

"That's it, Maddy, keep that honda secure but loose in your right hand," the fucking Romeo said as he eased both arms around her. One long-fingered hand slid the length of her slim arm. "Give enough slack to the coil in your other hand."

Hell, was he trying to climb into her skin? Holt braced one foot on the lower rail, poised to vault into the corral.

"Whoa, hoss." Will chuckled. "Your woman's safe. Slick knows better'n to rustle another man's brand."

Holt gave a sharp nod and forced himself to remain where he was. *Your woman.* In spite of the cowpoke jargon, Will had it right. Holt was acting engaged after all. Or was he acting? His feelings and his behavior didn't bear examination.

"And build my loop before I toss. I know." Maddy squinted, pursing her lips in a thoughtful pout. A maddeningly sexy pout, dammit. She adjusted her grasp of the honda, the eye the loop passed through. Slick stepped back out of the way and she swung her arm.

Holt let out the breath he wasn't conscious of holding.

Her rope whirred through the air toward the dummy. The leading edge snared one horn but slid to the ground.

"Whoa, you almost had 'er." Her hot-eyed teacher clapped her on the back. "That's the closest yet."

After retrieving her rope and her hat, she ruffled the boy Brian's curly hair. "Guess I need more practice to be as good a roper as you."

He grinned with his whole body, like an eager puppy wagging a stubby tail. "You keep trying. You'll get it too."

"Another time." She handed her rope to Slick and removed her gloves. "Thanks for all your help. That was fabulous."

When she pumped the cowboy's hand instead of giving him the expected hug, Holt relaxed. Nobody threw herself into a new experience more than Maddy. Nobody enjoyed it more. At times sadness clouded her eyes, but dark emotion couldn't repress her natural vivacity. In the child that mercurial personality had annoyed him. In the woman it captivated him.

When Maddy joined the other adults outside the corral, Holt was smiling at her. A surprise, but was the greeting welcome? Or pride? Though why he should be proud of her for playing with the kids while he slogged around the shooting scene with the deputies eluded her. Passing her time with the lasso had quelled her jittery nerves. Two confrontations with death in two days were two more than a person should have in a lifetime. At least the landslide had been an accident.

No remorse would chip at her pleasure in accomplishment. He'd wait until he found out what else she'd done with her time.

She gave Holt a bright smile as she joined Will, Faith, and him outside the corral.

"You're a quick study." Holt edged to her side and slid an arm around her shoulders. "Good control."

Maddy's breath caught on his masculine scent. She went as still as a fence post. A curl of heat slid through her. So much for control. "Thanks."

"Hey, you two, congratulations on your engagement," Will said. "That all got lost in the earlier to-do."

"Yes, when's the happy day?" Faith asked softly. She turned her walker to face them.

Maddy's shocked pleasure at Holt's affection thudded to a sudden stop. He was acting. It was the engagement pretext. Not her. Okay, let him answer the question.

"We have some things to figure out first. We haven't set a date yet." Holt's big hand squeezed her shoulder as though daring her to contradict him.

She nearly blurted out a date just to irk him, but just in time remembered that her big mouth and not his had dumped them into this fix.

She smiled at Faith. "Thanks for letting me in on the roping lesson. It was great fun." She winked at her friend. "I've been after Holt to let me help with the branding this weekend. Maybe I can rope calves with Bronc now."

"Branding weekend, huh?" Will asked. "You fixed for all the help you need?"

"We'll manage." Holt's expression slid from open to defensive. His hand stilled on her shoulder.

Maddy jabbed him with her elbow. "Barely. It's Espie's sons and me, but Holt and Bronc are the only ones who know one end of a branding iron from the other."

"I could spare a couple of guys for the day." Will took off his hat and resettled it on his head. "Luke's a fair hand with a reata."

Jaw working against his pride, Holt appeared to let the idea take root. "I don't like to be beholden, and I can't pay. Sure could use another roper though." He gave Maddy a rueful look. "One with experience."

Maddy shrugged, pleased Holt was considering the offer. She'd find some other way to edge into the action.

"Hell, I don't expect payment. In money." Will tilted his head back and laughed, an explosion of mirth as large as the man. "I hope you'll return the favor. Next weekend, hundreds of Cowboy Action shooters will descend on this place. I could use some extra hands then myself."

Holt let his hand drop, and Maddy rued the loss of his warmth. "I think I remember that. Don't the shooters use Old West style guns like Colt .45's?"

Will nodded. "Single-action revolvers and lever action rifles or vintage shotguns."

"Mounted competitions use blanks with black powder, but for the target shooting we use live ammunition. It's great fun," Faith added. "Everyone dresses in Old West outfits, and the contestants have colorful aliases like Comanche Sam or Deadeye Donovan." She sent Holt a tentative smile.

"Bronc Baker's your man, but that kind of play-acting's not for me," Holt said, holding up his hands in defense. "Those shooting scenarios remind me too much of the real thing." He offered the ranch manager his hand. "I'll take you up on your offer, then, Will. I won't shoot, but I don't mind helping out some other way next weekend."

"Count me in." Maddy stepped forward. "I wouldn't miss a great show for the world."

"But what about Bobby?" Holt cast her a puzzled look.

Faith chuckled. "Not a problem. We have

babysitting services all arranged. Do come."

"I even have a business deal for you, Maddy," Will said. "Word is you're a professional photographer. That right?"

"She has articles in international magazines," Holt announced.

Maddy blinked at the pride in his voice. Pride, not criticism. Peeling her gaze from him, she turned to Will. If his interest meant money, she was all ears. "What do you have in mind?"

"Next weekend's match is a tri-state competition. The organization's regional governor was sending a photographer, but he got sick. We need publicity shots. If you're game, we can pay you well."

When he named a generous fee, she said, "You bet. I'd love it." She glanced up at Holt. He probably suspected she'd bolt if she had enough money. Would he trust her with Bobby after next weekend? "How about it? I can take time out now and then to check in on the baby."

His expression didn't give away his thoughts, but he'd lowered his hat brim to shade his eyes. "Fine with me. You do what you want."

"Spending the day here will give you another chance to see the workings of the Circle-S. Get to know more about the investment you're considering." Will beamed at Maddy.

"Thanks. I appreciate it. You have a wonderful operation here." She turned to Holt, hoping he didn't construe her praise as a desire to leave his household. And Bobby. And him. "Ready to go?"

Holt nodded. After thanking Will for his help, he urged Maddy to prepare for the ride home.

"You sure you don't want someone to drive you? We can load up the horses in the van," Will said.

"We'll be fine."

Maddy squared her shoulders. She could be as stoic as Holt. "Now that the deputies have tramped all over the valley, that shooter's long gone."

Will and Faith remained with Slick and the kids, who continued their lasso lessons. One of the hands accompanied Holt and Maddy to the stable to retrieve their horses.

They rode in silence until they reached the valley. The afternoon sun cast long shadows across the grassy meadow, and Maddy snapped her collar against the cool air. A lone hawk piloted the air currents above Ghost Mountain.

"Tell me more about this investment in the Circle-S. You know I have concerns about some of the Raffertys. Does that put you in the middle?" He stared straight ahead, his back as stiff as his pride.

She edged her mare closer to him and described the terms of her grandparents' will. "I've made no decisions and I have no connection to the Raffertys themselves. The only home I have is a storage unit near my parents' condo." She paused, pondering, but opted for honesty. "I'd been thinking about a home base in this valley. If Faith hadn't contacted me about Rob's death, I'd have come anyway. To scope out the possibilities."

He cast her a cynical look. "The jet-set life losing its appeal?"

"Yes, as a matter of fact. I'm torn between wanting to help people with my skills and wanting my own home and family. The Circle-S seemed the logical place, but it might not work out."

"Living at the Circle-S." He seemed to mull that over. "Any reason you didn't mention it before?"

"I wasn't sure how you'd feel about it."

He made no response to that, walking his horse onward in silence.

His reticence made sense, but she desperately wanted his response. She had to say something to jar him out of his funk. "Too bad Luke is coming to help Bronc with the calf roping. I hoped to get in some practice."

"Branding is serious business. You can go back to your fast-handed pal if you want roping practice." His voice rasped like rocks on sandpaper.

Fast-handed? What in the world?

Little wings fluttered in her stomach. But no, Holt couldn't possibly be jealous. More likely he resented her being away from Bobby all this time. Best to change the subject. "Did you learn anything helpful about the man who ambushed us?"

"Some." As they approached the scene of the crime, he described the deputies' canvas of the area and the bullets they dislodged from the aspen. "And while you were playing around with Pretty Boy Slick, I learned more by downing a *cerveza* and touring the new stable with Will." He tilted his head and scowled at her.

So it was possessive sniping after all. A glow of warmth tingled in her belly and the wings beat faster. She gave him a slow wink. "Bet what I picked up dancing the lasso tango is juicier than you got swilling beer." She settled her hat firmly on her head.

Maybe it wasn't smart, given what had happened to them going the other direction, but she just couldn't help herself. "Race you."

As her mare lurched into action, her last glimpse of Holt was of his gaping mouth.

Chapter Fifteen

HOLT CAUGHT UP with Maddy in the barn as she was unsaddling Chica. He'd deliberately hung back to quell the storm raging inside him.

Her impetuosity had cornered him into accepting help. Or maybe she'd planned it. Maddy plan? Maybe. But that wasn't what put a burr under his saddle. She'd gone racing off across that field with no thought to the possibility of the gunman's return. Having her around would turn his hair white.

Once this custody problem with Bobby ended, she'd leave. But what if she went only as far as the Circle-S? Not that he ought to care. Aggravating woman. He shook his head.

Lust, on the other hand, was familiar and manageable, but he had to rein in unwanted possessive urges and protective instincts. If he'd jumped into the corral while that pimply-faced prick had his hands on Maddy, he'd have decked him. Not cool. Maybe acting engaged had simply confused his libido. Like hell.

He walked his horse into the stall and peered across at Maddy. "Okay, Sherlock, just what the hell did you find out?"

"Just a doggone minute, Donovan. I won our little horse race, so you have to wait. You go first."

He flipped up the stirrup and fender. Working his jaw, he loosened the cinch. Sensing the strain in his

150

hands, Bandito shook his head. Holt soothed a palm down the sleek neck. "Will told me about a hand they had who left the day after Rob and Sara died."

Maddy's single blink wasn't the reaction he expected. Not surprised? But she'd tell him her news in her own damn good time. The woman could give lessons in obstinate.

He explained the Circle-S boss's offer for Ghost Mountain. "I wonder if his stubborn pride got him killed."

Maddy shook her head. "I can't see Will Rafferty committing murder for Ghost Mountain. Hey, maybe there's silver in that old mine someone wants. But Will? No."

"What little silver there was played out long ago. But that wasn't what I meant. I don't know what I meant." He scrubbed a hand over his eyes.

Maddy lugged her saddle off the mare and deposited it beside the other. "Family pride might not have caused Rob's death, but it might've kept the ranch from prospering. Like his older brother, he didn't like accepting help from others. Even old friends."

She was something. Holt felt his mouth tilt in spite of his doldrums. "Think you're pretty smart herding me into having extra hands for the branding."

"Quid pro quo. The cowboy action shooting should be fun." She grinned and picked up a curry brush. Starting on her mount's coat, she said, "What did Will say about the drifter?"

"In March, he hired an extra hand to help finish the stable. Fellow named K.C. Riggs was thirty-six according to his driver's license. Drove a small RV and kept to himself."

"I imagine most of these drifters who sign on as temporary hands are loners. So what else?"

"After he left, Will checked out his Social Security number. No such animal. Keeping to yourself isn't damning, but high-tailing it when he did sure is suspicious."

"So's living under an assumed name. I read a mystery once where a woman used old obituaries to find aliases. She pretended to be the person and requested a card from Social Security to replace her lost one and used it to get a driver's license. Is it really that easy?"

"Unfortunately. Unless someone digs a little deeper, like Rafferty did. I'll phone the sheriff and grill Luke Saturday sometime during the branding."

"Do you suspect Luke?"

"Like I told Will, I suspect no one and everyone. I'm just asking questions."

He hauled the saddles over to the rack in the adjacent tack room. After placing the saddle blankets upside down on the saddles to dry out, he returned to slip the gelding's bridle free. "Your turn, McCoy."

Maddy had just finished placing buckets of water in both stalls. A mischievous grin curved her lips. "The cliché of the strong, silent type must have originated with the cowboy. It's like coaxing a wild animal to eat out of your hand. But he'll talk if he has something to argue or brag about."

"You mean Slick." Tension coiled in his gut, but he forced himself to relax.

"A pretty face, but easily blinded by a little flash." She sashayed closer to Holt, swaying her hips seductively.

He knew exactly what she meant by flash, and it

didn't come from a camera. Holt grabbed her upper arms and forced her to stand still before him. Her scent drifted through his senses, obliterating horse and leather smells.

"So you suckered him in." *Just like me. And Rob.* He drew his brows together into a scowl, his only shield. "Go on."

She smiled. "Slick boasted he could rope and wrangle better than anyone in three counties. Faith had told me about that drifter, so I let on I'd heard this Riggs was a fair hand with animals and a lasso."

"Are you getting to the point anytime soon?"

Her smile faded to a grim line. "After he finished sneering about the drifter not knowing a hammer from a horse, he dropped the big one. He saw Riggs in his camper cleaning a high-tech high-caliber rifle. Riggs slammed the door in his face."

His pulse spiked at her words. *High-caliber rifle.* Like the one that very morning that shot out Rob's tires and fired at Holt and Maddy.

"H-Holt. You're hurting me." She was prying at his fingers clamped on her arms.

Horrified, he relaxed his fingers and dropped his arms. He took a step back. "Shit. Sorry, Maddy."

"Slick didn't see anything else like a scope or ammunition, I'm afraid." Questions but not blame in her eyes, she rubbed her arms.

Holt stalked back and forth in front of the horse stalls. Flames of fury licked at him, but a cool head was the only recourse. He had to be an investigator, not a brother, and not a target. "Riggs had no motive for killing my family. According to Will, he didn't even know them."

But someone did. And that someone had wanted

153

them dead.

"Could he have met Sara when she went to the Circle-S to visit Faith?"

"By the time Riggs showed up, Rob was keeping Sara away from there."

"Ah, the Ghost Mountain thing. And you don't think he was just hunting that morning? Maybe after the truck crashed down the mountain, he took off because he was scared."

"Any hunter who shoots game with an exploding .50 caliber bullet won't have any trophy or meat to bring home. No, if he shot at their tires, it was deliberate."

"But why?" Her lower lip began to tremble, and she bit down on it.

"The only explanation is that someone hired Riggs to kill them."

And the one behind the murder has returned. Or hired another killer.

Fear for what could happen to Bobby edged into his brain, and he pushed it away. He'd telephone the sheriff right away. If that office had done nothing about finding Riggs, he knew a few guys in the Denver DEA office who'd help him.

He had to do something. And fast.

Horror darkened Maddy's eyes. "A paid killer? Like a…hit man?"

"If true, it about lets anyone at the Circle-S off the hook. That operation's in the black, but professional hired guns cost more than a gold-trimmed saddle. Even if Will Rafferty expected to dig ore out of Ghost Mountain, at the price of silver today, making any money would take years."

Gut as tight as a cinched saddle, he slammed a hand

against the wall. "No, if someone's paying this Riggs or whoever he is, they have more resources than anyone around here. Why? And who would have that kind of money to target Rob and Sara? And now maybe—"

"You…and me? Who indeed?" Tears glistened, and she hugged herself, but not because of bruised arms.

He drew her into his arms, and she came as willingly as she had by the stream. "I wouldn't blame you if you wanted to leave now. You signed on for baby care, not murder."

"I'll stick. If I leave, it will be because I'm no use to you. Or Bobby. And for no other reason." She trembled, but didn't raise her face for his kiss.

Thank God. If she had, he might not stop this time. Her warm curves fit him perfectly, and he could feel her contrasting textures against his chest—the softness of her breasts and the insistent hardness of her nipples. His need for her scraped at him with hot claws. He was no longer certain sex with Maddy would cleanse her from his system.

He had a plan for finding K.C. Riggs or whoever the shooter was, but what would he do about Madelyn McCoy?

****

The telephone receiver dropped into its cradle with a soft click. He spread his fingers on the polished mahogany of the desk, then picked up a custom-made silver-and-gold inlaid knife and scraped it beneath his polished fingernails.

The man standing before the desk took a cautious step closer. "Success, *jefe*?"

"The fool!" The long knife blade snapped shut and open again. "He has failed again."

His employee licked his lips. "If you will permit, perhaps it is just as well. Your enemy does not yet know why he should fear your vengeance."

His pulse faltered with sudden doubt, which he took care not to show. With deliberation, he closed the knife and placed it on the desktop. "Perhaps not." He reached once more for the telephone. "I shall make certain he does."

****

As if Bobby knew the day would bring excitement, he woke the household up long before dawn on Saturday. Maddy didn't mind. She was as eager as he to begin the biggest day in the life of a ranch. Billowy white clouds blocked the sun, but forecasters promised mild temperatures and no rain.

Esperanza and her sons, Danny and Sean, arrived as Holt and Bronc were starting the branding fire and readying the tools. Maddy held Bobby in her arms as she and Holt greeted them at the corral.

The two O'Grady boys looked like amalgams of their parents. They had the blue-black hair of their Ute ancestry, but the Celtic features and lanky build of their father. From the excited gleams in their brown eyes, they couldn't wait to be real cowboys, do real cowboy work. In well-worn boots and baggy jeans, they swaggered into the corral.

"You fellers ready to wrestle some calves?" Bronc said, with a sidewise wink to their mother.

"You bet. I been practicin' on little brother here," replied Danny, directing a punch at Sean's shoulder.

Apparently used to his brother's fists, Sean ducked. "Danny couldn't catch a calf if it sat on his feet, Mr. Bronc. I'm your man."

"In the old days," Bronc explained to the boys, "they heated the irons over a wood fire, but our fire's propane-fueled. More reliable." Spelling out their tasks for the day, he led them over to the pen where the calves had been separated from their mothers.

When Holt approached, Maddy turned Bobby toward him. Holt put a hand on her shoulder and bent to blow zerberts against Bobby's belly. She nearly purred at the warmth of his almost caress. The baby squealed with delight and waved his fists. *Your fan club.*

"As long as Espie's okay with both the cooking and my little buddy here, you're all set to do the vaccinations and ear notching," he said to Maddy.

"I can help Espie too if she needs me." Maddy raised her chin, ready to begin.

He tilted his hat to the women before disappearing into the barn.

Her heart thumped at the sight of his long-legged stride. He was every inch the proud rancher. The short chaps called chinks he wore were more practical for working on the ground to do the branding, and they accentuated his lean butt. And his denim shirt brought out the matching blue of his eyes, compelling against his tan. She sighed.

He was working so hard to make a go of this shoestring ranch, trying to be stoic and brave. Maybe he was even softening a little. After all, he'd accepted the extra help she finagled without blowing up at her.

"He's good with them, isn't he?" Espie said, a bemused expression on her broad face.

Maddy blinked in confusion. "Them?"

"My boys. Bronc's good with them."

Hoping Espie hadn't noticed her distraction, Maddy

forced her gaze to where the ranch hand was showing Espie's sons how to tackle a calf. "A kind man," she agreed. "He's as patient with them as he is with the horses. Do those boys know what they're in for with this operation?"

The housekeeper laughed. "I don't know. They've watched from atop a fence before, over at a friend's place, but there's nothing like the real thing."

The real thing. Today was the real thing, for sure—the real heart of ranch existence, rooted in tradition, branding the new spring animals as your own. Protecting the calves by identifying them and vaccinating them against diseases that could wipe out the herd.

Over the last few years, Maddy had pushed out of her head how much she missed this life—its rituals, its animals, its oneness with nature. Being part of it again brought home to her how artificial was her part in it. How temporary.

Yesterday's shooting had terrified her, for more than one reason. Holt seemed convinced the shooter was the same person who killed Rob. Slick's glimpse of the drifter's rifle seemed to support that. That the killer might be after her and Holt was chilling enough, but the experience had also forced her to face what lurked in her heart. And to see that she couldn't stay here.

She couldn't leave with no one to care for Bobby and with the grandparents' lawsuit hanging over Holt like an executioner's ax. Yet if she stayed much longer, she feared she wouldn't be able to leave at all. She had long ago given her heart to Bobby. With every shared moment, every small intimacy, every kiss, she felt herself falling in love with Holt.

He'd replaced sniping with pride in her

accomplishments. Whenever she looked into the banked fires of his cobalt gaze, his obvious desire kindled sparks deep within her and shunted aside the fact that he felt he couldn't trust her. His strength and relentless loyalty, his determination and pride gave her a sense of security and protection that she liked much too much. *Oh God, what am I going to do?*

She had no answer to the question.

After handing over the baby to Espie, Maddy ducked into the barn to help bring out the implements of their work for the day—bottles of vaccine, syringes, antiseptic sprays, and ear-notching and castrating tools.

As soon as they were ready, Luke Rafferty and another cowhand he introduced as Sonny arrived in a high-wheeled black pickup with the ranch brand, an *S* inside a circle, as a logo on the side panel. From the horse trailer behind, Luke unloaded his horse.

Holt circled the vehicle, scanning it up and down while Luke saddled up. When the deputy gazed at him quizzically, he said, "Nice truck. Do much off-roading in her?"

"A bit around the ranch is all. Why?"

Holt's lips curved briefly. "Thinking about new wheels."

Maddy shook her head at the odd exchange. She made a mental note to ask later.

After everyone was assembled inside the corral, Holt said, "Let's get to it, folks. We've got about a hundred of these little critters to tackle."

With that call of the ringmaster, the circus began. The day before, Holt and Bronc had gathered up the cattle and stashed them in the nearby meadow. About twenty of the brick-red-and-white calves had already been separated from their mothers and penned beside the corral. Mothers and calves mooed nervously to each other.

Bronc and Luke mounted up, ready to begin roping calves. Both riders wielded seventy-foot leather braided reatas, nothing like the simple rope Maddy had practiced with. She grabbed her camera from her case parked beside the corral fence so she could capture the action.

Bronc lassoed the first heifer's hind legs, and the O'Grady boys drag-carried the bawling animal over to the branding fire.

"That's it, boys. Danny, sit on her neck and grab onto that foreleg," Bronc yelled. "Sean, pin those hind legs or you'll catch it."

The calf and the boys struggled in the dust, and the humans almost lost the battle. Finally the calf lay on its side. Once immobilized, the animal quieted.

Maddy set aside her camera, ready to start her work for the day. She injected the first of three vaccinations.

"You do the ear notching next," Holt ordered. "The branding's last." Observing her every move, he rotated the branding iron in the propane fire.

The ear notching tool worked a little like a hole punch, and she'd done it before. But being so close to the red-hot branding iron tightened her stomach.

When she finished her tasks, he nodded his approval, then applied the Valley-D brand, a *V* overlaid with a *D*. She winced at the burnt hair smell and the calf's bellow for mama, but dug in her heels. She could do this. After she dusted the brand with antiseptic powder, the little heifer scrambled to her feet in a flurry of kicked dust.

From then on, the day was a blur of dust, the stench

of burned hide, and bawling calves. Bronc and Luke worked together as if they'd performed as a tag team for years, alternating loops to capture the calves. Then the O'Grady boys wrestled each wriggling calf over to the branding site and held it down for the duration.

Besides administering the Valley-D brand, Holt's job was to snip the testicles from the bull calves, determining their destiny as beef. Maddy covered the incision with antiseptic spray before the animal was released. Once the two of them eased into a rhythm, their part of the process took less than two minutes.

As soon as a calf was on its feet, Bronc herded it into the meadow to mother up, brief pain and indignities forgotten. The process began all over again with a new batch of calves.

Espie called them in for lunch at noon, and none too soon. Maddy had aches in places she didn't know she had muscles, and Danny and Sean looked like the entire adult herd had trampled them into the dirt.

"You ready to call it quits?" Holt said, eyeing her with skepticism.

She grinned at him. "When you are." No way was she yielding. A little nourishment and she'd be all set.

Espie had prepared a meal fit for a working crew—fried chicken, mashed potatoes, and a mountain of vegetables, followed by apple cobbler. Everyone fixed plates from the spread on the table and found a place to sit down and shovel it in.

Maddy observed Holt following Luke out to the porch. Interrogation time.

Chapter Sixteen

Holt collapsed into one of the rocking chairs. "I sure do appreciate your coming over to help out like this."

Luke placed his dusty Stetson on the small table beside him, then smoothed his blond hair. He forked up a mound of potato. "Ridin' and ropin' sure beat whatever my big brother would have come up with for me to do today. I might have to catch forty winks before riding patrol tonight, though."

Luke's relaxed demeanor and candid expression opened the door for Holt. "Sheriff tell you I called about K.C. Riggs?"

The deputy's candor vanished under a shuttered gaze. "He might have mentioned it."

"Any particular reason Foley or you didn't tell me about Riggs before?"

Luke shrugged. "No point. Until we had some information, there was nothing to tell. He's not a suspect. Officially."

"You had luck tracing him?"

"Sent his description out. The sheriff telephoned Sonora, where Riggs told one of the hands he was going next." He returned to his meal, biting into a chicken leg. "Too bad there's no more to go on."

"Description's not much help," Holt mused. "Brown hair and eyes, medium build fits half the men in the country." He laid his fork on his plate. Leaned forward.

"What about the gun?"

"Riggs's rifle?" Luke snorted. "Hell, that's even worse. Could've been a deer rifle for all I know. Slick's the only one who saw the weapon. He couldn't describe it worth shit."

Holt stirred around Espie's Parmesan tomatoes that usually vanished into his stomach first thing. He jabbed his fork into a crispy chicken thigh. "Did he see a scope?"

Chewing, the other man shook his head. "Even if we had this guy Riggs and his rifle, and he had opportunity, that still leaves motive."

That was the kicker. *Why.* The guarded aspect of Luke's expression nagged at Holt. "Motive indeed. Like the sheriff said, everyone around here liked Rob."

Indecision rippled across Luke's cool green eyes. He took his time chewing on his buttered roll. "Foley did say that. Fact is not everyone thought Rob walked on water. More than one caught the rough side of his temper."

"You one of them, Luke?"

****

At nine o'clock that evening, Maddy flopped on the enveloping silk cushions of the blue and mauve living-room sofa. Pretty and comfy but much too frilly and delicate for the rustic ranch house. She stuffed one of the brocade throw pillows behind her back and propped her feet on the mesquite-wood cocktail table.

They'd finished with the branding just before dark. After backslapping and handshakes all around, Luke and the other Circle-S cowboy loaded up the horse and left. Sean and Danny O'Grady collapsed bonelessly on hay bales, moaning they'd never be able to walk again. As soon as Holt waved paychecks at them, they kicked up their heels like colts in a pasture. Espie invited Bronc home to dinner, and to everyone's surprise, he accepted.

Maddy and Holt devoured the few leftovers for supper before she put Bobby to bed. Exhaustion engulfed every fiber of her body, but it was a good kind of tiredness, accompanied by the satisfaction of a job well done. Of participating in something permanent that went back generations, a ritual rooted in the soil as deeply as the surrounding mountains.

Holt came in and stretched out at the other end of the sofa. He too had showered and changed. He wore clean, worn jeans and a black tee shirt that proclaimed in red letters, "COWBOYS DO IT IN THE SADDLE."

Sandy hair frothed across the backs of his hands, and sinews defined his forearms. Maddy ogled his broad chest and narrow hips, but it was the intimacy of his bare feet and wet hair that had her swallowing hard.

"I have to hand it to you." Holt passed her a longneck.

"You just did," she quipped. "Thanks." The cold brew bit and soothed at the same time. She sighed and sank lower into the cushions.

"Smartass." He slugged back a long swallow of beer. "Seriously, Maddy, you did great out there. Without your help, I might not have finished all those calves today. The cow herd is ready to go to the upper pasture anytime."

"Thanks. It was fun." She shifted sideways and curled a leg beneath her. "Get back to what you were telling me about Luke. Did he and Rob have problems?"

He wagged his head. "I still don't know why Chris Hawke and Luke were shaking their horns at each other.

What you said about that, '*Cherchez la femme*,' applies here too."

"A woman? And Rob?"

"Sara. Seems Luke went out with her a few times before Rob horned in. He let Luke know in no uncertain terms he better butt out."

She'd been thinking about Rob's obsessive control over his wife. It was possible he was so controlling because of Maddy's leaving. She shook off the question. No way to know. Would he have become so overprotective of her? She'd not have let him get away with smothering her, but apparently Sara didn't mind. He seemed to have given in to her in other ways, indulging her whims and wishes. Jealousy of other men might've seemed the behavior of a loving husband to Sara, younger than Rob. But the other man—Luke or anyone else—reacting with murder? A stretch. She wouldn't reveal any of those suppositions to Holt. He'd had enough shocks about his brother.

"Not much of a motive for murder," she finally said.

"As a DEA agent, I've known people to kill for less." He closed his eyes and leaned against the sofa. "But in this case, I agree. I don't see Luke blowing Rob away—and Sara—because he's warned off after a few dates. And he hasn't the cash to hire out murder."

Sipping their beers, they sat in companionable, tired silence for a few moments.

"You know, when I came home and started all this," he said, his voice deep with intensity, "I never thought I'd be finding out things that made me ashamed of my brother."

She saw in his troubled gaze that he needed to cleanse the wounds Rob's vagaries had made, air them before they'd heal. "You knew he had flaws—his temper, for one."

"And his obsession with you—with Sara too." His jaw tightened, then eased. "My brother never really grew up, I reckon. I thought he'd learned to control his temper, but Luke implied Rob had alienated a few people around Rangewood."

He sat up straight and lowered his brows as he studied her face. "He never turned violent with you, did he? Abusive?"

Maddy laid a hand on his knee. "He never touched me except in affection. He may have been controlling, a good-time Charlie who wanted things his way, but physically abusive, no. That's something you don't need to worry about. Don't let yourself feel guilty for what you had no power over."

"So now you're reading minds." He turned his hand over and laced his fingers with hers.

The rough, callused texture of his big hand shimmered heat up her arm and through her body. "No mind-reading involved. You're a take-charge kind of guy. You pride yourself on being responsible for everything around you."

"I do that?" He shifted closer to her.

"You always have." She smiled, her heart squeezing at the sadness in his eyes. "You can't fix everybody. People are too complex. He was your brother and you loved him. Find his killer if you can, but don't feel ashamed that your loyalty doesn't extend to blindness."

"So I should let the rest go, huh, doc?" He sent her a crooked grin that softened his rugged features.

"At least don't think you're responsible for whatever faults Rob had." She winked at him, and then yawned. "Now take two aspirin and call me in the morning. But not too early."

"Thanks, McCoy." The tension in his jaw eased, and male awareness gleamed in his eyes. His gaze dropped to her mouth.

Her pulse jumped. It would be so easy to lean into his kiss, to block out problems with a night of mindless sex. Would a man so in control of his emotions use that control to give and prolong pleasure?

There lay inspiration.

Or would the rein he kept on himself be so tight, so stretched that it snapped?

And there lay temptation.

And way too much risk.

She placed her free hand on his chest. When she'd rather fist it in his shirt, breathe in his clean scent, and taste those sculpted lips, she pushed gently. "Whoa, boy. Things are already more complicated than a twin-lens reflex."

He released her hand and slid his arms around her. "At this moment I don't much care. What I want is damned simple."

"Holt, we—"

Sharp tapping at the kitchen door stunned them both.

Holt slumped. "Bronc must be back. I hope nothing's happened to any of the calves." He pushed to his feet and loped into the kitchen.

Three louder, peremptory knocks brought Maddy to her feet as well. When she saw Edgar and Phyllis Patterson in the open doorway, tension knotted her stomach. Whatever they wanted, their visit meant trouble.

Holt hung up their coats on the pegs by the door

before ushering Bobby's grandparents into the room. "Hour's a little late for a social visit," he said. "Is there a problem?"

Phyllis shielded her matronly stomach with her clutch purse. Her green polyester pantsuit was smooth as armor, but disapproval gathered more wrinkles around her pursed lips than on the Wicked Witch of the West.

If she didn't have such a strong portent of disaster, Maddy would've smiled at the image. "If you're worried about Bobby, you can go peek at him. He's sound asleep."

Phyllis scurried down the hall, her low-heeled pumps clicking on the worn oak floor.

Edgar Patterson had girded for battle in a charcoal gray business suit and a red power tie. He smoothed his wispy hair over his balding pate. "The county weekly came out this afternoon. The *Rangewood Messenger* contained some very disturbing news. Two days ago you two were shot at."

Holt had dreaded Patterson's reaction to the news. How would the wily banker turn the situation to his advantage? He began to explain, but Patterson cut him off.

"I know all about how it happened, young man. What disturbs me is what it means for the safety of my grandson."

"My nephew was perfectly safe. *Is* safe. He was here with Espie, not in the line of fire." But he realized what worried the Pattersons was exactly what worried him— what might happen if the killer returned for another try. The same thought must have crossed Maddy's mind, but thankfully she curbed any impulse to say so.

When Phyllis returned to the room, Maddy said,

"Let's go sit in the living room. We'll be much more comfortable."

The older couple took up positions on the sofa, and Holt and Maddy selected the opposite matching armchairs.

With a scornful glance at the half-empty beer bottles on the table, Phyllis said, "My Sara picked out this furniture. She was a good girl, a steady girl, my Sara." She plucked a tissue from her bag and dabbed at her nose.

"Yes, ma'am." Maddy scanned the room as if assessing the decor. "She had good taste."

The colors were all right, but not the puffy sofa and chairs. Or the silly pillows. Too flimsy-looking. The mesquite wood table was okay.

"Just what's your concern, Edgar?" Holt held himself still and composed, but his jaw ached, and double granny knots bound up his gut.

Patterson cast his wife a sideways glance. "We have more than one. Bobby's safety must come first and foremost, of course. Perhaps the shooting was merely a hunting accident. I have urged the sheriff to put his best men on the case."

"I appreciate that. An important man such as yourself can have more influence than I can." Flattering the enemy never hurt your cause.

The banker's chest puffed out with self-importance. He nodded. "We have nothing personal against Ms. McCoy here" —he studiously avoided Maddy's gaze— "but Phyllis and I have doubts about her reliability." He went on to enumerate her failings—leaving Rob at the altar and traipsing the globe, the very history that made Holt doubt her.

"I see you've done some checking on me." Maddy kept her voice neutral and her expression blank, but a wash of red on her fine cheekbones stood out in relief against a pale-as-bone complexion.

"I felt it was my obligation to know what sort of person was caring for my grandson." He still addressed only Holt as if Maddy wasn't there. "Instability is detrimental to a child's growth and well-being. We intend to assure that the judge is cognizant of Ms. McCoy's background, her penchant for, shall we say...flight."

"She ran away from one wedding. What's to say she won't do it again? Like the girl in that movie." Patting her tight gray curls, Phyllis sent a dagger glance Maddy's way.

"It was eight years ago. I was young and unsettled. I've matured. I've changed." It wasn't surprising that Maddy could contain herself no longer. Her expression bordered on mutinous.

"And the situation has changed." Holt reached across the magazine rack between their chairs and clasped Maddy's hand. When she held on tight, her trust reassured him. "Maddy's made herself an integral part of the ranch as well as an important part of Bobby's life. I trust her to stay."

At his hypocrisy, she dug her nails into his palm. If they were long instead of short and neat, she'd have drawn blood. He felt her eyes raking him, winced at their amethyst slice. Dammit. He didn't trust her, but by God, he wished he could.

"Be that as it may," Patterson said, apparently unaware of the undercurrent, "*we* don't trust her to stay, and neither will the judge." Eyes as gray and cold as gunmetal, he stood and took his wife's arm. "I can see we're at an impasse here."

Since they'd already made up their minds about her, why did they come, other than to reassure themselves of Bobby's safety? Holt had a nagging feeling the skirmish wasn't over.

In the kitchen, Patterson shrugged on his overcoat, then cleared his throat. "Finances can exacerbate instability in such a makeshift family. It would be a shame if the bank doubted your ability to repay the equity loan. The board might have to demand repayment early."

At the threat, Maddy exploded. She quivered with anger. "So that was the reason you came here tonight, to threaten Holt, you slimy—"

"Don't, Maddy." Holt wished he could tell them exactly what he thought. Slimy was too fucking mild. "Don't give them the satisfaction."

He turned to the Pattersons. "Bobby's a Donovan, and he'll be raised a Donovan. I take care of my own. From now on, I'll bring Bobby to town for your visits. You're not welcome on the Valley-D."

"Come, Edgar," Phyllis said on an imperious sniff. "We'll have our grandson out of this place soon enough."

"Have you heard?" Patterson straightened his shoulders for his final salvo. "Judge Gilbert set the court date for the custody hearing. May twenty-six. You have two weeks. Then our grandson comes home with us. For good."

Chapter Seventeen

THE NIGHTMARE PLAGUED Maddy again that night. With a change. This time, when Rob's ghost approached her, it was through a hail of bullets. When Bobby's wail summoned her, she moaned a relieved thanks. Holt's bedroom door stood open, his bed still made.

After the Pattersons had left, she and Holt hashed over what to do, but resolved nothing. Stiff-backed, he'd stomped off to his room, saying he intended to go over the books. To find extra money for the loan. Nothing she could do to help with that.

"But where is he now, pumpkin?" she asked the red-faced infant. "Bet I know. You mind a walk outside?"

A few minutes later, carrying a freshly diapered and blanketed Bobby and his bottle, she trailed Holt out to the barn. "The light's a dead giveaway," she whispered.

When she entered the tack room, Holt dropped the bridle he was mending and surged from the bench. "Something wrong with the baby?"

"Bobby's fine." She sat on another low bench and arranged Bobby on her lap. "We were worried about you." She spread the extra flap of blanket over her knees for warmth. Soon the comforting gurgles of the baby inhaling his bottle calmed both adults. A space unit in one corner heated the small room to a comfortable temperature.

Holt picked up the abandoned bridle, a hackamore. He heaved a deep sigh. "After I went over the books, I couldn't sleep."

"Could the bank really call in the loan early? That sounds fishy."

"I don't know. I'll call Chris Hawke tomorrow to find out. There's a clause in the loan agreement that might apply. Patterson's a greedy son of a bitch, but setting up his daughter's husband to lose his ranch would rank him lower than a snake's belly."

"Can you pay?"

"I've used up most of my savings keeping the place afloat as it is. I don't like to sell cattle before they fatten up in the summer, but I may have to. If I unload a few head, it might be enough for a couple of payments, to show good faith, but no way can I pay off the balance." He dragged a hand through his hair. "It would set back my long-term goals."

"Oh?" She waited, her gaze on him, hoping he'd trust her enough to elaborate.

"Not enough land here to make it a big-time beef herd. I'd like to have a breeding operation. That means keeping a small but prime herd of cow-calf pairs and a few top-of-the-line bulls. Building takes time and care. It means *not* selling animals for a quick infusion of cash."

"What about Will Rafferty's offer?"

"You mean sell Ghost Mountain?"

"Or the lease arrangement. Would that bring in enough to pay off the loan?"

"The sale would. And then some." His shoulders slumped, and he hung his head nearly between his knees as if the idea of selling land nauseated him. "I can't do it. I can't sell part of the ranch for any reason. It's all I have left, all Bobby and I have." When he raised his head, the pain in his gaze wrenched her nearly in two.

She had investments, but he was too proud to accept what he'd see as charity, especially from her. Not worth even asking. "So that means selling cattle."

"Looks like it." He fastened the last new leather piece in the hackamore. He cocked his head at her. "The custody suit worries me more. Patterson rode you pretty hard."

"Not anything you haven't said yourself." *And worse.* She propped Bobby on her shoulder. "I'm sorry my presence has made things worse for you. I only wanted to help."

"I don't know if you've made the situation worse. Interesting. More complicated. Asking you to stay was my idea."

Bobby made cooing noises as Maddy patted his back. Beyond the tack room, hooves stamped the floor as horses shifted in sleep. Smells of hay and horses flavored the air. Outside, a hunting owl hooted.

Holt blinked away fatigue from his gritty eyes. He'd sat out here working over the problems while working on the tack. He had an answer, but it wouldn't be what Maddy expected to hear. An off-the-wall suggestion worthy of her at her most inventive. A suggestion that shocked him, knotted his jaw—and filled a hollowness inside him he hadn't known was there.

He leaned forward. "If the judge thinks a family means two parents and the children, that's what we have to give him."

"What do you mean?"

"Marry me, Maddy."

She nearly dropped the baby. Bobby waved his arms and squealed with glee the same way he did when Holt blew zerberts on his belly. "It's okay, Bobby." She resumed patting his back, but with an erratic rhythm.

She gaped as if she hadn't heard right. Her eyes were wide as pansies. "Marry you? Now who's being impulsive?"

"How else could we prove your dependability? It's the only answer. We have to get married right away." He'd thought the words would choke in his throat, but they flowed out as natural as a mountain spring.

She pressed one palm to her forehead as if to calm a whirlwind inside. "The idea's preposterous, crazy. How could you even suggest such a thing? Maybe it's best if I leave. I could pack up and be out of here tomorrow. I could use my credit card to rent a car."

He shook his head. "If you leave now, it looks bad for us both. You prove your flightiness, and I look weak for choosing such an unstable woman."

"It's not safe around here anyway, with someone shooting at us. Why on earth would anyone stay?"

"True enough. That's not your battle. But if you go, I still have no one to help care for Bobby. I see no other solution."

As if to punctuate his uncle's statement, Bobby delivered the goods, loud and clear.

Maddy mopped Bobby's milky mouth, nuzzled his dandelion fluff hair, and settled him on her lap. Keeping her head down, she cuddled his warmth. Seeing her like that, Holt recalled the softness, the silkiness of her skin and felt a twinge of envy at his nephew's privileged seat.

"I know there's not much time until the court date. But there must be something else we can do. Couldn't we just fake it?" When she looked up, emotion sheeted her gaze. Sorrow at the thought of leaving? Or fear of the idea of marriage?

"Fake it, for a judge?" He snorted his disdain. "Great way to lose the case, lose Bobby, and get clobbered with a fine."

"But marriage, Holt. Mr. and Mrs. Holt Donovan?" Anguish and indecision filled her eyes. Edging forward, she passed the goggle-eyed baby to Holt. To Bobby's giggling delight, she stalked back and forth like a caged cat.

Most women longed for love in their marriage. She'd fled a wedding to a man she didn't love. How could he expect her to accommodate him now? Even temporarily. "After custody and adoption are final, we can get an annulment."

"A marriage in name only. Is that it?"

"You're under no obligation, Maddy. Bobby has no connection to you. He's my family, my responsibility. You can leave tomorrow if you want. If you care about Bobby, marry me." Best to limit her caring to the baby. No way he could suggest she might care enough about him to stay, let alone marry him. He held his breath.

Narrowing her eyes, she stopped before him, arms folded beneath her breasts. The close-up view of their perfect roundness shot heat right to his groin. "So I can leave tomorrow. Does that mean you'll drive me to town?"

"If I have time."

"If I go, how will you manage with the baby?"

"Damned if I know." His nephew was his final card, his only leverage.

Fury fired her expression, and she sputtered like oil

on hot coals. She was magnificent. "Guilt-trip me, will you? No connection. *No connection.* I couldn't be more connected to this precious babe here if he was my own. Damn you, Donovan, you're as big a manipulator as Edgar Patterson. Bigger."

"I'll do whatever it takes. I make no apologies."

"So cold and calculating. You claim to have such responsibility for this sweet little boy, but how much do you love him? With your heart encased in rock as hard as these mountains, how much *can* you love?"

His gut tightened as if she'd punched him. He rocked his nephew. "Bobby knows I love him. You and I could do the deed on Monday. The state of Colorado has no wait and no blood test requirement."

She eyed him with suspicion. "And how do you know that?"

"When Rob and Sara were planning to get married, they talked about eloping. He checked into it. Reckon he didn't want to take a chance on another bride skipping a big wedding."

"Har de har har." She collapsed on the bench.

"We can drive to Denver. A buddy of mine from law school's a superior court judge there. He'll marry us, and we can drive back with a license to wave at the Pattersons."

"Get married and make it home by supper. It might work." The words came out slowly, as if she tasted each one, mulled its meaning.

The tension in Holt's jaw eased. He had her. Then why did he feel as if he'd lassoed a mustang? One who'd run away at the first chance—and drag him in the dirt to boot. This temporary solution gave him a very dangerous bride.

****

Maddy squinted through the moonless gloom at the road sign. Ten miles to Rangewood. Rain had herded them all the way from Denver. It sheeted a waterfall against the windows.

"Ten seems too late to pick up Bobby at Espie's." The three-hour drive seemed interminable in an already endless day. She rolled her shoulders and glanced sideways at Holt.

He nodded. "We'll go straight to the ranch. She'll bring him over in the morning."

In profile, his flattened nose gave him a fiercer look than usual, pugnacious as a boxer. Her...husband. Intense, tenacious, proud, powerfully male, and devastatingly sexy.

She knew his feelings—concern for his nephew's fate and little or nothing for her. Except desire. But that was just chemistry. She ought to feel trapped, though the marriage was temporary. She ought to feel anger for Holt's coercing her into this sham, but she had herself to blame in large part. Instead, she felt warmth, anticipation, even...joy.

Her heart thumped, and she pressed a hand over it to keep the agitated organ inside her chest. Surreptitiously she glanced at the circle of gold on her left hand. Holt's grandmother's wedding ring. *Her* wedding ring. And it fit. Perfectly. An omen? For good or ill?

She averted her gaze to the window and the black nothingness occasionally spangled by headlights. Rain blurred even the dark. The windshield wipers seemed to be wagging fingers berating her. A second promise to herself was shattered. Her throat clogged, and she fought tears.

I love him. She'd fallen in love with Holt.

The marriage—charade though it was—embedded her more deeply in his and Bobby's lives and sank tendrils into the soil of the Valley-D. Yet she had to go on as they planned. She would leave in June, ripping up roots that would were part of her now. She couldn't invest and build on the Circle-S or ever return again. Either would cleave her in even more pieces.

"We'll have to convince everyone we're truly married," Holt said in an even tone.

"We *are* truly married," she snapped at his seeming sangfroid. He was planning and organizing as if this were a DEA case or a cattle sale.

The truck stopped at the turn from the highway onto the ranch road. He hopped out to retrieve the mail from the box. When he returned, he raised a shaggy eyebrow at her. "Tired, Maddy? So am I. Unfortunate that the court had a full docket today and the judge couldn't marry us until tonight. We'll be home in a few minutes." He clicked the wipers to low as the rain dwindled to a drizzle.

She stared through the mist at the dark road. Home. And what did that mean? She blinked at him when he placed a hand on her arm. Liquid warmth suffused her belly at the softness in his gaze. "What do you mean, *appear* truly married?"

"I don't like lying, but we have to convince everyone this is for real. That means Espie and Bronc too. They could be called to testify."

Her heart sank. Fool. What had she hoped he meant? "Oh." Rallying, she hopped on his train of thought. "Then you'll have to move your things into the master bedroom so she thinks we're sleeping together."

He turned her toward him and tugged her arms around his neck. His hand made gentle circles on her shoulders. Raindrops slicked his hair and beaded his lashes. By the dashboard light she saw the dark flame of desire in his eyes. "We don't need to pretend that part."

"Holt, you were the first one to say—"

He touched a broad finger to her lips. "I know. Too complicated. And you think it's not complicated already?"

He bent his head and pressed his lips to hers. His touch sparked instantaneous need. Before he pulled away, his tongue traced the seam of her lips, creating currents of electricity. He removed her arms from their lasso around his neck.

"It's our wedding night after all." He hooked her camera case from behind the seats and dropped it in her lap. Putting the engine in gear, he headed down the drive toward the house. "You're the photographer, sweetheart. Let's go home and see what develops."

She slapped her forehead in reaction. "Mega corny. That line must date back to the daguerreotype." But her thoughts were serious. Tearing herself away from Bobby and him would break her heart. If she and Holt made love, leaving him would smash it completely. But how could she reject her only chance with him? Better to have loved and lost...or something like that. And she would have the memories, mind snapshots instead of the reality.

A truck with no headlights barreled out of the night toward them. "*Look out!*"

"What the hell!" Holt swerved to the right. He slammed on the brakes.

The vehicle nearly sideswiped them as it careened past on a tidal-wave splash. It vanished behind them down the black road.

"Are you all right?" Holt put his hand on her arm.

"F-fine." She inhaled to control her tumbling heart. "Who on earth was that?"

"A damned good question." He accelerated ahead. "We'd better get to the house and check things out pronto."

No porch lights or spotlight by the barn greeted them. Only an eerie orange glow on the right side of the barn.

Maddy peered into the misty darkness. "What's that funny light?"

What had appeared a hazy glow at first, bloomed into shooting crimson flames. Smoke billowed like a storm cloud. Her pulse kicked like a maverick.

"Fire!"

Chapter Eighteen

THE SIGHT OF flames eating through the barn wall and climbing to the roof stabbed Holt's chest. He bounded from the truck. "The horses!"

"I'll get water!" Maddy ran for the hose.

"Too late. Help me with the horses." He dashed into the barn and slapped on the lights.

Ears flattened, the three horses whinnied and tossed their heads. Acrid smoke filled the air and stung his throat. He grabbed the towel by the utility sink, dunked it in a bucket and held it over his mouth and nose.

Maddy did the same. They unlatched the stalls and led each horse out. Screaming and rearing, the terrified beasts allowed the two humans to herd them away from the billowing smoke and to the corral on the safe side of the barn.

After the horses were safe, Maddy ran to connect the hose. She aimed a stream of water at the barn wall, but it barely reached the flaming roof.

After Holt settled the horses, he used his cell phone to call for help. Then he clicked on the outside spotlight and joined her. Neither the rain nor the rush of water from the hose was drowning the fire or calming the horses' whinnies at the pungent scent of smoke.

"Too late to save the barn. You'd do better to wet down the house roof." A muscle in his jaw spasmed as he gazed around at the muddy ground. "Bastard couldn't have picked a better night. The rain's wiped away any tire tracks or footprints. Or he parked on the cement by the bunkhouse."

Black clouds rolled from the conflagration and were knocked down and diffused by the return of hard rain. The barn wall and roof were caving, but the rain seemed to contain the flames to the one building.

Now that the danger was passing, his chest warmed at Maddy's courage and strength. "Quick thinking. Thanks for your help."

"The truck that passed us," she said, still soaking the house with the hose. "Whoever was in that truck started this blaze. Thank God for the rain."

"Looked like he ignited the hay bales against that wall. I'll lose the barn, but insurance will replace it." Rob had let insurance lapse, but with the equity loan, the bank had insisted on his reinstating it. Hell of a thing, being grateful to Edgar Patterson, even for that.

She turned to him as if at a sudden thought. "Bronc! Where is he? Could he be hurt?"

"He's not here." That had been his first concern too. He jerked a nod toward the bunkhouse. "His truck's gone. To know that, somebody was watching the place real close."

"Not here?" She blinked into the night. The drizzle had increased to a downpour. "But where could he have gone?"

He had an idea, but heaved a shrug as his only response.

The last barn wall collapsed in on itself, and the flames began to sputter in the heavy rain.

"Edgar Patterson will use this to his advantage."

He nodded. "Endangerment of a minor child or

something like that."

Maddy shut off the water and wiped her hands on the wet grass. She started to the porch. "I'll see if the house is okay."

"No. Don't go in by yourself."

Reaching in the truck for the shotgun he kept in the gun rack, he drew deep breaths to calm his racing heart and focused on what he had to do. He climbed the porch steps. Stopped and tried the door. Maddy came up beside him but he shoved her to one side. "Unlocked. Wait here. Don't come in until I call you."

Bent low, he pushed the door inward until it hit the wall.

Darkness cloaked the kitchen. Not a light, not even a faint glimmer from the hallway night lights. Danger pricked the air with dagger points. "When I give you the word, reach inside and flip on all the lights."

"Got it." Her voice was raspy but firm. Good, she'd hold together.

Holt edged inside. Their unknown assailant was getting bolder. Thank God Bobby wasn't here. He held his breath and listened. Nothing. Crouching, he scuttled to the hallway entrance and listened. "Hit it."

Clicks while she flicked up all three switches. Brilliant white flooded the kitchen and hallway.

Blinking at the brightness, he crouched, listening, shotgun braced. The house appeared empty. Slapping on lights as he went, he checked the living room, then the bedrooms.

He returned and uncocked the shotgun. "It's all right. They've gone." His surveying gaze cataloged the damage.

She stepped inside and gasped at the devastation.

Drawers lay on the floor, their contents strewn around them. All the cupboard doors stood open. Cornflakes, rice, and lord knew what else spilled across the counters. "What on earth?"

Shotgun still in hand, he jerked a nod at the other rooms. "They hit the living room, but the baby's room looks untouched. And the bedrooms. I'll give them one more look."

When he returned to the kitchen, he found her on a chair, hugging herself and rocking. The sight of her pale and strained features squeezed a band around his chest. She was a sensitive creature of strong emotions, but he thought of her as indomitable as well.

For so long he'd hated her, hated what she'd done to his brother, hated his own attraction to her. When she'd first arrived, he treated her like a rabid coyote, but her bold spirit and generosity gradually dissipated his misplaced anger.

And now where was he? Married to her. For Bobby. That was all. Or everything.

The adrenaline rush of the excitement past, he found his hands were shaking and his heart doing more than a fast trot. For him, hot entries and armed targets were the DEA's normal business. Her adventurous life had shown her danger, but tonight must have made her feel she'd been tossed onto a bucking mustang. She looked vulnerable, brave, and beautiful.

He lifted her gently to her feet. For such a tall, strong woman, she felt soft and delicate in his arms. As always, she fit perfectly against him. Her head rested against his neck.

"Hell, Maddy, could've been worse. The horses are safe, we can rebuild the barn and he did no real damage in here. He didn't slash the mattresses, only those damned ugly chairs and sofa. I hated them anyway."

When she gave a watery sigh against his chest, he continued, "It doesn't look like robbery. Not that I have anything valuable. And you had your camera stuff with you."

Maddy went stiff as a board. "Could he have been after the pictures?" She sounded skeptical.

"Someone afraid of what's in your shots of the crime scene? Doubtful. The destruction looks more like deliberate vandalism than a search."

"Maybe." She clutched his coat like a lifeline. When at last she stepped back, she pointed to the table. "There's more. He left a note."

His pulse scrambled, and hairs rose on his nape. The sheet of cream-colored vellum lay flat on the worn wooden surface. The vandal had written his message in flowing black script.

You have not suffered enough.
****

When the sheriff's men and the fire department left, it was past midnight. Exhaustion flooded every fiber of Holt's body. He and Maddy had risen before dawn.

He tunneled fingers through his hair and massaged his temples. This was the second attack. He ought to be able to identify the enemy. "Why? Why set the barn on fire and trash the house just to leave that note? Why shoot at us?"

Across the kitchen table, she sipped water and sighed. "The other day, he aimed that first shot at me. Why me unless it's the pictures? Even then…" She lifted her shoulders in bafflement.

His lips curved in a wry smile. "So you didn't buy

my analysis that the shot was to scare us. I can't make sense out of it. And what the hell does that note mean? '*You have not suffered enough.*' It sounds like…like some melodrama or—"

"Foreign phrasing." She nodded grimly, her complexion pale ivory. She rubbed the bridge of her nose. "And the handwriting, all loopy with curlicues."

"Old-fashioned."

She shook her head as if clearing the cobwebs. Damp curls from her recent shower clung to her nape and cheeks. His fingers itched to touch them. "Old-fashioned maybe. Or foreign."

"What do you mean? Where?"

"It didn't hit me at first, but now I remember seeing handwriting like that in Central America." As if she could sit still no longer, she carried their glasses to the sink.

Holt's heart raced, and threads of alarm wound through his brain. *No, it can't be.*

He rose unsteadily and went to stand beside her. "Central America. Are you certain?"

"The schools down there stress handwriting. Especially the older generation writes like that." She placed the mugs in the drainer and draped the dishcloth over the faucet. "I spent a lot of time in small villages in Guatemala and Honduras. People often gave me letters for their relatives in the next village. It was faster than the postal service." She smiled, a soft, sad smile.

He put his hands on her shoulders and kneaded gently, but he wasn't sure if it was to soothe the tension he felt in her muscles or if he needed an anchor in the rock-tumbled rapids of reality. "What about Mexico?"

She tilted her head back and let his hands ease her

aches. "Mexico? I'm sure of it, but I haven't spent much time there. The drug cartels. I don't have to tell you about that."

He went numb as the pieces of the puzzle clicked into place. The high-powered rifle. The hired killer. The lack of motive. "No. I know more than you can imagine about Mexican drug trafficking."

As if in a video, his last confrontation with El Águila played out in his head. The bodyguards' guns shooting at him. His return fire. The young lieutenant's body on the ground. The drug lord's cries of grief. The hatred in his sunken eyes.

"El Águila."

Maddy lifted his limp hands from her shoulders. "The eagle? What are you getting at?"

"I just *got* the message he left." He wrenched away from her, his heart a lifeless stone. "I have to make some phone calls." He snatched the phone receiver from its base and stalked away to his bedroom.

At the sight of Holt's grim cop face, laser eyed and impassive, Maddy snapped her mouth shut instead of pelleting him with questions. Though he seemed to have a lead, he wasn't happy about it. Now that she'd recovered from the initial shocks, she couldn't just stand around. She had to *do* something, so she shrugged into her jacket and went outside.

The past few days had dumped more danger on her than she'd ever experienced in her eight years of traveling. Even in the Balkans, she hadn't felt bull's-eyes painted on her body. After this Holt would probably expect her to pack up and run, but she wouldn't leave him in the lurch. He needed her. And not just for Bobby.

She jogged to the corral. The scent of smoke, still

rank in the air, continued to spook the animals. Quickstep and Chica rolled their eyes and tossed their heads, but calmed when she talked to them and petted them.

Bandito reared and pawed at the air. Maddy was able to grab his bridle and ease him back down. She walked him around the corral and talked softly. She gave them all fresh water and hay from a covered stack outside before returning to the house.

Once back inside, she exchanged her boots for sneakers and hung her coat on the hook. She washed up while listening for Holt's voice. Nothing. She found him sitting on his bed, his head in his hands.

"Holt?"

The eyes he raised to her were as bleak and pale as November skies in a face ashen with grief. "You know that old saying, 'Be careful what you wish for'?" He barked a bitter laugh and passed a hand over his eyes.

She sat beside him on the bed and curled a hand on his knee.

"I know now who's behind it all. But when I searched for a monster, I should have looked in the mirror."

His face was a mask of pain, and she ached for him. Whatever it was, he blamed himself. No surprise in a man who took on the world's responsibilities. "Tell me."

He pushed himself upright and paced the length of the room. "The message made everything clear. Rob wasn't killed because his temper pissed off a cowboy. Or because the Raffertys wanted to buy Ghost Mountain. Or because a damned hunter shot wild." He was nearly shouting at her. "He and Sara were killed to punish me."

"Who, Holt? Who?"

"El Águila. He's a Mexican drug lord. Not just drugs, but illegal arms." Spitting out the words like bullets, he laid out a tale of intrigue that would have staggered her if she weren't already so shaken.

Though she knew such standoffs went on, to Maddy it seemed more like Movie of the Week than reality. She shuddered to think of Holt facing down such a soulless gangster. "And you think this El Águila had Rob and Sara killed because you killed one of his men, the one the bodyguard carried off?"

"Not just one of his men—his heir apparent. His *only son*." He swore and pounded his right fist against his palm. "Word is he paid to have anyone close to me killed. So I would suffer."

"Like he did." She still couldn't fathom the gangster's long arm of vengeance. For an evil man like him, having Rob and Sara killed added only one more crime to a long list, but equally monstrous was saddling Holt with the burden of guilt. "You killed that man in self-defense. In the line of duty."

"To hell with the line of duty. Being twice a target makes it personal. I never dreamed my work could harm my family. I might as well have put that bullet into Rob instead of into the man in Tijuana. And now El Águila has taken aim at *you*." He strode toward the kitchen door. "I need some air."

She followed only as far as the door. Coatless, oblivious to the icy drizzle, he loped to the corral. Repairing tack always seemed his remedy to a problem. But the tack was gone, all the saddles and bridles burned or charred unusable in the fire.

She'd leave him alone this time, let him work it out his way. For a while.

Chapter Nineteen

HOLT DRAGGED HIMSELF back to the house two hours later. His muscles ached almost as much as his head, but he felt better. Every nail he'd pounded to rig up a makeshift horse shelter was a nail driven into El Águila's coffin.

When the answers had fallen into place, his throat had clogged as if he'd lost Rob all over again. A little focused violence out in the corral sweated out the misguided guilt. He let fury harden him, give him a focus, a direction.

The puzzle had a shape, a form, a pattern. The senseless murders had a motive. The killer had a face. A face he had seen. Now that he knew who committed this cowardly crime, he would get the bastard and those he hired if it was the last thing he ever did.

He left his reeking shirt and dirty boots in the laundry room off the kitchen and rinsed off the worst of the sweat and smoke. The house was quiet and dim, with only one light over the kitchen sink and the night lights in the hallway. Only a couple of hours until dawn, but he might as well try to grab some sleep. If he could.

"You okay?" Maddy came out of her room as he padded down the hall in his bare feet. Even in the semi-dark, he could see the deep shadows beneath her eyes. Her hair stuck out over one ear where she'd been lying on her side. He wanted to go smooth it, kiss the shell of her ear.

Then he saw she wore jeans, and her denim jacket. His heart slammed against his ribs. She was leaving. Damn, he should have known. But he'd already said his piece about her running, so he held his tongue.

Her eyes narrowed as if she read his expression, and she cocked a hip. "Maybe it's better if I leave. What if tomorrow when I'm holding Bobby, El Águila's hit man blows us both away?"

"That bastard would've killed my horses and burned my barn. And he tried to kill you. He'll try again. Because of me. But now that he knows we're married, he'll find you anywhere—New York or L.A. or between. If you stay, I can protect you."

She skewered him with a skeptical gaze. "But who'll protect you and Bobby?"

His concern so far had been for her, but now his gut clenched for his nephew. So far El Águila hadn't targeted the baby, but that was no guarantee. "The Denver DEA office will send a team pronto. Fight or flight, those are your choices, McCoy."

"I choose fight. Besides, I can't leave now. We just got married."

The sinking feeling in his gut told him he'd stepped in Rocky Mountain meadow muffins—up to his hips. "Hell. You weren't leaving anyway, were you?"

Her angelic smile contained a dollop of deviltry. "Not unless I hitchhike or hotwire your truck. I was headed out to see if you were all right."

Something warm and liquid unfurled inside him. "Thanks for worrying. No one ever worried about me before. Reckon I jumped to conclusions."

"Now who's the impulsive one?" She grinned, her

gaze cruising his bare torso. "You got your head on straight so you're ready to find this El Águila?"

Damn, she knew him too well. He gave up on maintaining distance and closed the space between them. "Sounds like you knew I would. That was grief talking. I'm well aware of where to hang the blame. If I ever face the son of a bitch again with a gun in my hand, he won't walk away."

"And the DEA will help put a stop to this terror?" Her earlier tears had dried, but her eyes were bleak with fear.

She needed protection. And he needed—*wanted* her so much his body shook with it. He placed his hands on her shoulders. "I'll do everything I can to keep you safe. I promise."

When he felt her trembling—or was it him?—he pulled her closer. He needed to feel her soft curves against him. He still couldn't bring himself to trust her to stay, but his distrust didn't stop him from a near savage longing for her. And a powerful desire to protect her. "I'm surprised you aren't yelling at me for putting you in the middle of this danger."

She shook her head and struggled in his embrace. "I have no cause to blame you any more than you should blame yourself."

Stubborn as a filly in a windstorm. He held her fast, needed the satisfaction of having her in his arms. She'd turned water on the fire, tended the horses afterward. No tenderfoot.

"You were courageous and resourceful tonight. And I thank you for that." He kissed her forehead and tucked her beneath an arm as he began walking her down the hall.

He didn't mention his suspicions about Luke Rafferty. Troubled and a loner, Luke didn't evoke trust in Holt. The DEA could check him out thoroughly. Maybe the man had no grudge against Rob, but he might not have resisted a generous offer to eliminate him. Or Maddy if the absent Riggs was the first shooter.

Since no one new had hired on at any of the Rock County ranches, this shooter was probably a local. As a deputy sheriff, Luke had the contacts, the skill, and the mobility to have carried out both shootings. And he had that Circle-S custom black pickup. Holt wished he'd gotten a better look at the truck tonight.

He squeezed Maddy's shoulders. What had he done, putting her in such danger? He wouldn't let her out of his sight tonight. God, if anything had happened to her...

She hauled on the reins. "Holt, what are you doing? We need to go to bed."

"Exactly. It's our wedding night. What's left of it." He released her and trailed a finger along her chin and over her mouth. Her full lower lip was smooth as velvet, and he had to taste her again. To taste her all over, to drive into her welcoming body and blast all their problems into temporary oblivion.

He needed sleep, but he needed her more.

"I know this is bad timing. But you know I've wanted you since you arrived. Hell, I've wanted you for years. Come to bed with me, Maddy."

At his blatant invitation, she didn't flinch, only watched him, her eyes wide and somber. The same hunger he felt shimmered in her hot gaze. Then she smoothed a hand across his belly. She opened her mouth and flicked her tongue over his fingertip. Slowly she sucked his finger into the warm moisture of her mouth and swirled her tongue around it.

Lust slammed into him with the heat of a branding iron. His body hardened with a rush that made him light-headed.

"Make love with me, Holt."

"Maddy." His mouth on hers, he scooped her up and carried her into his darkened bedroom. They shouldn't do this. He knew a thousand reasons it was a bad idea and he'd regret it later, but with her soft and clinging in his arms, to hell with them.

All he could think of was Maddy. Her taste. Her sleek curves. Her generous spirit that might offer him solace. The roaring in his blood was a hunger for her that wouldn't abate.

He lowered her to the bedspread and followed her down, cradling her in his arms, reveling in her sweetness. He tugged her T-shirt hem from her jeans. "I need to see you," he gritted out as he punched the bedside lamp button.

She wrenched the shirt over her head, then fumbled with his jean buttons. "I want to see you too. I want to feel you against me."

He shimmied out of the jeans and flung them into a far corner of the room. He sprawled half over her, savoring the shivery sensation of her nipples against his skin, in the wildflower scent that was Maddy. He trembled, struggling to keep his hand gentle on her breast. When he closed his mouth over her budding nipple, he moaned with the intense pleasure.

She arched beneath him, yearning for more. "I need you inside me. I need you now."

"Easy, easy. We'll get there."

She kicked off her sneakers, and he helped her skin

off her jeans and panties before he stripped away his boxers. This was the first time he'd seen her naked body, taut and fit, yet curved in all the right places.

"The hallway light frames your body," she murmured, "hard muscles and strength from ranch work. If I wasn't so aroused, I'd run for my Nikon."

"X-rated for damn sure." He chuckled, then knelt above her, aching to be inside her. He dug a condom from the bedside table and ripped it open.

Her eyes were dark plum and languorous with desire. She closed her soft, warm hand around him, streaking a hungry blaze through his body.

Moaning with desperation, he lowered himself to her. She felt so good, so damn perfect it ought to scare the bejeezus out of him, but he banished the thought and let his senses hold sway. He focused on her, inhaled the essence of her skin, absorbed every line and curve, every nuance down to his soul. He wanted her to cry out his name, to explode in his arms.

He swept his hands over her, kissed and licked his way over her delectable body and then returned to her mouth for a stunning kiss that was unbearably sweet and slow.

"Now, Holt, now!"

Heat danced over his skin with bursts of lightning-bolt pleasure. As he surged into her, a rush of excitement ripped the breath from his lungs. His soul expanded at this possession, with each drive of his body into her tight heat. She writhed beneath him, meeting him stroke for stroke, climbing an impossible slope propelled by his molten body and frantic heartbeat. He felt her body shimmer with the first twinges of release. When he reached between them, his intimate caress sent her shimmering and bucking against and around him. She cried out his name.

Holt closed his eyes in fierce control as his own release clawed at him. The joy of being inside her was so exquisite it was almost painful. She was wonderful, fiery and uninhibited, moving with him in undulations that drove him faster, deeper. Her inner muscles clenched around him, knifing shock waves through his loins and coiling tension inside him tighter and tighter. All too soon, he felt himself stiffen, poised on the edge, and then a huge, rocking kick of pleasure slammed him in a wrenching release as he poured himself into her.

****

When Maddy woke, sunlight streamed through the lace curtains. She rolled over, but found on the soft cotton sheets only a trace of warmth from Holt's body and the mingled scents of their lovemaking. Sensations of his loving wove through her mind and ghosted across her skin. Longing for him made her shudder.

He didn't love her no matter how much he desired her. She wouldn't let him send her away now, but she'd have to go eventually. Away from Holt. And Bobby. She choked up at the thought of little Bobby—his cooing laugh, his bright eyes, how he waved his little hands, and put out his pudgy arms when she picked him up.

At the thought of someone threatening him, her heart stumbled. She had to help catch this monster. She had to do whatever she could.

Resolved, she forced herself to rise and begin the day. Holt would return from the animals and need breakfast. After a quick shower, she made coffee and popped Espie's leftover corn muffins in the oven to warm. She was searching for the eggs in the refrigerator when Holt opened the door.

He looked wonderful, sleep rumpled with a beard-stippled chin. Sexy as hell. She wanted to jump him all over again.

"I tried not to wake you. You needed some sleep."

"Neither of us has had much sleep."

He headed for her, determination in his eyes. His kiss was tender, so gentle it brought tears to her eyes.

"Everything will be okay. We'll get this guy." His voice softened, deepened to a seductive velvet rumble. His blue eyes glided over her body as if seeing her naked.

"I'm not afraid for myself. It's Bobby...and you." Pierced to her core, she rested her head against his chest. "I was wondering about something you said last night. About the DEA."

"The Denver office will organize a team."

"No, not Denver. The Tijuana task force. If the DEA knew you had killed the drug lord's son and he was after you, why didn't they warn you?"

"A hell of a good question." He raised his hands as if in surrender. "You want to hear the answer? Last week after an informant told them, the special agent in charge decided to send agents to trap El Águila's killer when he came for me."

"But they didn't tell you about this great plan."

"Bull's-eye. I'm now out of the loop, a civilian."

"And these are the guys you intend to trust with our lives—and Bobby's?" Wrapping her arms around him, she shivered. She didn't need much reflection to decide who she'd trust with her life.

He was right here.

****

When Espie and Bronc arrived an hour later in a

two-truck procession, the mystery of Bronc's disappearance was solved. He'd spent the night with Espie. Holt didn't seem surprised, but the older couple's blooming romance left Maddy speechless.

Agog, she opened her arms for Bobby, who came to her with squealing giggles. She cuddled him and nuzzled his softness, breathed in his baby scent. After last night's events, she needed to embrace innocence.

Espie shrugged off her surprise. "My boys had an overnight with the basketball team," she said, as if that explained everything.

Bronc stuttered an apology when Holt told him about the break-in and the cause of the fire, but Holt brushed it away. "You might have been killed if you'd tried to stop them."

While they checked out the soggy ruin in the brilliant spring sunshine, Holt and Maddy disclosed everything—their reasons for eloping, the killing in Tijuana, their conclusions about the killer's identity and motives.

"When I was in the DEA's Boston office," Holt explained in conclusion, "we broke up one of El Águila's smuggling operations in the Northeast. In the middle of that, we got word about his hiding out in Tijuana."

"Why'd they send *you* all that way?" Bronc kicked at clumps of sodden, burnt straw.

"Since I spoke passable Spanish and knew something of his operation, they sent me to join the task force."

"How did this gangster find you?" Espie asked.

"What happened to that Mexican feller's body?" Bronc demanded.

A barrage of questions ensued that made Maddy feel

like a politician on *Meet the Press*. She and Holt answered the ones they could and said they hoped for answers soon for the rest. Finally the older couple seemed satisfied.

"If you can nail this gangster, it will shut down his dirty business," Espie declared.

Maddy jiggled Bobby. He happily gummed his fist.

Holt shook his head. "Until the next petty drug emperor takes over. The drug and arms smuggling trade is like the mythical Hydra. Every time we lop off a head, a new one grows."

Bronc gestured toward the corral, where the three horses were peacefully soaking up the sunshine. "Horses don't look too stove up from the fire."

"Holt got them out quickly." Maddy considered Holt's harsh expression, the way his jaw worked. He stared toward the meadow beyond the corral, but from his expression, he didn't see the green.

Espie clucked at the baby's yawns and whisked him inside for a nap. Bronc headed to the barn to begin his day's chores.

Maddy remained beside Holt at the corral. "Something else is eating at you. That note, does it mean El Águila is here?"

He hooked a boot heel on the lower fence rail. "The way it was folded, it looks like he could've mailed it to his man here."

"So we still don't know who we're up against."

He removed his hat and turned it around a few times in his hands. "Here's how I think it went down. That drifter Riggs was the shooter who killed Rob and Sara. His disappearance the day after the crash can't be coincidence. Nobody new has signed on at any of the valley ranches. Strangers would stand out like saguaro cactus. Whoever is in El Águila's pay now has to be local."

Their stalker might be a man they knew? She shivered. "But that's not what's bothering you."

He ran a hand through his hair and resettled his hat. His hard features turned cool and analytical. "This sort of revenge intrigue is unusual. Damned strange."

"Because El Águila involved himself personally by sending that note?"

"That and why a powerful Mexican cartel lord would go to the trouble to concoct such an intricate plot."

"I see what you mean. It's more subtle than you'd expect from guys who blow up judges and whole police departments for no reason at all." The freshening breeze sneaked down her collar, and she tugged it tighter.

His gaze, hard and assessing, narrowed. "It's as if he's lost his edge and doesn't command his usual army of thugs."

Chapter Twenty

LATER WHILE THE men worked clearing away smoldered rubble of the barn, Maddy and Espie straightened the house under Bobby's alert gaze. Insisting that the first room they complete be the master bedroom, Espie carted Holt's clothing from his old room and stowed it in the highboy. Later they dragged into the living room the dark-green plaid sofa and chairs. A few worn spots marred the wood-frame furniture but the older set was more suitable to the ranch house than Sara's fancy ones.

The check Maddy'd awaited arrived in the morning mail along with a check from the sale of her dead Rover, and she saw no reason to wait to spend some money. As she stood staring at the check, she speculated on Holt's attitude. Would he return to his hands-off stance? Or would his eyes smolder with desire, and would he take her in his arms? The mere thought of the heat between them last night had the power to melt her insides.

He had given her his body and some small measure of affection and comfort, but she couldn't expect to win his love or trust. He held himself separate from everyone but Bobby, retaining his wariness and distrust as armor.

No matter the outcome, whatever the DEA accomplished, she had to leave for her calendar gig at the beginning of June. In the meantime, she meant to squeeze out every moment of happiness she could. The footloose life was what she knew best, what she wanted. Wasn't it? Was June coming too soon...or not soon enough? She huffed a bitter laugh.

She sought Holt outside the barn, where he was filling the back of the truck with debris. The stench of wet soot accented the breeze.

He nodded toward stacks of black asphalt shingles on the ground beside a tool shed. "If the barn hadn't burned to the ground, yesterday's rain would've soaked the horses through the leaky roof," he said, his expression rueful. "Now I can use these shingles on a new roof."

The barn roof was another example of Rob's neglect. Wiser not to comment. "Could I use the pickup to drive to Fort Adams? Now that I have funds, I need to buy wheels. And I'm supposed to pick up the enlarged crime-scene shots."

Slowly he raised his head, his eyes a wintry blue. He pinned her with a narrowed gaze so full of cold fury that she retreated a step.

She wasn't afraid of him, but she should have known what he'd think. She straightened her shoulders and glared right back. "I'm not going to steal your truck and hit the road, Holt Donovan. I promised to stay, didn't I?"

"That's reassuring. Thank you very much." He rubbed the back of his neck and drew a deep breath, control on his temper clearly tenuous. He didn't take his eyes off her. "El Águila's hired killer would be grateful for such a nice fat target."

Maddy blinked at him, nonplussed. He was worried not that she might flee but for her safety. For years she'd looked out for herself. The awareness that Holt would shield her fluttered her stomach. Knowing his sense of loyalty and honor, she shouldn't wonder that he'd include her in his protective circle. If not in his heart.

He hesitated, hope and apprehension chasing across his taut features. "The DEA team of special agents won't set up shop here today, so you're stuck with me. I can't go. This mess has to be cleared and ready to start the new framing."

"I'll stay on the main roads. I'll be careful."

"No, you'll be escorted." Shaking his head, he marched to the shed door. "Bronc, you finished stowing the grain?"

The hired man appeared in the opening. "All set. Want some help hauling the debris?" His weathered face wreathed in wrinkles, he looked dubious.

"I can handle it. How'd you like to ride shotgun for Maddy? You can order the lumber we need for the new barn."

Bronc's eyes twinkled at the prospect, and it was settled. They made the drive to Ponderosa Photo Lab in Bronc's red truck, with Maddy sitting on the floor until they put several miles between them and the ranch.

After a stop at a bank, she found a second-hand black Range Rover one year newer than the other. While the dealer prepared the paperwork, she picked up the eight-by-ten enlargements of the crime scene. Holt's friend at the lab blushed from his neck to his hair line when she gushed about the quality of his work. She and Bronc returned in time for her to feed Bobby and tuck him in for a nap before Espie left in the late afternoon.

At suppertime, when she spied Holt striding toward the house, she scrubbed clammy palms on her jeans and geared up for which man came through the door—

protective Holt or lover Holt.

****

Holt rolled his shoulders after a long afternoon of physical labor. Clouds roiled in a gigantic pillow fight over the surrounding peaks, but forecasters predicted no more rain. Temperatures rising into the sixties had alleviated some of the discomfort inherent in the demolition job, but he'd rather climb on a horse any day.

Or on Maddy.

For the forty-seventh time that day, the image of her naked and warm and soft in his bed branded his brain and sizzled his loins. He'd been an idiot for believing one passionate night could satisfy his craving for her. His desire for her smoothed the pretense that their marriage was real, but it confused the issues. It jammed up his concentration. It distracted him from his real objectives.

He was right to begin with. Sex complicated the situation too much.

He'd do better to rein in his libido and back off from her—at least in private. His priorities ought to be catching El Águila and his hired killers and keeping his nephew and the ranch, not sating himself on a female who was leaving soon. Now that she had her own transportation, he trusted her even less to stay.

Even if she did need his protection at present. Even if kissing her was the tart sweetness of an apple and holding her was the first warmth of summer. Even if making love to her was soul-deep, mind-blowing sorcery—

Damn! Sex had never before made him poetic. That wasn't him. Another reason to keep his hands off her.

He cleaned up before entering, and once inside the kitchen, sensed her presence in the room. He hung his jacket on a hook and turned to find her at the stove. She wore jeans and her customary souvenir shirt, without a bra like last night. His loins tightened at the faint shadow of her nipples through the cotton fabric. He dragged his gaze up to her amused face.

She was stirring something in a big pot on the stove. Maybe the scent that teased his nose wasn't pheromones after all. "What delicacy has Espie left for us tonight?"

"*I* am your chef for this evening, I'll have you know." She cocked a hip and winked as she tasted broth from a teaspoon. She licked away the dab of sauce remaining on her lower lip. "Thought it might make me appear more wifely."

The sight of her moist tongue seized him by the crotch. He nearly bolted over and grabbed her, but he forced himself to remain rooted by the door. The stiffness in his jaw radiated downward. He rubbed his nape. "Wifely. Maddy, don't—"

"Donovan, don't you even say it." She shook her wooden stirring spoon at him like a mother shaking her finger. "I'm not presuming anything. I know good and well this is for show. Oh, it's fine for you to wave the marriage license when it suits you. Like last night."

"Ouch." She was right. He'd sure as hell used the marriage bit to lure her into bed. Before he got himself in deep enough to need a shovel, he'd better change the subject. "So Maddy McCoy cooks. Did you buy a casserole kit with the grocery money I gave you?"

She snorted her disdain. "That's Maddy *Donovan* to you, *Mister* Donovan." The spoon plunged into the Dutch oven. "I don't cook much, but I do have a few specialties. This is a Turkish lamb stew my friend Karen makes. I found the lamb in your freezer, and Bronc picked up the rest of the ingredients while he waited for me." She gave him a sassy smile and held out a brimming teaspoon. "Want a taste?"

The aromas wafting to him, redolent with garlic and oregano, had him salivating. It was Maddy's tempting mouth he wanted to taste at the moment, but stew was safer. He stepped closer and started to take the spoon. The broth might not be too hot for his mouth, but the brush of her finger singed him.

"Ah, ah, ah, might spill." Not relinquishing the spoon, she grinned wickedly.

First cooking for him, now feeding him. The woman was trying to seduce him. That insight only intensified his desire. He slurped up the smidgeon of stew fast enough to nick a tooth. He shied away like a Pinto pony from a cougar.

"Too hot?" Her voice was sweet and smoky, sliding down his spine smooth as honey and whiskey.

He ran his tongue over his teeth to check for chips. All whole. "Delicious." It was, hearty and flavorful with lamb and onions.

Still grinning, she wagged her head. "Look around. Espie and I made a few changes." She spread her arms in demonstration. "I hope you don't mind."

Some trained investigator. Until now he hadn't noticed the china cabinet had been moved to the wall backing onto the living room. And in its former location was the old wood cook stove that had ruled there for as long as he could remember. Until Sara redecorated.

Maddy darted to the old stove. "When Espie and I moved in the original living room furniture, I thought this ought to come back in the house too." She gazed at him, her smile faltering. Unease crimped the corners of her violet eyes.

Shaking his head, he crossed to her. "How could you think I wouldn't approve?" He ran a palm over the cool iron surface of the old griddle top. "The kitchen didn't seem right without it. Now the stove is home again."

"It's not ready to use, of course," she rattled on. "It needs new stove pipe, and the flue has to be cleaned, and—"

He pressed two fingers to her mouth and left them there, enjoying the soft resilience of her lips, the perfume of her breath. "All in good time. Relax."

He couldn't help but glide his fingers over her glowing cheeks, across the impossible softness of her temple. Of their own volition, his fingers trailed upward to soothe the worry lines from her brow. Wisps of hair curled around her face. The scent of shampoo mingled with her own to cloud his senses and make him forget everything but silken skin and her sigh as her eyelashes drifted lower.

Damn, he had to stop or he'd thrust into her right now. He plucked back his hand and edged around the stove.

Straining for control, he peered closely at the stove's rear opening. "Easy enough to attach new stove pipe and clean the flue. This baby'll come in handy when a winter storm knocks out the power. Generator's had it."

Eyeing him with cool appraisal and a trace of hurt at his withdrawal, she folded her arms. "Rob again?"

He shrugged instead of answering. "The old stove hasn't gotten much use in many years. Dad kept it blacked and polished. Used it to make griddle cakes on Sundays."

"Your dad did the maintenance, not Bonnie," she

observed. "I remember Espie did most of the cleaning then too. Seems like Rob inherited the neglect gene from your mother."

He began to see just how much alike Rob and their mother were. "Got his temper from her too. I recall some shouting matches. Miracle she stuck around long as she did."

"And you keep beating yourself up for not reconciling with her." Maddy returned to the electric range. After covering the pot, she set the burner on simmer.

"I never once heard her apologize. Dad was always the peacemaker, the one to make up." He parked a hip on the old woodstove and worked his jaw.

"And when she left the family behind, you were a boy. She was the adult. It's her loss, not your fault."

Hot damn, she was beautiful with her dander up. Full of fire and quivering with passion, defending *him*, of all things. "I didn't tell you before. I telephoned her. About Rob."

"Ha. So you did make the first move. And?"

"She came to the funeral. We talked for a few minutes." He didn't know if he wanted to see her again or not. It had been so long. They were strangers.

"So it's up to her to keep communication open." Cheeks pink with indignation, she stalked closer, brandishing the spoon.

"If that was a sword, I shudder to think what you'd do if one of our bad guys walked through that door. Thanks."

Flushing even deeper, she bowed. "You're entirely welcome, sir." Then she planted her feet in the classic fencing stance and circled her spoon cum rapier. "Just let that El Águila walk in here. *En garde*, you scum of the earth."

Giving up his fight, Holt captured the spoon and yanked her between his thighs. "Come here, warrior princess."

The pressure of Maddy's flat belly against the straining bulge in Holt's jeans assuaged his pain only momentarily. The hell with it. He had to hold her, to feel her against him, to sheathe himself in her. "Maddy."

He slid his hand around to cup the back of her head and wrapped his other arm around her, pulling her flush against him. He felt her trembling with the same urgency that shafted through him. "Wanting you has tormented me all day. Tell me now if I should stop." Every muscle tensed, rigid and edgy.

"No, don't," she whispered.

"Don't?" He was so hard he might explode if he didn't get inside her, and she wanted him to stop?

"Don't stop. I want you too." She clung to him, nipping his neck, laving it with her hot little tongue.

He stood up and turned them around. Lifting her curvy backside onto the stove top, he shuddered. She wanted him, as much as he wanted her. Feverishly, he kissed her with his mouth, his teeth, his tongue, savored her textures, her taste.

Control, restraint, you're no teenager. But control had already burned away in the furnace of passion. She'd leave him before long, and he needed the feel and the scent of her branded into him.

"Holt." She writhed against him. Her hand tortured him where he strained against his fly. She slipped a foil packet from her jeans pocket and handed it to him.

"Oh, yeah." He skimmed one hand beneath her shirt

to cup a firm breast. He tugged away the offending fabric to give him access to those strawberry-pink nipples, taut and eager for his attention. So sweet.

He fumbled with her zipper, and in a flash, he had her naked and her sexy long legs wrapped around him. Her breath hitching, she started on his clothing, snapping off buttons in her haste.

"Let me, sweetheart. I don't want to have to explain ripped-off buttons to Espie." When his shirt fell open, the pleasure of her breasts pressed against his chest had him gasping. She shuddered, her mouth seeking his.

Once he'd understood the danger he'd placed her in, he'd been terrified for her. Covering her with his body, joining with her held panic at bay, reassured him in a way he scarcely comprehended. His fingers found her, wet and sleek and ready. As she welcomed him into her body, his soul expanded.

Chapter Twenty-One

WHEN HE ENTERED her, Maddy arched and sighed with the satisfaction she felt only with him. Her body was on fire, her pulse scrambling. She bent to taste his lips, salty with passion, as the deep thrill sparked within her, rocketed her to white-hot stars. She may never feel this soul-deep connection again, and she wanted it to last forever.

He bucked against her, pulled her closer as he let go and joined her in a cascading release.

Long moments afterward, Maddy stirred, squirmed against Holt. "It's hard."

He chuckled. "Not at the moment. But give me a little while."

She erupted in giggles against his chest. "No, silly, the stove. It's very hard. And cold."

"Oh." He separated them and lifted her to her feet.

After they rearranged their clothing, she kissed him. "I'll take you up on the offer—later. Hear the Bobby Alarm?"

Intermittent fussing squawks emitted from the nursery, indicating the baby was cranking up.

"I'll go." He stuffed his shirt into his jeans. "I haven't seen my little buddy all day."

While he tended the baby, Maddy sat at the table. She felt contented and sated and smug. He wanted her. And he cared enough to ensure her pleasure before he brought her to climax and sought his own satisfaction. Sex had never been a priority for her, but maybe that was because no one had ever made her feel the way Holt did.

Maybe it was because she loved him, but he dazzled her with a mix of tenderness and sensuality that thrilled her from the deep recesses of her soul to her fingertips. Heat crept through her at the thought of the approaching night. She had time to make a few more memories. More than that, she wouldn't let herself hope.

Banishing further romantic dreams, she began examining the prints of the crime scene photos. One by one, she pored over each square inch. The close-up of the shooter's hiding place, an angled shot of the roadway, the steep hillside showing the mangled trees. Nothing betrayed a hint of a clue.

She slumped in the chair. Even if Holt hadn't dared to hope, she had longed to find something. Anything.

She peered closer at the two blowups of the landslide aftermath. Those weren't for evidence, but to indulge herself. The composition of the shadows and textures in the jumble of boulders had intrigued her at the time and still did.

Frowning, she peered at a section of the rock slide. What was the odd-looking object protruding from the rocks? A branch? She rooted in her camera case for a magnifying glass.

When the wide convex lens framed that section of the picture, what Maddy saw skittered a shiver down her spine. She opened her laptop, on the kitchen table where she'd placed it for checking e-mail. A few clicks took her to the same photo. She framed and cropped the section showing the jutting object.

A few adjustments with the resolution clarified what

she'd suspected. She could only stare, heart pounding like a tom-tom, at her discovery.

"If you find anything important in those pictures, I'll eat it," he said, cool derision in his voice. "Right, Bobby?"

Bobby wore a one-piece pajama patterned with bucking broncos. He waved his arms in glee. The duck down that passed for his hair made him look like a surprised angel. He gave a juicy lip-smacking reply.

"Did you ever see that old movie *Blow-Up*?" she said.

Holt adjusted the baby to a more upright position and dangled a stuffed cow in front of him. "You mean the one where the photographer blows up his pictures and finds a—" Shock, then steely concentration hardened his features.

"Body."

Gripping the baby tightly to him, he sat down heavily beside her. "Show me."

"I thought this was a stick at first." She slid the laptop over to him. Clamping her lips together, she waited.

Removing a tasty hand from his mouth, Bobby voiced a complaint at the tension he clearly felt in the adults.

Holt rocked him and edged the computer out of reach of chubby, wet digits. He leaned closer to the screen. When he looked up at her, his eyes were hard with determination and bright with triumph.

"It's an arm." He threaded a hand through his hair. "Or what's left of it. Someone is buried under that rock pile."

****

After a phone call to the authorities, discussing the possible meanings of a body beneath the landslide calmed Maddy's nerves to a manageable level, but she still picked at her dinner. Holt, on the other hand, concentrated on the lamb stew with all the fervor of a restaurant reviewer. What that meant she had no idea.

Afterward, he gave Bobby his bath and put him to bed. When he returned to the kitchen, she was just stowing the leftover stew in the fridge.

"There's enough for another meal," she said. "I don't cook often, so I tend to overdo. You don't mind leftovers, do you?" She smiled, her heart tripping on itself at his sexy lean body and brooding eyes.

He rubbed his jaw, the only betrayal of emotion he seemed to allow himself. "Leftovers? No, I don't mind. Thanks for the great dinner. Sorry I teased you about it earlier. Give Espie that recipe. Maybe she can make it after you leave."

A frisson swept through her. She watched his expression harden. What was going on? Was it the body beneath the rocks or something else? She stepped closer, held out a hand. "Holt, I'm not leaving until this is over." *Not even then if you want me to stay.*

His gaze fixed, he held up his hands. "I believe you. And I appreciate it. But let's not let sex make us pretend this marriage is more than a pretext. Because you will be leaving."

Heart sliding downward, she could think of no good reply to that frank statement.

He plunged his hands into his pockets as if avoiding touching her. "I'm damned beat. Gonna turn in now. I need a solid night's sleep."

With those words, he turned and strode down the

hall to his old room, not the master bedroom where the king-sized bed awaited the newlyweds.

Maddy stood in the kitchen, her heart torn and bloody at her feet.

The door clicked shut behind him.

****

Sheriff Foley's crime scene crew kibitzed by two DEA agents uncovered the body beneath the slide. Foley wouldn't permit Holt to be present, but under pressure from the Denver DEA office, conceded his participation in a strategy meeting on Thursday morning.

Holt and Maddy were the first to enter the Rock County Sheriff's Department conference room. Wanted posters and yellow sticky notes peppered a nicked cork bulletin board. A photograph of the governor on the far wall completed the room's limited décor. He held out a wooden chair for her at the long metal table, then took the next seat.

She sat silent and stiff beside him. Mouth tight, she stared straight ahead at the jumbled bulletin board as if it held the answer to their problems. The sheriff and the DEA agents might not approve of her presence, but Holt wouldn't be the one to deny her. In her present mood, she'd probably flay more than one strip from his hide.

He didn't blame her for being ticked off. After their spectacular kitchen fireworks, he'd been as smooth as an earthquake at dousing the flames. He hadn't come up with the right words, but hell, how could he have stated his case? That preoccupation with sex interfered with their real problems? That it made him feel guilty? Nothing would have sounded any damned better than what he did say.

That prissy iron bed felt even lonelier now that it

held her scent. Damn. A shaft of sunlight filtered through the conference room's dusty window and glinted on Maddy's wedding ring. Double damn.

After two restless nights alone, he was primed for a fight if the DEA and the sheriff tried to keep him on the fringes of their investigation. He meant to make fucking sure they got this hired killer and protected Maddy and Bobby. He'd feel a hell of a lot better if El Águila would come out in the open and fight him instead of stalking innocent bystanders.

In the hallway a murmur of voices superimposed by the sheriff's booming intonations announced arrivals.

Jarvis Foley entered first, a bulging file beneath his arm. While the others streamed in and settled around the table, he stopped to shake Holt's hand and greet Maddy.

"Ms. McCoy, I'm right pleased to make your acquaintance."

"It's Mrs. Donovan now, Sheriff," Holt said. "We were married the other day." Apparently the deputies investigating the fire and the break-in hadn't apprised their boss of that news tidbit.

"My congratulations to you both," Foley inserted smoothly. "Burglary and bullets don't make an auspicious beginning for a marriage, Mrs. Donovan."

"Call me Maddy, Sheriff." She flashed the man a warm smile.

"You just make yourself comfortable." Beaming from his bushy eyebrows to both ends of his handlebar mustache, he took her proffered hand and made a small bow over it.

Chris Hawke entered bearing a tray with a carafe and paper coffee cups. He wore his customary Anasazi amulet at the neck of a denim shirt, but topped with a corduroy jacket. In deference to the meeting's gravity, Holt surmised.

Luke Rafferty, seated already near the sheriff, snorted a laugh. "Didn't know the Legal Eagle moonlighted as waitress."

Chris spread his lips in a smile as cold as a rattler's. He eased the tray onto the table and sat on Maddy's other side. "Sheriff, your secretary seemed hassled, so I offered to bring in the refreshments. I can take them back if Rafferty here objects to the quality of service."

"Foley, I asked Mr. Hawke to join me in case Maddy or I needed counsel," Holt put in. The Denver SAC had probably wised up his agents to the enmity between these two. Maybe it had nothing to do with murder, but he wanted all bases covered.

"Of course." The sheriff gave his deputy a pointed glare.

Luke shrugged and reached for the carafe and a cup. "Appreciate your help, Hawke."

Foley stood at the end of the table and made a production of arranging his documents. "Teller County had those escaped Texas convicts a while back, but this is the most excitement Rock County's seen since the Indian Wars. No offense meant, Hawke."

"None taken." Cold-blooded smile smoothed to a neutral expression, Chris extracted a yellow legal pad from his briefcase and set it on the table before him.

Foley's barrel chest expanded with such self-importance, he looked like a courting pigeon. He introduced the two DEA agents seated opposite Holt and Maddy.

Special Agent Georgia Bonnyman's red hair and freckles made her look too young for her senior status.

Big boned and rangy, she gave a stern and efficient impression. Probably an effect cultivated to offset her baby face.

Special Agent John Salazar was his partner's physical opposite. Dark and of average height, he would blend in anywhere. He smiled congenially. "We'll catch this killer before El Águila can extract further revenge, Mrs. Donovan."

"I hope your plan suits the confidence of your words," Maddy said.

Although her features were composed, Holt detected a waver in her voice and saw her hands gripped tightly in her lap. He wanted to reach out to reassure her, but he didn't think she'd welcome the gesture. When Chris covered her hand with his, Holt suppressed a spurt of anger.

He turned his attention from his friend and his…wife. "Sheriff, what can you tell us about the body you dug up yesterday?"

Foley folded himself into his chair and donned reading glasses. He lifted one of the reports before him. "First time I ever heard of a rock slide *un*covering a body." He shook his head. "Lab and autopsy reports won't be ready right away, and decomposition makes visual ID difficult."

"Any credit cards, driver's license?" Holt asked.

"No papers of any kind. No wallet. Nothing. The general build, coloring and clothing fit the description of that drifter who disappeared from the Circle-S back in March."

"K.C. Riggs?"

"As it turns out," Bonnyman said, "that's one of the names used by a professional hit man who's been working out of California. The FBI has been on his trail. The suspect got careless, whacked innocent bystanders who crossed him. Very unprofessional. The FBI lost track a few months ago, and now we may know why. They're sending more information."

Luke Rafferty nodded thoughtfully. He looked up from the doodles and notes on his small notebook. "Pro, huh? That makes a strong case for him being the one who killed Rob and Sara."

"If K.C. Riggs, or whoever he was, was the one who shot out Rob's tires, what happened to his camper?" Holt asked. "Sheriff, how did the man get under those rocks? In March that area was snow covered and frozen."

Casting Maddy a glance, the sheriff shifted in his chair. "Looked like he was buried deliberately. Wrapped in a tarp. Someone worked their butt off to hide him good."

Chris Hawke leaned forward, as intent as Holt. "I suppose it's too much to ask for the high-powered rifle used to shoot at Rob Donovan."

Foley pushed his glasses to the end of his nose, a move that made him resemble a beardless Saint Nick. "There's nothing near the body. I have some men digging around, but the hillside's shaky." He sighed. "Even if he's ID'd as this hit man, we still have nothing solid to connect him with the crash. Merely the coincidences that he disappeared the next day and was found in the same location as Rob's truck."

"Two coincidences too many, Sheriff." Holt caught Special Agent Salazar's eye. The genial man wasn't smiling anymore. "The cause of death, then. Any educated guesses?"

"It was clearly murder." Foley frowned at his

papers.

"Was he shot?" Maddy asked.

In her lap, the knuckles of her knotted fingers were white with tension. This time Holt enfolded her hand. She cast him a wisp of a smile.

"I think the sheriff's aiming to shield you," Bonnyman said to Maddy. "Considering your profession, I reckon you're tougher than you look." The agent's stern expression softened. "The man's abdomen was sliced open from sternum to pelvis. Whoever killed him was making a definite point."

Color drained from Maddy's cheeks as if imagining herself the victim. "Because he might tell who hired him?" She gripped Holt's hand.

Foley cleared his throat. "That's one viable theory. I'd prefer not to speculate until we have more information. My concern now is stopping the second man before he makes another attempt on Mrs. Dono—Maddy's life."

Holt rotated his jaw. "We're thinking alike, Sheriff." He had more faith in the DEA agents, however. Even if they hadn't included him in their information loop. The toughest cases Foley was used to handling consisted of the occasional cattle rustler and rowdies at the Ski and Saddle.

"Maddy, you're photographing the shooting matches on Saturday," Luke said, his gaze keen with speculation.

Holt bolted to his feet. "She's not going, Rafferty. You're *not* setting her up as bait. In a crowd like that? Too risky."

Maddy placed her hand firmly on his forearm. "There may be no other choice. How else can we trap this guy?" Her voice was calm, her chin tilted with bravado.

"No way, not an option." He sat down and curved his arm around her.

"Mr. Donovan," Bonnyman began, "we can have a team of agents undercover in the crowd. I'll look pretty good as Annie Oakley." She patted her auburn waves.

The discussion grew more heated as plans bounced around the table. Holt dug in his heels a while longer but knew he'd lost as soon as Maddy'd declared her willingness. He might be her husband, but he'd squandered what little influence he'd had on her by ignoring her these past two days. Hell, Maddy McCoy—Donovan—was her own person anyway.

But what she was planning was damned dangerous.

How the hell could he keep her safe in a mob of more than a hundred people armed with six-shooters and shotguns?

Chapter Twenty-Two

"TAKE ONE OF these, *jefe*. You will feel *mejor*." The man handed his employer a glass and a large yellow capsule.

"Better? No, it is too late for that...and other things." The gray-faced man reclining on the chaise swallowed the capsule. "Eliminating the woman is taking too long. Exacting vengeance is taking too long. There is not enough time."

"Then perhaps it is wise to let the quest end."

A muscle in his jaw leapt. "Let it end? No, *I* shall end it. Holt Donovan took from me. I shall take from him. Myself."

The fierce brow and cold glint in the hooded eyes reminded his employee why he was the Eagle. "What do you want me to do, *jefe*?"

The one called El Águila smiled. "Pack a suitcase."

****

Maddy leaned her cheek against the gelding's silken one and breathed in the earthy scents of horse and hay. She stroked his muzzle, soothing her spirit as much as that of the animal. Holt didn't think she should act as bait. He'd made that point forcefully at least twenty times since they'd left Fort Adams yesterday afternoon, yet she remained resolved to go through with the plan. She had to.

Before El Águila became impatient for vengeance

and decided to move on to a new target—Holt. Or, God forbid, Bobby.

"You keep pettin' Bandito like that, he'll think he's a lap dog," Bronc said from the rear of the makeshift stall in the corral. "He's doin' fine. Aren't you, big fella?"

As if he understood, the horse whickered softly.

Somehow during the day, Bandito had skinned his left rear cannon bone, and the injury had swollen. Maddy turned to glance at Bronc as he doctored the leg.

"Horses panic easy." The cowboy applied an antibiotic ointment to the wound. "A noise, even a mouse could have spooked him, made him kick up his heels in his jug. Or maybe he done it out in the corral." He grumbled on about the dangers of splinters and sharp edges in horse stalls.

She listened half-heartedly. Sleepless, she'd seen the barn light at midnight and come out to help.

That afternoon, she and Holt had delivered Bobby to the Pattersons' house. Rangewood seemed a safer location for him for the time being. Convincing Phyllis they needed honeymoon time alone was easy. She sure missed the little guy, though.

And leave him? A fissure opened in her chest at the thought. His inquisitive blue eyes, his satiny skin, the bow mouth that more often widened in a happy smile. Now that his digestive problems had ended, his sunny personality shone through. How could she go?

Earlier that evening after one last harangue, Holt had stormed down the road for a last-minute meeting with the DEA agents. His absence gave her a chance to gather her courage.

Once again, he had withdrawn from her. Except for nagging her about being a sitting duck, he was avoiding her. Was he afraid of his feelings? Sometimes she glimpsed a deeper emotion in his eyes, but then his damn control kicked in and rendered his expression opaque.

If there were a chance he might return the love she felt for him, she'd find a way to stick around. The open road no longer had the same appeal. Leaving would tear her away from the ones she loved. Staying would mean heartache if Holt couldn't believe in her loyalty and love. Anticipating either deepened the rift in her to a mineshaft.

Was his problem his damn pride, or did he still not trust her?

When he returned, she would try to reach him, to convince him of her steadfastness. Would he believe her if she confessed the depth of her feelings for him? Probably not.

"All done here. Bandito'll be fine." Bronc smoothed a gnarled brown hand over the horse's flank and followed Maddy out of the stall. "You missin' Holt? He'll be back soon."

Can the man read my mind? "Um, just daydreaming."

Bronc grinned, clearly aware he'd nailed it. "The boy needs you to keep him from bein' so goldarned serious all the time." He cast her a sly look as he walked her to the porch. "And if an old man ain't mistaken, you need him just as bad."

Before she could counter that perceptive comment, Holt's truck pulled into the drive.

****

As Holt braked to a stop, he spotted Maddy and Bronc outside. His pulse soared skyward. What the hell was going on? Why were they out here so late?

He jumped out and strode over, concern lowering his brow. "Everything all right out here?"

Bronc winked at Maddy for some reason. "Doctorin' Bandito's leg is all."

The tightness in Holt's gut eased. Nodding, he tossed Maddy a brown envelope. "Pictures you might want to take a look at."

He knew her well enough to see the tangled emotions in her eyes, the worry at the edges of her mouth. He wanted to pull her into his arms, to reassure her he'd look out for her even if he'd prefer she'd stay here and not go to the Cowboy Action Shooting.

She wore the denim jacket she'd arrived in. The reminder she'd be leaving soon racked his chest with a stony ache. Better to worry about Bobby.

A wry smile quirked her solemn mouth when she slid out the eight-by-ten sheets. "Is this a picture of El Águila?"

Bronc ambled closer. He studied the sunken eyes, scarred cheeks, and cruel mouth. "Kinda puny, ain't he? Don't look strong enough to cause all the trouble you say he's done."

Holt snorted his disgust. "A man like that wields his power through other people. He rarely gets his hands dirty."

"It's a telephoto lens. But nice and clear." Maddy slid the second sheet to the top. It was a long-range shot of a city street with scattered pedestrians. "What's this?"

"A police surveillance photo. The man in the middle is our first shooter, K.C. Riggs, or whatever he was calling himself in L.A. The next one's a blowup."

She blinked at him. "Why do you have these?"

He shrugged. "They had extras." He'd bulled his

way into the team with pseudo-DEA status and requested the copies. In case the trap fizzled, he wanted a starting point.

Bronc peered over Maddy's shoulder at the enlargement. Wearing a tan jogging suit and a Padres cap, the professional killer strolled unconcerned down a city street. Bronc jabbed a gnarled finger at the man, who had prominent ears and a blade of a nose. "I seen this man arguin' with Rob."

Holt's pulse jumped. "Are you sure? When?"

The wrangler nodded emphatically. "Sure as spring rains. Was a day or two before Rob was killed. In Rangewood. Him and this feller had a shoutin' match outside the Ski and Saddle."

"Whoa," Maddy said. "Why didn't we know this before?"

"Nobody never asked me. That's why. I didn't know who the feller was 'til now." Bronc folded his arms.

"What did they argue about?" Holt asked. The reason might shed light on the killer's actions.

"Dunno. I was across the street at the feed store." Bronc shook his head sadly. "Rob almost threw a punch at him. Then this feller just smiled and walked away. Why do you reckon he did that?"

"That's a puzzle, all right. What did Rob say about it?"

"He wouldn't talk about it. Said it was nothin'." Bronc yawned. "Big day tomorrow. I'm hittin' the sack."

He headed to the bunkhouse, a sickle moon above the high hills dimly lighting his way.

As Holt and Maddy entered the house, she asked, "What do you think Rob and that man could have been arguing about?"

"That's an answer we may never know." He hung his jacket on the coat hook beside hers. "Given Rob's temper, it could have been anything. Doesn't seem very chill of a hired killer to mix it up with a target."

Her violet eyes widened and she rubbed her nose in her familiar thoughtful gesture. "Better to keep a low profile?"

"Right." He preferred not to speculate more with her. She'd be no safer if she left, but he'd wrap her in a cocoon for the next few days if he could.

"What's that?" She jerked a nod toward a florist's paper sleeve on the kitchen counter.

"A peace offering." Holt rubbed his nape. "I've been too hard on you about photographing the shooting matches. I understand why you have to go through with it." Still didn't like it. Every muscle in his body seized up at the prospect of her vulnerability in the middle of the action.

He ought to plant himself on the other side of the room. Instead he leaned on the counter beside her, close enough to reach out and touch her.

Too close. He hooked one thumb in a belt loop.

"Flowers! Irises. They're beautiful." She buried her nose in the bouquet.

"The Mountain Market in Fort Adams had them." Mingled with the flower scent, her unique springtime fragrance eddied to him. A pang of longing rocked him, longing to have his mouth replace the flowers, to sample every inch of her skin. He managed a casual shrug. "They're the color of your eyes."

Her smile lit the room and heated his insides. Pleasure heightened the color in her cheeks. "I love Siberian irises. Not as showy as the bearded ones, but elegant and with this rich, bold color."

Like you. The slim blooms suited her better than pansies. With her creamy, pale skin that flushed rosy with emotion, with her eyes that iris color, and hair the color of honey, she was elegant even in jeans and a cotton shirt. And bold at whatever she did.

She set to arranging the flowers in a tall vase she pulled from a cabinet. Burying her nose in them, she made little purrs of ecstasy in her throat.

Nonchalance was a tough order with her nearly coming over flowers he didn't think had a scent. Every sensual sound reminded him of her uninhibited responses in bed. Blood roared through his veins, firing lust he might not be able to hide.

Lashes lowered, she slipped her arms around his neck and pressed her lips to his. "Thank you for the flowers. It was very sweet." She nibbled at his lower lip and teased the corners with her tongue.

He sweated, but made himself drag her hands down. "Maddy, we were right. Sex complicates things too much. I have to focus on the dangers tomorrow. On catching the shooter. On protecting you."

She stepped back, sparks of anger flashing in her eyes. She folded her arms under her breasts. "Well, that's dandy. And just why do you have to protect me?"

He blinked at her. "You're not stupid. The killer could be anyone in the crowd. All it takes is one loaded gun when they're supposed to be empty."

"Not what I mean. Why are *you* my designated protector?"

"Because you're my responsibility."

She rolled her eyes. "I've been responsible for myself for a long time, but never mind that. Okay, Mr.

Loyal-to-a-Fault, why am I *your* responsibility?"

He gritted his teeth against her grilling. She was doing it to him again, backing him into a corner. "Dammit, because, well...because you're my wife. That's why."

She tilted her head and smiled, a seductive, pouting smile that rushed every corpuscle to his groin. "Your wife. Exactly." She stepped close and slithered against him, her eyes daring him to accept her offer.

When he didn't, she continued. "We talked before about my leaving Rob—*before* the wedding. I didn't love Rob the way he wanted me to. I told you that. I didn't tell you the whole reason. It was *you*. And not only because of that kiss in the moonlight. There was more."

He remembered her that summer, so full of vitality, she gleamed like Midas's daughter with a fresh beauty that nearly blinded him. He'd tried not to act on his attraction to her. Until that last night. "I came home for the wedding. That's all I did. I never meant—"

"Yes, you came home. And you rode with me and you talked with me." He watched her expression turn dreamy.

"And Rob." They hadn't been alone. Except that once. He didn't trust himself with her. Not then. Not now. He took advantage of his brother's girl and the guilt had eaten at him ever since.

"You were grown up and strong and in charge of your life. You were a man, to Rob's boy. I couldn't take my eyes off you. He was the volatile good-time Charlie. You were the steady, responsible man."

He loved seeing her blush, the glow tinting her high cheekbones. "Sounds boring."

"I suppose, but I found your quiet strength

incredibly sexy and moving. That and the way you take responsibility for everything and everyone."

"I never meant to seduce you."

She waved off his rebuttal. "Do you remember the rehearsal dinner, our dance together?"

"Before Rob crashed and we went outside. I remember. Rob pushed you at me while he went to play drums with the band for a set." He shifted his stance, hitched his thumbs in his belt loops.

She gave him an enigmatic smile, the kind that said she knew what he was thinking. "You held me in your arms for one dance. I don't know how I stayed on my feet. Your nearness reduced me to a puddle of lust. When the music stopped, you could have spooned me off the floor. Later when you kissed me, I knew I couldn't go through with the wedding. I couldn't marry Rob."

That dance had done him in too. Set him up for what happened later. And for what almost happened. As if branded, he'd felt the imprint of her breasts on his torso, her hips and thighs against him, and her soft hand on his shoulder.

He burned just remembering. And from the amused curve of her lips, she knew.

Her expression softened and her eyes turned misty. "I told you I was having doubts about the marriage being what I really wanted, but that dance and the kiss later cinched it. How could I tell Rob I couldn't marry him because I had the hots for his brother? I couldn't look him in the face and explain without divulging the truth."

"So you wrote that cowardly note and left."

"But this time is different. We're—"

"Sure as hell is. You have a job to go to. A life away from this valley. A career. No reason to stay here as soon as Bobby's custody's all set with me and we catch this killer."

"If you believe that, you weren't listening when I told you why I thought about investing in the Circle-S."

"You say you want a home and a family, but for how long?"

Tomorrow he'd need all his professional senses tuned if the trap they'd devised were to work. How could he wall off his emotions from duty if he spent the night in her bed? She'd be leaving, not tomorrow, but soon, and he needed more entanglement with her like he needed a kick in the head.

"Good night, Maddy." He turned and walked away. It was one of the hardest things he'd ever done. A small voice in his head asked if it was also the stupidest.

****

An hour later, Maddy tossed, awake and aching with emptiness in the king-sized bed. He wanted her. She knew it. But something—his overinflated sense of responsibility and pride—had stopped him. And his embedded distrust of her had sunk deeper than she could root out.

Too much stood between them. When she left, she couldn't return. Ever.

Good thing she'd already telephoned her agent and arranged for a flight from New York to Paris in two weeks. She curled into a ball in the dark. The hurt grabbed at her throat, suffocated her.

The bedroom door swung inward, shafting light across the foot of the bed. Holt stood in the opening. Barefoot, he wore only boxers. His hair stood on end as if he'd tortured his pillow the same way she had.

"If I can't sleep for wanting you, I'll be no good to

you tomorrow."

She couldn't see his face, but every muscle gilded by the hall light bulged with strain, radiated tension. The ache in Maddy's chest eased a notch, and her heart throbbed an erratic beat. He may not love her, but she'd have one more night, one more memory, by heaven.

She sat up and peeled off her sleepshirt. She summoned a welcoming smile. "Come here. You can get some sleep—later."

Chapter Twenty-Three

SATURDAY'S BLUE SKY provided the perfect
weather for the Cowboy Action Shooting matches at the
Circle-S. When Holt wasn't looking, spring had slipped
over the Rockies with soft air and green leaves. The only
ominous darkness existed inside him. He and Maddy
arrived at nine-thirty, in time to observe competitors sign
in.

"Except for the registration packets, you'd think
we'd stepped into the Old West," she said. "And the lack
of horses." Which were all safely stabled far beyond the
action and noise.

The porch on the main house now sported a false-
front street scene with a saloon's swinging door and a
general store. Several dozen people in period and
Western movie attire milled around before it on the
broad lawn. Welcoming everyone, Will Rafferty glad-
handed his way through the crowd.

Holt watched Maddy eye the six-guns strapped on
every hip and the standing racks full of lever-guns and
double-barrel and pump shotguns. It was obvious what
she was thinking. Whether replica or refurbished
antique, every firearm was deadly. And anyone here,
even Will Rafferty, could be the person hired to kill her.

Those around the sheriff's conference room had
agreed the killer was someone local. Some uncertainty
about that ate at him. No one had been seen in the high

meadow or near the Valley-D. And here was Maddy in a crowd of both locals and strangers. Her shoulders shook in a small shudder before she focused her camera on the colorful crowd.

A woman in a divided skirt and leather vest regaled a huge, mustached man in the blue and gold uniform of the United States Cavalry with her exploits at the last match. A tinhorn gambler in a black Western-cut jacket and string tie stood to one side and surveyed the crowd. Maddy scowled at him as if imagining him plotting his opportunity. Holt could put her mind at rest on that one, at least.

"Those two are probably swapping lies," he whispered. "And the gambler's Doc Warner, Bobby's pediatrician."

"The pediatrician, really? Paranoid, that's me, seeing bad guys everywhere." She lifted her chin. "I need to get a grip, think about my job today, whether the three different lenses I brought are adequate."

He'd make damned certain she made it through the day alive, even if it meant hovering over her like a Secret Service Agent protecting the First Lady.

While they people-watched, a Rock County cruiser pulled up and disgorged Sheriff Foley and Luke Rafferty. Agents Bonnyman and Salazar arrived separately and threaded into the crowd. Even Chris Hawke in cavalry scout garb appeared and waved to them. Another undercover DEA agent was supposed to keep an eye on Luke, although Holt had suggested they confront the deputy with their suspicions.

When Maddy spied Luke, she nudged Holt. "You were going to tell me what the DEA uncovered about him."

"He didn't leave Denver in disgrace after all. Luke's partner was killed during a raid on a gas station stick-up suspect. No one but Luke blamed Luke for his partner's death, although that's why he resigned and came home."

"And why he doesn't talk about it." Sadness overlaid the anxiety in her eyes. "Doesn't seem like much of a reason to suspect him."

For now. Holt rotated the tension from his jaw. "Guilt and self-loathing can send a man down the wrong road for no good reason at all."

"Suspect everyone. Trust no one. Is that your motto?" Her tone and smile didn't match. On a sigh, she turned her camera toward the assortment of vendors setting up stands.

He blinked at the cynicism. "In this situation, it sure as hell is."

Signs hawked local crafts, food, "Authentic Western Duds," and supplies for antique guns. Will hadn't mentioned vendors. Another set of possibilities. The pressure in Holt's jaw shot warning salvos down his spine.

"I've photographed a few historical re-enactments and Renaissance festivals," Maddy said. "Those enthusiasts staged a rehearsed show. The competition here adds a layer of excitement and realism the others lacked."

Babbling, talking too fast. "You okay, Maddy?"

"I've had photo gigs in many dangerous spots before—war-ravaged countries and earthquake-leveled cities where aftershocks could slam you at any minute. I've never deliberately set myself up as a target. But I can do this."

"Like you said, immerse yourself in taking your

pictures and forget about the danger," he said. "Trust me and the others to do our jobs."

A wistful smile quirked her mouth. She placed a soft hand on his cheek. "Trust. That's what it's all about, isn't it?"

Huh. She was no longer talking about letting him protect her. "Maddy, I trust you in lots of ways. You've saved my ass in more ways than one by staying to look after Bobby. Not to mention ranch work. You put yourself in the crosshairs of a killer in a fight that never should've been yours. I trust your courage. I trust you to take care of my nephew. I trust you to see this through."

"But even though we're married, you don't trust me to stay with *you*. You can't let go of the past. I see it in your eyes." In hers, tears glistened. "Is it guilt, Holt? Is it doubt about my character? Or do you simply not love me?"

Before he could reply, Will Rafferty joined them.

"Hey, lovebirds," Will called. "Heard you eloped. You should've told us. Too bad about the barn. But we could throw a wedding party and barn raising all in one." He clapped Holt on the back.

Holt straightened his hat brim and rubbed his nape. Will knew nothing of the joint DEA-sheriff's office plan. Once he found out—supposing his innocence—would he remain the genial host? "Seems like everyone knows already. No need to send out engraved announcements."

Will's jovial guffaw had bystanders smiling. He handed them each a booklet of the day's shooting events. "Let me take you away from this unromantic bum, ma'am. I'll show you around, explain the stages and the layout for the day."

Holt was supposed to keep his distance while

coordinating props for the stages of shooting. Maddy ought to be safe until the matches started with their noisy cover of gunfire, smoke, and hullabaloo, but he didn't like sending her off alone with anyone. Even their host.

"Holt?" Her pansy eyes widened with anxiety before she caught herself and smiled.

"I'll be around...if you need me."

She dropped her camera case and flung her arms around his neck. "I'll always need you," she whispered. "You'd better get used to it. But I'll be fine for now."

She kissed him deeply. He hesitated, but then his arms went around her, crushing her to him as he returned the embrace, physically communicating all the passion and conflicting emotions he couldn't otherwise express.

Making love with her had shown him how much he needed her. It had fanned his feelings into such a swirl he might never sort them out. He had to stop that whirlwind and steel himself to be the professional she needed to protect her. But for now, he was enjoying losing himself in her.

"If this goes on any longer, I'm going to sell tickets," Will said.

Grinning, Maddy backed away and slung her case over her shoulder.

"See you later," Holt muttered.

She waved and strode away with the rancher.

Holt meandered along at a distance while Will showed her each of the six one-to-four-gun "stages," or competitive courses of fire. The stages were placed around the outbuildings, in the corral and in one meadow. Each stage required the shooters to act out a scenario by blasting steel targets in a prescribed sequence with pre-1899-style weapons. Scoring was based on timing and accuracy. For that day, about eighty shooters had registered, and they would rotate among the stages in "posses" of eight or ten.

Excusing himself to go check on some of the props, Will left her at the first stage, outside the hay barn.

Holt hung back as she focused and began capturing the scene on film. Neither of them had dressed for this time-machine trip. Her denim jacket and faded jeans weren't out of place, but the Notre Dame cap didn't quite cut it. She bent and twisted to snap pictures. He couldn't stop a grin. She was already deep into it, unaware of his surveillance as he gathered props for the next stage.

The front of the barn had been transformed into the inside of a saloon, complete with card table and dummy gamblers. The scenario involved a crooked game and an escape, the booklet said. It required the shooter to use both a pistol and a rifle. Six-guns held only five rounds, with one chamber left empty for safety. Wooden silhouettes of other gamblers blocked the path to a steel-drum horse. Smaller targets designated as "vultures" completed the stage.

Bronc was in the first posse to compete. As he prepared to shoot, he grinned at Maddy and tipped an enormous black hat made even more towering with an eagle feather. His bib-front flannel shirt, leather gauntlets, homespun trousers, and high black boots fit his alias of "Buffalo Bronc." Most of the shooters looked too twenty-first-century well fed to be authentic, but Bronc's wiry form and weathered face made him kin to Buffalo Bill's prairie marksmen.

Buffalo Bronc took his place at the card table, and a beep began the timing. Acting outraged, Bronc leaped to his feet, and his six-gun blazed at the two cheating cardsharps still seated opposite him.

The metal targets rang like bells as they were hit, and gun smoke hung in the crisp morning air. Its acrid smell drifted to Holt with the usual scents of hay and dust. Maddy clicked at Bronc shooting the prescribed targets in sequence.

She knelt in front of the smattering of colorfully dressed onlookers and waiting shooters. A prime target. Dammit.

Holt swept a gaze around the vicinity of the barn. Any guns visible were holstered or carried with the action open. The club members were fiercely rigid about safety, thank God. But might someone *pretend* to be careless?

Gunfire erupted again as Bronc dashed out onto the "street" and blasted the three "gamblers" in his way. Holstering his pistol, he mounted the "horse." From the saddlebag, he withdrew a rifle and shells. On another beep from the timer, he loaded a round and leveled one vulture, reloaded, and wasted the other vulture. A final beep ended the shoot.

After collecting his spent shells, Buffalo Bronc swaggered over to Maddy. Holt couldn't hear their words, but he'd bet the old cowboy was downplaying how well he'd done and expounding on how hard the next stages would be.

She photographed two more shooters before she moved on to another stage. Will had said he wanted pictures of the action at all six stages as well as the winners and the team shoot at the end.

Holt's other duties called him to the opposite side of the ranch compound. He helped settle a dispute between two vendors about a prime location. Then he and Chris

Hawke carried new dummies to a stage where a novice shooter had pulverized the wrong targets.

Chris nodded toward where Maddy was snapping the adjacent stage. "Looks like your lady's having a blast," he said as they entered the corral.

Holt winced. She crouched nearly in the line of fire. Anything for a good angle. "Very funny choice of words."

His friend's ebony eyes gleamed. "You spotted the undercover agents?" He set the ranch-wife dummy in the wagon.

"A few. Bonnyman's competing in two of the stages and the team shoot. Talked the Denver club into including her. The sheriff and Luke are just patrolling."

Chris frowned. "Making their presence obvious may be too much of a deterrent. You're hoping to invite an attack, or am I mistaken?"

"That's the plan." Holt's spine tingled from neck to butt. "My sixth sense tells me the shooter's here. Whether he'll try anything is anyone's guess. I'm surprised you're part of this shindig. Not your sort of thing."

Chris's Indian scout outfit consisted of cavalry trousers and a fringed shirt topped with a beaded headband. He shook his head. "Faith asked me to come. Said they needed the help. This is the biggest match the Circle-S has ever hosted." His opaque gaze invited no more questions.

Chris and Faith Rafferty had dated for a time before her injury. But what happened to the relationship was a mystery. Holt wouldn't ask now.

The shooting events progressed through the day and wore on his nerves. He gritted his teeth and tried to remain calm for Maddy's sake. She appeared to be having the time of her life, laughing and joking with the costumed shooters, changing filters and lenses as fast as she could click through the frames.

By mid-afternoon, all the shooters had finished the six stages. While the officials tallied the results, a team shoot between two of the clubs would take place. In the meadow, Holt and Chris hung two thick wooden posts horizontally between supports. Each team would race to cut their post in two with a blast of firepower from all their weapons—pistols, rifles, shotguns.

Two-by-tens formed three tiers of a makeshift grandstand against the barn, and chattering shooters filed into them for the rest of the entertainment. An empty corral joined the barn at its far end along with a jumble of small sheds at both ends. A light breeze blew across the meadow, bringing with it the scents of new grass and meadow muffins.

Maddy rushed to him and hugged him around the waist. "This has been such fun. I totally forgot about the danger." She glanced around conspiratorially. "Looks like our shooter chickened out."

Because others were watching the honeymooners and to please himself, he flipped off her cap and kissed the top of her head. "I hope you're right. But the horses aren't all in the barn yet."

She sputtered a laugh. "How folksy. Or is that secret agent code?"

He swatted at her shapely bottom as she danced away to take up a good viewing position.

He shook off the grin their banter had inspired. Shadows slanted across the spectators and crept toward the meadow. The sun would be to one side of the team shooters, but in his eyes when he turned to scrutinize the crowd. Salazar sat in the back row. Other agents were scattered through the crowd and lounging on the fringes, but he didn't see the sheriff or Luke or Chris.

He started to leave, to search for them. Will's booming voice stopped him.

"Gunfighters, duelists, renegades, and buckaroos, I congratulate you on a successful day of single-action shooting."

His words met with hoorahs, whistles, and applause. "Hey, Will, let's get to the barbecue," shouted a gray-bearded man in a silver-studded white suit.

"You can fill your belly soon, Hiram," Will said. "If you folks can be patient a few moments longer, the officials will have the points tallied. In the meantime, two teams of our finest marksmen and women have agreed to show off—I mean demonstrate—their prowess." He introduced the two groups, who spread out twenty-five feet from their respective targets. Some wore a double-holster set of pistols. Others carried either a shotgun or a rifle. The massive mustachioed cavalryman wielded all three.

Bonnyman was the last to line up and don her hearing protectors. The agent's ginger braids and fringed, pink skirt and vest had transformed her into the Annie Oakley she'd promised—in glorious color. She positioned herself with her team on the end near where Maddy waited with her camera.

Good strategy. If anything happened, Bonnyman could rush Maddy out of harm's way.

Maddy eased down on one knee a little in front and in alignment with the shooters, so that her camera had a perfect shot of the action and the weapons.

Her open position made her a perfect target.

Shit. His gut clenched, but a scan around noted nothing out of the ordinary. Only a hundred or so folks bristling with guns.

"No limit on bullets," Will announced. "No fanning or fast draw with pistols is permitted. Aim only at your designated target. On my signal, commence shooting."

He blew a whistle. Team members slipped their weapons free and blasted away at their targets. Cracks from the assorted weaponry boomed like cannon fire. Gunsmoke blued the air, and wood chips sprayed as bullets rammed the posts.

Maddy clicked away.

Holt scanned the cheering crowd and the outbuildings. In the front row of seats, a trio of teenaged girls covered their ears and giggled. The bearded man tossed his ten-gallon hat into the air. No signs of danger. Only folks having a good time.

He slid his gaze back to Maddy. The haze of blue smoke drifted to cloud around her. Coughing at the stench, she batted at it and covered her camera lens.

Out on the field, one target post sagged from the onslaught. The earsplitting barrage like a roaring avalanche blocked all other sound.

Maddy pushed to her feet, then jerked like a marionette whose puppet master had yanked her strings with vicious force. As if released, she crumpled to the ground.

Chapter Twenty-Four

HOLT STARED, FROZEN.

Oh, God, please no! The prayer stuck in his throat. She wasn't moving. Adrenaline pumped through his system like a geyser.

He pivoted, drew his 9mm from beneath his vest, searched for the shooter. Saw only the crowd staring at the field, the team shooters aiming at their targets, the cloud of smoke a pall over the festivities.

He yanked out his cell phone. An ambulance was on site, a safety requirement of Cowboy Action Shooting. Neither the DEA nor the sheriff's department had seen fit to equip him with the communication devices they all wore. He'd fumed but met only shrugs and excuses he wasn't law enforcement anymore.

Hell, fuck, damn, he'd been watching Maddy instead of the crowd. He raced across the field. "Woman down, shot on the grandstand field. Get here stat!"

The team shoot continued as if nothing had happened. Alert to Maddy's plight, Special Agent Bonnyman stood over her. She'd dropped her competition pistol and held her 9mm as she scanned the crowd.

Will's whistle shrieked to stop the din of gunfire. A woman in the stand screamed. Apparently now aware a disaster had happened, the crowd surged to their feet with a collective gasp. Slowly the pop and crack of pistols and rifles ceased. The acrid smell hung in the air as the smoke from the team shoot spread across the field and the grandstand.

"See anything?" Holt yelled to Bonnyman as he reached Maddy.

"Too much smoke." The agent turned away as she spoke into the small mic hidden on her collar.

"Maddy! Sweetheart, talk to me." He sank to his knees and cradled her head.

The only response was a soft moan. Her chest rose and fell with shallow breaths. *Thank God she's alive.* But how bad was she hurt?

Blood covered her left side beneath her arm, pooling on the dirt and grass beneath her. He tore off his shirt and wadded it up. Pressed it against the wound to staunch the flow of blood. *So much blood.*

"EMTs are here," Bonnyman said, her hand on his shoulder. "Let them do their work."

He forced himself up but his legs felt as unsteady as little Bobby's. He moved aside as the two emergency technicians bent to care for Maddy. He stayed with her until the EMTs trundled her onto a gurney and moved her into the waiting ambulance.

"She's lost some blood," one tech said as he closed the doors. "She's in shock. That's all I can tell you. You can call County later for more."

Holt followed the ambulance across the field as far as the dirt track leading through the pseudo Old West town. As soon as the vehicle bore the unconscious Maddy away to the hospital, he bent over, hands propped on his knees and dragged in air. He hadn't drawn a good breath since he saw her fall. His heart was pounding out of his chest.

"Go to her." Bonnyman spoke behind him. "We've got things covered here."

He ached to go, to see she would be all right, to— Shit, he didn't know what other than pace and drive himself crazier than he already was. But he'd be more use to her here. Maybe he'd have good news when she woke up. She had to wake up. She had to be all right.

"No. I'll stay. Help find the fucking shooter." He turned toward the red-haired agent. "What's the plan?"

"Sheriff assigned deputies to keep the viewers in the stands until they can be interviewed. My agents are questioning the team shooters now. Next is a search of the grounds."

He pondered places other than the grandstand for the shooter to set up. "I'll start searching the outbuildings near the grandstand."

"I'll go with you." Luke Rafferty jogged from the grandstand gate to join him.

****

"See if you can sit up now, hon," said the nurse, a maddeningly cheerful woman with brown hair in a frizzy halo. "It'll take the pressure off those ribs."

"I'll try." Maddy rolled over on the padded table to her uninjured right side. How could she possibly move at all with ten of Lucifer's demons jabbing pitchforks into her ribs? Anything but a shallow breath scraped her side like a scythe, despite the painkillers that fuzzed her brain so she could barely think. She closed her eyes and concentrated.

Metallic clangs of gurneys and the squeak of rubber soles filtered into the small treatment room along with medicinal and disinfectant odors.

"You're all wrapped up, and the stitches are

protected," the nurse babbled in her irritating, jolly manner as she rearranged bandages on a tray. "The bullet nicked two ribs, so the surgeon had to remove bone chips. In no time you'll be dancin' the two-step."

Sweat broke out on Maddy's brow. Pain was a gorilla squeezing her chest, but she made it to an upright position by levering on an elbow.

She didn't want good cheer. She didn't want consoling. She wanted answers. "Do I have to stay here? How late is it?"

"Oh, no, hon, you can go as soon as the chair arrives. A volunteer will wheel you right to the door." The nurse helped her into her shirt and jacket. "It's seven o'clock. You can go home for supper."

The movements required to slide her arms into sleeves irritated the demons into a frenzy of pitchfork jabs. She mentally thanked Holt for bringing a button-up shirt not a pullover. No telling what mischief the demons would have caused. By the time she was dressed, perspiration rolled down her spine and her breathing came in shallow gasps.

The nurse bent closer and winked. "There's one large, anxious cowboy pacing out in the hall. If I had that gorgeous guy to go home to, I'd be ready to leave too."

"Holt?" He was still here? Oh, my. She pressed a hand to her lips. When the bullet from nowhere had slammed into her side, her last thought before she blacked out was that she'd never get to tell him she loved him.

Opening her heart to him again would have to wait. He wasn't ready. He'd made that painfully clear. In any case, inroads in his stubborn pride would also have to wait until the danger was eliminated.

The nurse bustled out to the hall and ushered in Holt before she left.

He took one slow step and then another toward the gurney. A fierce scowl drew his sandy brows together, and he gripped his hat tightly with both hands. He looked enraged and wretched.

"You didn't...get him." Every breath stabbed a new sliver in her side.

Shaking his head, he worked his way around the hat brim like a kid molding a clay ashtray. "Dammit, Maddy. I didn't protect you like I promised."

Her heart swelled with love for him. That was her Holt, taking responsibility for everything. Never mind all the deputies and DEA agents surrounding the place. "Dicey situation. You couldn't...be everywhere. Tell...me about it."

"When you were shot, all hell broke loose. Bonnyman was right there beside you. She drew her sidearm, but we saw no one to shoot at." He slapped his hat against his pants leg as if to punish it. "If you hadn't stood up at that moment, the shot might have—" His voice broke, and he kneaded the hat even harder.

"You're going to...ruin your favorite hat." She tried a smile. No pain there. But no laughing allowed.

He jammed the tortured headgear on his head and his hands in his jeans pockets. Used to competence and control, the poor man felt so furious at being powerless.

"The sheriff and Special Agent Salazar found a spent shell from a rifle in one of the outbuildings. That shed was supposed to be locked. The shooter fired through a crack in the wall."

"What about the gun? Did they find it?"

"Hell, no. A near impossible job. One of the gun

racks stood next to the shed. If the shooter brought his own load, he could've picked any rifle off the rack, shot at you, and replaced it with none the wiser. They all appeared to have been fired recently. Probably used for the team shoot. Do you have any idea how damned long it'll take to test the dozen or so firearms in that rack? And all the others. And forget fingerprints."

"If that's what he did." Talking didn't rile the demons as much now. Painkillers were doing their job.

He nodded morosely. "Many folks—vendors mostly—were still around, but the deputies and the DEA cleared the people in the stands."

"Including Will, I assume." When Holt nodded, she asked, "How did he react?"

"Shook his horns like one of those steers he used to tackle, but after we explained, he understood. What riled him was somebody ruining the safety record of the shooting clubs."

The wheelchair arrived, guided by a sweet-faced grandmother in a pink smock.

With one last look that told her he doubted granny could protect her, Holt trudged out to fetch the pickup.

Maddy edged off the table to a standing position. Pain radiated through her torso and dizziness rocked her head, but she made it into the chair.

At the patient exit, the pickup was waiting, door open, but she didn't see Holt at first. Night surrounded the hospital except for pools of safety lighting. One of those spotlighted Holt talking with Luke Rafferty beside a Circle-S truck. Maddy stood and dismissed the volunteer.

"I'm awful relieved you're going to be okay." Luke strode to meet her. "I apologize for lying down on the job instead of keeping an eye out for the bastard who shot you."

What might be humor tilted Holt's mouth. "He's not kidding about the lying down part."

He offered her his arm, and she held on. Through the canvas jacket, she felt his solid muscular presence, a mountain of stability. Luke was one of Holt's prime suspects, so what was going on? "What do you mean, lying down?"

"You might have noticed some tension between Hawke and me." He thumbed back the brim of his black hat.

"A bit." She leaned against the side of the truck. The dizziness abated, and she was only a little winded from the walk. "Only thick enough to slice with a machete. Something about Faith, wasn't it?" For the first time, she noticed Luke's lower lip was swollen and red as a tomato.

"How the hell did you figure that out?" Holt blurted. He stood beside her, arms loose, as if to catch her if she fell.

"I thought it was obvious. Will and Luke are very protective of their sister. She used to date Chris." She shrugged, then winced at the careless movement.

Luke kicked his boot heel on the pavement. "Instead of doing my job this afternoon, I had it out with Hawke. We pounded on each other for a few minutes before Faith broke us up. Then what he's been trying to tell me for months finally got through my cement skull."

"And what was that?"

"See, all this time, I counted him lower than the underside of a rock for ending it with her because she was crippled. He didn't dump her. She ended it with him.

Something about not wanting to burden him with a gimpy woman. But that's another whole set of problems."

"And you never asked Faith about it?"

Luke shook his head, a rueful twist to his puffy mouth. "So Hawke pummeled some sense into me." He quirked a crooked grin. "But I gave him a shiner that'll rival the full moon."

His phone beeped, and he walked aside to take the call.

"Then he's out of the running as shooter?" she asked.

"Reckon so. While you were being shot, those two were pounding each other. Our trap failed all around."

The deputy returned, his expression as grim as Holt's. "I hate to be the one to tell you bad news. Bobby's missing."

"Missing?" she said. "Oh no, he's okay. He's staying with the Pattersons for a few days." A chill slid down her spine at the hollow optimism in her voice.

Regret darkened Luke's gaze. "Edgar Patterson just phoned the sheriff's office. Sometime between five-thirty and six-thirty, someone pried open the bedroom window and snatched the baby from his crib."

Maddy's throat seized up. The pool of light she stood in shrank to a shimmering, formless whirl. She squeezed her eyes closed. *"No! Oh, no, dear God...Bobby!"*

Beside her, Holt stiffened. His features hardened, and he gripped Luke's arm. "Is there more?" His voice chilled her.

"There was a note." Luke's gaze shifted back to her. "Block print on ordinary white stock. It wasn't signed, but they want to make an exchange. The baby for—"

"Me." She fought back the clawed at her chest. No, no, no. That innocent child. Fear was a living thing that threatened to consume her, to paralyze her if she let it. "Me. He wants me. To get at you. I—"

Holt sidled away from her, his eyes narrowed to hard chips of ice, the crystalline blue of the coldest snow. "So here's your big chance to run. To escape."

Tears stung her eyes, and she clutched the passenger door handle for support. How could he not trust her still? Pain suffocated her. She couldn't draw enough breath to respond.

His countenance as hard as iron, he turned away from her and to Luke. "Take her back to the Valley-D, will you? I'm headed to the sheriff's office."

"Holt?" she said weakly.

"You keep the hell out of it." He paused, his jaw working. "You've done nothing but cause problems ever since you arrived. If you're well enough to leave the hospital, you're well enough to leave, period. Isn't running what you do best? You can pack up and fly to that European gig anytime."

Chapter Twenty-Five

AFTER HOLT'S SHOCKING dismissal, Maddy sat numbly in Luke's truck for the ride to the Valley-D. Tears threatened every time she allowed her fears for Bobby to surface.

To add to her sore ribs, her stomach cramped. Who could have him? Where was he? Was he warm and fed? Did the kidnappers know to rub his back when he fretted in his sleep? Did they know that his little wrinkled brow meant he was wet? Did they care?

Oh, God! Bobby!

At the ranch, she began to pack her duffel, but then little things seeped into her wooly brain.

Holt's initial concern for her at the hospital, his gentle caring. His relentless nobility and damned sense of responsibility.

The fury in his eyes hid a deeper fear, for her as well as for his nephew. He'd ordered her to keep out of it not to get rid of her, not because he could no longer stand the sight of her, but because he loved her.

He was sending her away to protect her.

That perception gave her the strength she needed. She couldn't leave Holt any more than she could leave before she knew Bobby was safe and sound and home.

Impetuosity might be such an integral part of her nature she couldn't change. She could change in another way. Holt had accused her of running whenever things got rough. Fight or flight, was it?

Maybe he was right about the past, but this time she chose fight.

****

When Holt returned after midnight, he found Maddy asleep in the kitchen rocking chair. He fisted his hands at his sides, steeling himself.

She startled awake with the click of the door. Blinking, she sat up. A fleeting grimace told of the pain in her ribs. "Bobby?"

He shook his head. "No news. Writing on this note was different from the other one."

Her breath hitched as she seemed to suppress a sob. "What will you do?"

"We're setting a trap for him. Beyond that…" He shrugged, his throat too tight to find words. His jaw tensed at what he was bound to say next. "You packed and ready to go?"

She scooted forward and pushed to her feet. Perspiration beaded her forehead. In spite of pain that had to be like a knife in her side, her stare was determined and level if her stance was not. She crossed to the table and gripped a chair back for support. "I'm not leaving."

"Your calendar job starts in less than a week."

"I cancelled that. And the rest of my contracts. You're stuck with me. For better or worse. Isn't that what we vowed? I want to help. I can take Bobby's place." Her chin took on that stubborn cant.

What was she saying? His heart raced at the possibilities. The impossibility. And a trade was out of the question. The kidnapper wouldn't trade. He'd have them both.

The leather of his boots creaked as he shifted back and forth a couple times. He paced to the cold woodstove, unable to stand still. "God, Maddy, your offer to trade yourself is braver than I can ask. I'm more grateful than I can express for your help, but your part in this is done. You...you can't stay. The marriage was just for the baby's sake."

"Maybe at first. No more. I'm in love with you."

"In love with me? Love *me*?"

Her words wrapped around his heart like a warm blanket. He shoved them away before he could let himself believe them. "Like you loved Rob? And we know how long that 'life together' lasted."

"By now I'd think you'd understand Rob and I weren't meant to be. If you keep looking over your shoulder at the past, you'll miss your whole life. *Our whole life together*. I believe you love me too. We have a chance to make a future as a family, and I won't let you throw it away."

He watched the determination in her features, but couldn't make the leap. "I know you've changed, matured. But it doesn't change who you are. You're a nomad."

In the coolness of the late hour, boards creaked in the old house. The wall clock seemed to tick louder to make up for the lack of a baby's cries.

Maddy wanted to weep. She wanted to scream at Holt for being so blind. So proud and stubborn. But that pride and tenacity were part of what she loved in him.

She tried to speak clearly over the tension in her throat. "I've *been* a nomad, but it's not who I am. You refuse to see the truth."

"And that truth is?"

"I've been running from my feelings for you for eight years. Maybe we wouldn't have had a chance together then but we do now. I love you. I love Bobby and the babies we can have together. And I love this ranch. My roots in these mountains aren't as deep as yours. *Yet*. But I'm *not* leaving."

"Maybe not today. Maybe not next month. But you're used to the jet-set life, to taking off to all parts of the globe."

"Been there, done that. Freelance photography helped me grow. But I can take pictures anywhere. Even here."

An inarticulate humph was his only reply.

She gazed at the ceiling, seeing their crazy situation as a whole. "Ironic, isn't it? You fought loving a woman you don't trust, and I fought loving a man who won't let himself trust me."

He folded his arms over his chest and narrowed his eyes. "There's more to a marriage than love. I need a wife to help run the ranch. In good times and bad. You've spent only summers here, the easy time. No winters when you might have to slog through deep snow to rescue damn fool cows that wander off. Nor when a blizzard might strand you, limit you to between the house and the barn for days at a time. Nor—"

"Early spring calving when you might be up every night for a week doctoring newborns with scours and coaxing new heifer moms to nurse their babies. I know all about that," she added softly. "And I'm *not* Bonnie."

He sagged, looking bushed, his features tight with anxiety. "Knowing isn't doing. How could I be sure you'll stay?"

"You can't be sure." She edged toward the hallway.

"Then what do I do?" Exhaustion and worry etched deep lines in his face and honed his voice to razor sharpness.

Time to play her trump card. "Take me on faith. Your brother doesn't need your guilt trip any more, but *your wife* needs your loyalty."

"Maddy, it's not a real marriage." His tone bordered on desperate, as if he needed her to convince him he was wrong.

She tossed her head, would flounce around if not for the pain. "It's real if we make it real. Sometimes I wonder if your blindness is guilt or just pigheadedness. You who pride yourself on family loyalty will have to trust my word I feel that same family loyalty. I love you and I will stay with you. Forever."

Twitching her hips, and with a show of confidence she didn't really feel, she headed to the bedroom. With every step, every twitch, the demons stabbed spears at her ribs.

She turned to find Holt staring after her with hungry eyes.

"I'll be right here if you think of some way I can help bring Bobby home." Her lips curved in what better look like a sensual smile, and she lowered one eyelid in a slow wink. "Oh, and I notice you didn't deny that you love me too."

****

By the time the sun climbed above Ghost Mountain's rugged slopes, Holt and the others had settled into hiding places in and around the old silver mine. Sheriff's department vans dropped them off on the old trail, and they'd hiked up in the dark.

The mineshaft was little more than a gaping maw in

the cliff with three tumbledown sheds to its right, just enough to qualify as a ghost town.

Holt tried not to dwell on what could happen to Bobby if something, *anything* went wrong. Delivering Maddy to El Águila, which he would not do under any circumstances, wouldn't ensure the baby's safety. Surrounding the drop the kidnapper chose seemed the only alternative. "We still have a while to wait."

"The note said nine A.M." Luke hunkered down in the rocks beside him. He eyed Holt doubtfully. "You were awful hard on Maddy last night. Have you talked to her?"

"Back off. That subject's off limits." He wouldn't talk to anyone about Maddy.

He turned away and held binoculars to his gritty eyes. Shadows laced the rocky path leading to the mine. The trail was empty except for darting songbirds. A flock of chattering nuthatches settled on a low-growing juniper. The sparse Ponderosa pines and other evergreens would provide little cover for anyone climbing the trail—or avoiding the trail.

The mountainside surrounding the mine was a litter of boulders, smaller rock piles, and scrub. He couldn't spot the other watchers.

A good thing.

If he couldn't detect the sheriff's bulky form to his right on the slope or the several deputies and DEA agents scattered around in the sheds and behind boulders, neither could the bad guy—or guys.

Even old Bronc had stashed himself somewhere on this mountain to aid in rescuing the helpless baby.

They didn't have much of a plan. The drug lord would send one—maybe more—of his goons. Their main hope was to snatch the man and grill him before he realized Maddy wasn't here. Force him to disclose where they were holding their hostage. *Bobby.* Those thoughts would paralyze him. Holt focused on the hillside.

Shivering in the early morning chill, he snugged his sheepskin collar tighter. After Maddy'd gone to bed, he spent a restless night on Chris Hawke's recliner.

Ten times he rose to telephone her.

Ten times he stopped himself, telling himself he didn't want to wake Bronc, who'd volunteered to bed down in the living room with his rifle. The old man said she was still in the bedroom when he left the house.

Maybe she'd be gone by the time this was over, and the twin agonies of wanting her and not trusting her would end.

Sure.

Even injured, her first impulse had been to say she'd give herself up for the baby. If he'd learned anything about Maddy in the last month, it was that she wasn't selfish or pampered. And at the darkest point in that long night, he admitted to himself that he'd fallen in love with her. But ask her to stay? No, he couldn't set himself up to be bucked onto his ass when she decided to kick up her heels and gallop away.

She'd changed, was it enough that she'd stay with him? Did she really love him like she said? Take her on faith? Hell, how could he know? Better she leave now than later. Get it over with. Rip out his heart instead of picking at it little by little.

He had Bobby to worry about. That was all. That was everything. Had to be.

****

"Thanks, Chris. I needed to know what was going

on." Maddy disconnected. She glanced at the kitchen clock. Less than two hours until the deadline, the drop, as Chris Hawke had termed it. In her stiff and sore condition, she might need every minute of it to reach the mine on time. She swallowed one of the painkillers, less than the prescribed dose, but she needed to be alert.

No telling who she'd have to face when she got there—El Águila or some of his henchmen—or what she could do. But she had to help. She had to try. Perhaps she could distract them to give Holt and the others an edge.

Panting shallow breaths against the pain, she donned the sheepskin jacket. Stomping her feet into the riding boots was less painful than bending to tie sneakers, but just barely.

In the barn, she contemplated how to manage saddling Chica. The buckskin watched her patiently, with apparently less apprehension than Maddy felt about the process. "Yes, I know, girl. It's impulsive of me to do this, but I have to. That's me—impetuous, impulsive Madelyn McCoy...Donovan. Don't forget the Donovan. I sure as hell won't."

Today she felt better, but sagged when she saw Holt's bed hadn't been slept in. She'd spent the night in the house alone. Then she'd telephoned Chris Hawke.

The pitchfork-wielding demons had departed during her drug-induced but fretful sleep. The wrestling gorilla, however, had not. Tossing the saddle blanket over the mare's back prompted him to squeeze her ribs a good one. The racking pain bent her double, and she propped her hands on her knees and breathed with deliberate slowness until she could straighten again.

Good. The pain would focus her, help her concentrate on what she had to do for Bobby. She could crash once he was safe.

Now for the saddle…

Maybe she'd slip on the bridle first.

****

By nine o'clock the sun soared high over Ghost Mountain. Holt loosened his coat and turned his face to the sun. The time Maddy was supposed to surrender. Unless the bad guys knew she wasn't coming, they should have arrived by now.

He pursed his lips and frowned. "It prods me like a rock in my boot why El Águila would choose this old mine."

Luke turned to face him and propped his rifle across his knees. "Remote. Difficult access. Maybe he figures we can't chase his man or find him if he bolts."

"But how'd he know about it? It's not public knowledge."

"Ah, we're back to the local gun theory."

"Not a theory I first put a loop on, but it's looking better."

Down the mountain out of sight, stones clattered.

Holt focused the binoculars. "Someone's coming."

Ducking lower behind his rock, Luke checked his rifle. "I didn't take part in the investigation of the meadow shooting, so I don't know the details. Seems like the sheriff should've found that black truck you saw when you and Maddy were shot at."

Reality tilted. Holt's breath clogged his throat. In two powerful moves, he knocked Luke's gun to one side and slammed him face down onto the hard ground. He twisted his right arm behind him and held on. He knelt on the other arm.

"Hey! What the hell!" Luke struggled to wrench

away from the body pinning him. "Donovan!"

"How do you know about the black truck? How?" Adrenaline fueled his blood, as if acid filled his veins. Everything inside him screamed to beat it out of this guy, but he held on. He had to know the truth.

"It was in the report, maybe, or I heard it in the office. What's the big deal?"

"I never got a look at that truck. Once or twice a black pickup followed me on the highway, but I never mentioned that to the detectives." He leaned harder on his prisoner. "Maybe it was a Circle-S truck. Maybe it was you."

"You're crazy! Why the hell would I sit here with you if I was involved in this business?"

The rage died as cold reason and memory returned. Luke had an alibi for yesterday's attempt on Maddy. And that morning a week ago, he'd been on duty, driving an official department vehicle in another part of the county.

Holt sat back and released Luke. "I believe you, Rafferty. Had to be sure. I apologize."

"It's okay, man. I understand." Luke rotated his shoulder, then sat up, brushing dirt and pine needles from his chin and jacket.

"The black truck. It's the key. Who told you?" Holt subsided into his former position. He glanced down the trail. At what he saw, the blood froze in his veins. He had to act fast. "Think, Luke. I see who's coming up the mountain, and it's not fucking El Águila."

Chapter Twenty-Six

MADDY'S HANDS WERE icy beneath a layer of sweat. The demons had awoken, and this time they wore spurs. She should've brought the freaking pills with her. Every step the smooth-gaited mare took over the rough slope ripped agony through her torso.

Holding the reins took all her strength, all her focus. She had to trust the horse. "Good girl, Chica. Just keep going up this damn hill."

She glanced at her watch. Nearly nine.

She had to make it in time. Had to. Spasms clutched at her chest, making her breathing shallower than did the pain.

Bobby, where are you? Are you all right? If she focused on him, she could do it.

The mare brought her over the last rise, and the mine entrance lay ahead. All was quiet and undisturbed. Not even bird twitters drifted to her ears. She imagined hunting rifles and assault rifles and RPGs aimed at her from every rock and tree and shed. Ice-edged shards scraped up and down her spine.

But she saw no sign of Holt and Luke and the agents. They were supposed to be surrounding the place. Nor did she see El Águila's man or men.

And where was Bobby?

She urged the mare onward.

****

He removed the black metal components from the small backpack. So easy a child could do it. Not quite. But after he snapped and rotated the parts together, the powerful sniper rifle was ready. He attached the telescopic sight and inserted the bullet.

He'd have time for only one.

If he screwed up this time, he'd be chewing dirt from six feet under. If she didn't come, he didn't know what that crazy Mexican would do. He'd seen eyes like that before, not alert and piercing like the hunting bird the man was named for, but flat and emotionless like a damn shark's.

He knew death waited behind them. His death.

Donovan had warned her away, but she would come. She was one tough cookie. And she loved that baby.

He counted on it.

Guilt nibbled at the edges of his brain, but he shoved it away. His own life was on the line. He had no choice.

The clatter of stones pricked up his ears. A kick of adrenaline set his heart racing like a formula engine. Willing his hands steady, he raised the rifle and adjusted the sight.

****

Holt sidled bent over around the clump of rocks. He could see no movement behind the boulder that was his target. Luke should be in position and ready. He stretched up enough to view the trail.

Maddy sat stiffly, pale as ashes. She gripped the saddle horn as Chica picked her way along the rough trail.

Oh, God, she must be in terrible pain. Fear and pride and—in spite of himself—love roiled in his bloodstream.

Dammit, he should have known she wouldn't fucking listen.

He checked his watch. Time to make their move.

Side arms drawn, Holt and Luke dove in tandem around either side of the boulder.

Nobody.

Frustration knotted Holt's gut. He wanted to punch someone. "Where did the fucking son of a bitch go?"

Luke squatted down and peered at the ground. He pointed to fresh digs in the hard soil, scrabbled pebbles a few feet farther uphill. "Up there," he whispered. "About thirty feet. The two boulders close together."

"Keep low and keep quiet. Maybe he won't spot us. Same drill." Holt waved Luke around to the other side of their quarry. They had to make it in time. They had to stop him before he could fire.

Holt crept uphill, placing his booted feet on hummocks of greening grass to minimize the sound. From the corner of his eye, he spotted Luke doing the same.

A few more steps took him to the lower side of the smaller boulder. He slipped the safety off his SIG. Crouching low, he edged along its perimeter until he could see his man.

The shooter knelt between the two rocks with the powerful rifle aimed at the trail.

At Maddy.

No time to wait for Luke. "Freeze, Foley. You fire that gun and you're a dead man."

"*NO!*" The sheriff swung the sniper barrel toward Holt. He started to push to his feet.

Holt lunged forward and tackled the off-balance man. He hit him square in the numbers.

Luke snatched the rifle from Foley's hand as the the sheriff and Holt slammed to the rocky ground.

Foley grabbed for Holt's automatic, struggling to wrench it from his grasp. They grappled, rolling over and over, scattering pebbles and small rocks.

The older man might be less fit, but he was desperate. Holt slammed a left hook into his jaw.

"Give it up, Jarvis," Luke said. He held his .38 to the sheriff's temple.

Another deputy, Bronc, and Special Agent Salazar ran forward with their pistols drawn.

With a moan, Foley sagged into the dust and stayed there.

****

"Whoa, girl." Maddy halted Chica at the mine entrance. She pushed back her baseball cap and gawked at the people making their way toward her. Bonnyman and three deputies popped out of the timber-propped mine and its ramshackle sheds. Others traipsed down the slope above the shaft.

Holt and Bronc were among them. She blew out the breath she'd been holding and nearly sagged, but anything other than remaining poker stiff hurt too much. Holt's jacket was torn and his jeans grimy. She'd seen him so angry he nearly steamed, but coming off that mountain he emanated pure danger.

Behind him came Luke and Salazar dragging Sheriff Foley between them. In handcuffs. *Foley?*

"Here's your shooter," Luke said. "Dirty slime took blood money to kill you."

Foley looked at the ground. His tan uniform as well as his chin bore the dirt and grime of a struggle. The handlebar mustache he was so proud of drooped like the rest of him.

Holt's gaze radiated rage and relief. He laid his hand on her knee. "Dammit, Maddy. He nearly got you this time. He had the sniper rifle. I sent you away."

She smiled. "I know why you told me to leave. You wanted to protect me. It didn't work, Holt. I had to come. For the baby." She cast an anxious glance around. "What about Bobby?"

"Foley, tell her." Holt's voice was menacing.

"Bobby's all right. He should be back at the Valley-D by now. In his own bed." The disgraced sheriff raised his head. Maddy expected to see guilt and fear in his eyes, but not bravado. "He promised me he wouldn't touch him. Snatching him was just my means to get you here. My idea."

Holt wheeled on the man. If the two men had been alone, he would no doubt have continued the beating it looked like he'd begun earlier. "*Promised* you? And you believe him, a drug dealer? A man who traffics in death and deception. What possible motive could he have to lie to you?"

"He promised," Foley repeated, but less certain.

"Why, Sher—uh, Foley? Why?" Maddy asked. "You've been a public servant all your life. Why dishonor that record now?"

He shrugged. "That's just it, don't you see? A damned public *servant*. Do you know what the pension is for a sheriff these days? Not enough to keep me in beer. With his money I'd be set up for life, on a beach somewhere, maybe Tahiti."

"He's been a very clever boy, our sheriff." Bonnyman approached Maddy. She stroked the mare's neck. "Kept one step ahead of us the whole time.

Yesterday he did what we deduced. He fired a rifle from one of the racks, then replaced it. Being Johnny-on-the-Spot with Salazar here to 'find' the shell casing made him look good."

"Planned something on that order for today too, I bet. Shoot Maddy with that high-tech rifle. Then pretend to be the first one on the scene to find that the shooter had fled." As if itching to bloody the man's face, Holt took himself out of reach. He returned to Maddy's side.

"You missed yesterday, just wounded me." Maddy lifted her chin in challenge. "Did you really have the nerve to go through with it?"

"We'll never know now." Foley licked his lips and slid his gaze from her to Bonnyman. With him out of commission, the agent was in charge. "How did you figure out it was me? Did I give myself away?"

"Holt?" Bonnyman said. "You and Luke broke this puzzle. How did you do it?"

"I got detoured with the Circle-S trucks awhile, but Luke and I sorted it out. He remembered Foley told him I saw a black truck that day in the meadow. He couldn't have known the color unless he drove it. Then Luke recalled a black pickup that was impounded, but disappeared."

Foley gave a bitter laugh. "Reckon this blows my cushy retirement."

Bronc spit into the dust beside the man's boot. "Feller makes a pact with the devil, he's gotta know he ain't made a hell of a bargain."

Maddy turned Chica and adjusted the reins. "I'm heading back to see about Bobby."

Dammit. Holt sagged watching her struggle to stay erect in the seat. Exhaustion and pain made dark smudges beneath her eyes and she was too damned pale. Hiking down the mountain with the rest of them would drive daggers into her ribs. He couldn't keep up with her on foot., and riding double was out of the question. The mare couldn't carry them both. She had to ride back alone, but every step must be agony.

He wanted to wrap her up and carry her down. That would probably hurt too. The less contact between them the better. She said she wouldn't, but she'd leave. His gut ached with it.

"You can't go alone. El Águila or some of his goons may be waiting at the house. You'll only endanger yourself. Then how could you help Bobby?"

"I have to go." She kicked the mare into a walk.

"I'll meet you there," he called. "Promise you'll wait for me. Don't go inside alone."

She made no reply, but the painfully stiff set of her shoulders told him the answer. He'd sure as hell hurry.

"Radio for a couple of units to get to the Valley-D pronto," Luke said to one of the other deputies. "Let's get started hiking out of here."

"You can't call," Foley said. "I knocked out the radio. Didn't want you in too much of a hurry to track the shooter."

"No wonder you insisted that for security reasons we bring only one unit. We'd better get a move on." Bonnyman motioned to the group.

"You bastard." Holt swung a fist at the air. "If that drug-pushing monster has harmed my nephew, you'd better hope the jail has security strong enough to keep out an army."

"I'll take my chances with you…and jail. Better than El Águila's punishment. I saw what he did to the first guy." Beside Luke, he trudged downhill, his cuffed hands behind him.

Holt hurried ahead, scattering rocks beneath his boots as he scrambled down the trail. He had to get to the Valley-D. And Bobby. And Maddy.

The two people he loved.

What else would Maddy find when she got there? And who?

Chapter Twenty-Seven

HOW THE HELL she made it to the ranch house she had no idea. She could barely summon the energy to slide off her horse's back.

The late morning sunshine lay quietly on the house and yard. She saw no vehicles, no one. They were radioing for patrol cars as she left. Where was Bobby? "Where is everyone, girl?" she said to the tired mare.

Feet dragging, she led the patient animal into the corral. She unfastened the saddle and dumped it on the ground by the fence before ensuring the mare had water. "You're a wonder. I'll tend to you in a little while."

Her nerves thrummed as she approached the kitchen door. At the thought of who or what she'd find, her stomach churned. She opened the door and stepped in.

She hadn't believed Holt's prediction. The last person she expected to see seated at the table was the dark man.

El Águila.

She stifled a shudder. This was the ruthless gangster who had arranged Rob's and Sara's deaths as indifferently as those of rodents in a pantry.

And on his lap lay Bobby.

The baby seemed content, propped against the man's stomach. Bobby waved his arms and squealed when he saw her.

"*Buenos días, señorita*—or rather *señora*. Finally

we meet," the cartel kingpin said in barely accented English. "Since you have returned safely from Ghost Mountain, I know that Foley has failed. Again. I salute your husband."

He held Bobby securely with his right arm. In his right hand he gripped a short-barreled automatic pistol.

Bobby bounced excitedly, his plump hands batting at the lethal steel.

Her mouth was suddenly dry, but she managed to swallow past the lump in her throat. Pain and exhaustion receded, and her entire being focused on the baby. He was helpless and trusting, cradled in the arms of a killer. Her hands itched to snatch him away, but she had to act cautiously. Impulsivity in this case might mean disaster.

She pushed the door closed behind her and leaned against it. "*Señor*, I am grateful you have not harmed the child."

A sneer contorted his harsh, pockmarked face. He snorted his disdain. "I am not a baby killer."

Perhaps not directly, she nearly retorted, *but how many babies have died because of their parents' addiction?* She'd have angered him and he probably believed deaths the fault of the drug users, not himself. To an extent, he would be correct.

Determination kept her knees from wobbling, and she inched toward him, an eye on the gun. "I'm told that in Tijuana you used the name Perez. I prefer that to *El Águila*."

His sunken-eyed gaze flat and unreadable, he made a small bow with his head. "It is my name."

She doubted that, but it didn't matter. "How did you get here? I saw no car."

His cold and lethal smile showed two gold teeth.

"My driver has hidden himself well. He will return for me soon."

Her heart throbbed painfully against her poor ribs. She took another step closer. "*Señor* Perez, may I take the baby from you? I should feed him."

With his free hand, he stroked Bobby's head tenderly. He laid his long fingers over the vulnerable soft spot on top. "You took so long to return. He was indeed hungry. I found formula and fed him, just as I have fed my grandson. He is a fine boy."

The sight of the cartel leader's hand on the baby's head riveted her gaze. Her breath stilled and she forced herself to raise her eyes.

Perez spread his lips again in that shark's smile. He caressed the downy head once more. "I think he may need a nap." He supported Bobby's head and held him out to her.

"Gah!" Bobby waved his arms and gurgled. In his wriggling, he kicked her side.

She inhaled a painful breath, but held on. She cuddled him close. Thank God he was whole. She pressed her lips to his soft forehead and breathed in his sweet milky scent.

As if he knew cooperation was imperative, the baby rubbed one eye and yawned.

Anything to get him out of this man's reach. "I believe you're right. I'll go put him down."

Perez pushed slowly to his feet. He held the gun pointed at the floor, but followed her, watching her like the eagle of his nickname while she laid the sleepy infant in his crib.

When they returned to the kitchen, leaving Bobby out of harm's way, she said, "If not the baby, have you come to kill *me*, to finish the job others have botched?"

"Pah, the fools." He sank heavily onto a chair. His tone was tight and sharp as a dagger, but his blunt features remained impassive. He gestured to the other chair. "Sit down, please. I dislike people standing over me."

She sat. Whatever he wanted. She had to keep him talking until Holt and the others arrived. What was keeping them? And what if this man's driver came first?

"*Señora*, I have been the fool, for trusting lesser men to carry out my orders. To answer your question, I came to see that this affair is finished."

That this affair is finished. Did he mean to kill her or not? Her heart tumbled. "How did you track Holt? He was based in the Boston DEA office."

"Computers are wonderful instruments. My Tijuana police connection was most efficient in tracing his family ties to this valley. The rest was up to the man I hired. He was what you n*orteamericanos* call a loose cannon. He overstepped."

She frowned in confusion. "That man Riggs was supposed to murder Rob, but not Sara?"

"He was supposed to be discreet. Riggs had a capricious temperament. In a professional, a disadvantage. He made an unwise remark on a public street to the hot-tempered *Señor* Donovan about his beautiful wife."

"I learned of that only the other day."

"When Donovan threatened him, Riggs unfortunately chose to eliminate them both in a spectacular way. An unauthorized, brash move that invited attention to my plan too soon. I do not, as St. Paul says in Corinthians, 'suffer fools gladly.' A couple of my men were observing. When I learned of Riggs's foolhardiness, I had them eliminate him."

In this case it was the fool who suffered. This powerful man who organized murder as easily as he ordered lunch quoted the Bible. She suppressed a shudder.

But she needed to know more. "You put yourself in considerable danger to cross the border, to come here personally. Why?"

"I came to meet the man who killed my son and to finish what he began. The man who kept me in hiding across the border until it became too late." His dark eyes narrowed and his breathing became shallow, gasping.

Only too well she recognized the signs of pain. She remembered his shuffling walk when he accompanied her to the nursery. His shark-gray complexion reflected not his character, but his health. "You're ill."

"I am beyond ill, *señora*." From a pocket he extracted a small pill bottle.

She rose and poured him a glass of water. She waited for him to elaborate.

After swallowing two tablets with the contents of the glass, Perez leaned back and sighed. "That encounter in March prevented me from entering the U.S. for treatments to combat the cancer that eats at my liver. The doctors tell me that it has now spread throughout my body."

She stared at him in dawning comprehension. "That's why you went to Tijuana. To get into California for cancer treatments." She was looking at a dying man. A dying man nevertheless bent on revenge.

"We will wait for *Señor* Donovan together." Clutching his belly, Perez struggled to his feet. "I will witness his knowledge of the debt his loved ones have paid."

"But you—"

"Federal agents. Come out with your hands up."

At last! Maddy had heard nothing, but agents and deputies must have surrounded the house. She should be grateful, but the possibilities of a shoot-out tightened the gorilla grip around her ribs. Gasping a painful breath, she started to the door.

Perez grabbed her elbow and pulled her backward. "No, *señora*." With surprising strength, he banded an arm around her. He held the shiny barrel of his pistol to her head. "We go out there together."

****

Holt knelt between his truck and one of the sheriff's department SUVs. Four vehicles in all blocked their quarry's exit, and eight agents and deputies encircled the house. Bonnyman had taken Foley into custody, but Salazar stood with Luke.

Where the hell was Maddy? He couldn't see the corral or inside the makeshift shelter to know if she'd made it back. And the baby, where was he? Was Bobby safe? Barbed wire coiled around his gut, sharp and spiked.

"We are coming out," a man's accented voice called.

The door opened, and two figures shaded by the porch roof appeared in the opening.

The barbed wire coiled tighter. He flattened himself against the truck. "Don't shoot. He's got Maddy."

"If you allow me to leave, I will not hurt the woman." The leather-jacketed man walked his hostage to the porch steps. He held her tight against his body with one arm. His other hand pressed a .357 Magnum snub to her temple.

The drug lord seemed to have shrunk since March. Thinner in a leather jacket that hung loosely on his frame. The scarred face, the hooded eyes that hid his intent but not his corruption—those had not changed.

"*Señor* Águila, you're not going anywhere," Luke called. "Your driver has been detained. Let Mrs. Donovan come to us."

"She remains with me." He forced her down the steps with him. He edged them to the right, as if headed to the barn.

"Does he think he can escape on horseback?" one of the deputies whispered.

"How many horses you got?" Salazar asked.

"Three." If he rode across the hills, they might not catch him. He could head any direction. What if he forced Maddy to go with him? Holt's lungs ached so he could barely breathe.

"Holt, Bobby's all right," she called in a strained voice. She grimaced with the pain of being gripped around her injured ribcage. "He's safe in his crib."

Thank you, God. He fought down the urge to leap from cover and tackle the man. He inched ahead, ready to dash forward if he saw an opening.

Maddy lunged to one side. For a long moment, she struggled with her captor. He wrestled with her. He held the high-powered pistol high, then between them. With a sudden shove at him, she dropped to the ground and rolled away.

Holt vaulted to his feet and started forward. He raised his weapon with both hands. "Put down your gun!"

El Águila fired three quick bursts toward the trucks.

As Holt squeezed off a carefully aimed shot, a bullet slammed into his thigh and knocked him to the ground. *"Noooo!"*

El Águila staggered. He clutched his shoulder. The pistol dangled loosely from his bloodied arm.

Two deputies slipped from around the house and tackled the gangster. One grappled him to the ground. The other stripped him of the weapon.

Before Holt could drag himself closer, Maddy was at his side, pressing on his wound. She dragged off her flannel shirt and held it to the wound. Then she slid off her belt and wrapped that around the thigh.

He felt no pain yet, only weakness. "Maddy, you're safe."

Tears stained her beautiful pale face. "So much blood, oh, dear God. Luke, call an ambulance."

"On the way." Luke directed the deputies to get the man to his feet. One of them read him his rights.

"He says Juan Perez is his real name." She sat, with her arms supporting Holt.

"Whatever you say your name is…you bastard, you're nothing but filth." Pain was setting his leg on fire, but it couldn't match the hatred burning inside him. "You killed my family. You took my nephew and threatened my wife. You can never pay enough."

"You killed my son, my Ernesto. He was my hope for the future. All that I built is lost, torn limb from limb by my enemies." Perez's mouth twisted with the fervor of his words.

"I shot a dirty drug-dealing, gun-smuggling snake who would have killed me. If I'd had one second more, I'd have sent you to Hell like you deserve."

"Give the word, Holt," Luke said, "and I'll send these guys away. You can finish it your way. He shot you. It'd be self-defense. Nobody here will say any different."

The temptation of vengeance vibrated the air, a resolution to months of horror and grief.

Holt wrapped his hand around his gun, in the dirt beside him. He lifted it, pointed the cold steel barrel at his enemy. "I could snuff out your life with one bullet. But would that end it? Or only cause more grief? Unlike you, *Señor* Perez, I am no cold-blooded killer."

Juan Perez angled his head in a courtly bow. "The *señor* is a cruel man. You have won even if you do not know it."

The deputies led the notorious El Águila to one of the police vans. In the distance an ambulance siren wailed.

Once they were alone, Maddy kissed Holt's hot forehead.

"What did he mean...I've won?" he said.

"He knew there was no escape. I think he was taunting you only to lure you into shooting him. I didn't pull away from him. He pushed me down. A quick death is what he wanted."

"A quick death?" Holt visualized his enemy, his ashen visage and sunken eyes. He began to comprehend the meaning of the man's enigmatic last words to him.

"When a body is riddled with cancer, an agonizing, slow death beckons," Maddy said. "A bullet to the heart would end his life too soon. While the wheels of justice turn, let the devil wait for him a while longer."

Holt nodded. Savage pain seared his wound, shot up his entire leg. He turned his face to her soft breast, absorbed her comfort and breathed in her fragrance one last time as the blackness pulled him under. "Maddy, it's...over," he gritted out. "Don't...leave...me."

Chapter Twenty-Eight

DURING THE SURGERY on Holt's leg and the next few days of recuperation in intensive care, Maddy spent more time at the hospital than at home. She couldn't bear to be parted from Bobby again, so she kept him snuggled against her in the sling carrier, or she carried him in the car seat.

The big-bore bullet had torn through muscle, but mercifully missed the bone, major blood vessels, and nerves. The surgeon said he would have a nasty scar on both entry and exit sides, but no limp after some therapy. Holt's only reaction was a thunderous complaint about having to remain in the hospital.

"The bigger the man, the bigger the baby," Espie said after a quick visit with him.

Maddy tried to make light of his attitude, but optimism was difficult when monosyllables comprised his only utterances. Before passing out, he'd asked her not to leave him. What did he mean? He'd said nothing more since, only terse requests for water and food, anything other than gelatin and soup.

The pain in her ribs was an itch compared to the bed of nails she walked waiting for him to find more words. She loved him and she owed him so much. He captured a killer and took a bullet in her defense.

For eight years, she'd wandered the globe, running from her feelings for him, searching for a future anywhere but here. When tragedy finally sent her back to him, she found the love she feared she could never have, the love that gave meaning to her life.

He'd hardly spoken to her since Sunday and glared at her when he did. Was he so afraid to trust? Would he again ask her to go?

He couldn't force her to leave, could he? She needed a plan for when he came home.

****

On Wednesday Holt badgered the doctors into sending him home. He was supposed to keep his leg elevated and let it heal, but that sort of confinement felt like prison. Even in his own house he felt like a bear in a cage. A wounded bear.

Maddy insisted he stay in the master bedroom with its own bath. Dammit, lounging in the king-sized bed or on the sofa in the living room seemed to be all he was good for. He read *Western Horseman* magazines and watched old movies and even a damn soap opera while she flitted around fluffing pillows and fussing over him like he was Bobby.

She nursed him and tormented him with her damn breezy energy and smile that always brightened the dark corners of his soul. Her sore ribs had healed enough for her to perform light ranch chores. As if tending Bobby wasn't enough for her to do, she took over care of the horses so Bronc could ride fence and check on the herd.

All day long, even late at night, she dashed in and out of the bedroom because her clothes were in the closet and her shampoo in the bathroom. In his weakened condition, he shouldn't be thinking about sex. When she popped in wearing nothing but that damn short silk thing she slept in, it just about drove him over the edge.

For the first time, he noticed smudges beneath her eyes. A haunted sleep wasn't surprising after what she'd been through. So some of her flip cheer was bravado. Maybe for his sake.

He tossed and turned with images of her long legs wrapped around him. He ached for her, but his other aches made any moves as stupid as tickling a bull. Then there were her injured ribs. How could he even think of sex?

Thinking was all he *could* do.

And he hadn't admitted it to her, but he had nightmares. Of *El Águila* holding that deadly big-bore pistol to her temple.

When the nightmares woke him in a cold sweat, he thought about her.

His wife.

She was all he thought about all day as well. Her and where his loyalties lay. She was bold and courageous and full of a zest for life. Somehow along the way his desire for her had grown into more. Much more. She'd nailed it. He couldn't deny he loved her.

He couldn't deny she loved the ranch and these mountains. And Bobby. A thrill coursed through him at the thought of her having his baby, their babies. With all his heart and soul, he wanted a life with her.

It all boiled down to one question. Could he shake off the mistrust and guilt of the past and believe in her?

In us?

****

By Friday morning, he itched to get outside and back to work, but every time he tried hobbling around on those fucking instruments of torture called crutches, he broke out in a sweat and nearly collapsed from the pain.

Instead he sat in bed and caught up on the bookkeeping and other ranch business.

Maddy came in with a mug of steaming coffee as he hung up the phone. "Kind of early for phone calls."

He grabbed the mug and gulped down a swallow. The brew burned his tongue, but he gritted his teeth.

"The coffee's hot, but I see you've discovered that," she said sweetly, folding her arms beneath her breasts. Her perfect breasts.

"If you must know, I was calling Will. While the guests are having breakfast is a good time to catch him in the house. I decided to take him up on his offer to lease trail rights to Ghost Mountain."

Her smile began with her eyes and curved her full mouth in a way that had him craving a taste. "Fantastic! Keeping it in the family." She cocked her head. "What else?"

"The barn. Will's sending a crew over next week to frame out the new barn. I won't be in shape to do more'n supervise, but if they get a skeleton up, Bronc and I can do the rest soon enough. Before snowfall anyway."

She beamed an even sunnier smile. "I'm glad to see your stubborn streak's faded a tad. Neighbors helping each other is a good thing, Holt."

"Seems like it." He sipped his coffee, but it was her smile that warmed him. "While we're having True Confessions, I might as well tell you I'm giving Bronc and Espie a little land to build a house on."

"Down that side road off the drive."

"I should have known those two would blab." He set his mug on the bedside table. "Dad cleared that land the year before he died. Thought Rob or I would build there."

"It's perfect. Sean and Danny will love being on the ranch." She cocked a hip. "You know what today is?"

"It's Friday, five days, a hundred eighteen hours and twenty-five minutes since I got shot."

"To be precise, it's Friday, May 26, the date set for the custody hearing. And speaking of phone calls, Edgar Patterson telephoned you yesterday. Will you tell me about that, or do I have to call Chris Hawke?"

A cry came from the nursery, and she whisked off. A moment later, she returned with the baby. She laid him on the blanket on his tummy.

Bobby squirmed and smacked his lips, blowing bubbles. Holt put aside his coffee and tugged the little guy onto his chest. Clutching at his uncle's shirtfront, the baby lifted his head. "Look at that. And at barely three months."

When she didn't react, he jerked a nod at the bedside stand. "I found this book about a baby's first months. All kinds of helpful stuff in there." He gave her a deadpan look.

"Okay, you've found my secret to child care expertise. I confess. Now it's your turn. The Pattersons?" Maddy sat on the bed and gazed at him like a young robin waiting for a worm. Her honey-colored hair and smooth skin were magnets to his lonely fingers.

He folded his hands on Bobby's padded rump. "I should have told you right away. I was just…"

"Feeling grouchy? Out of sorts?" She smiled. And waited.

"They're dropping the custody suit."

Her eyes closed in thanks. When she opened them, tears welled. "There has to be more to it."

"Edgar was ticked as a milked mule we didn't tell

them the truth from the beginning. Then he said that if a kidnapper could steal the baby from their home so easily, they weren't fit to keep him."

"So they'll make no more trouble?"

"And he won't call in the loan." Holt rubbed his chin in thought. "He did mention two o'clock feedings and nonstop care being more taxing than he remembered. I get the feeling exhaustion played a big part in their decision."

"Then you can start the adoption proceedings." She sucked in a breath, her lower lip quivering. "We'll be his parents."

"Maddy," he began. How the hell would he breach the wall he'd erected around himself?

The phone rang, and she picked up. "Sure, just a minute." Her hair flipping about with her energy, she carried a yawning Bobby to his crib, then dashed to the kitchen.

At first, Holt heard only a muffled conversation until one sentence nearly stopped his heart.

"Holt won't even miss me."

"*Won't miss me.*" Won't miss her? If she left, she'd tear his heart out. And leave a hollow in his chest for the rest of his empty life. He'd ignored her, trying to get his bearings, trying to find the words, but his temper was running her off.

In a few days, it would be June first, the day she was to start her calendar contract in Europe. She canceled that, she said, so what the hell was going on? "Yes, I'm all set to start the job. Should be a lot of fun. I'll see you there soon."

She was leaving. Holt's heart stopped, then thumped painfully against his chest.

Twice he'd tried to send her away, and twice she'd stuck it out. How blind a jerk could he be? Was it too late?

He swung his legs to the floor and grabbed his crutches.

When Maddy spotted Holt hobbling toward the bedroom doorway, her pulse pinged. She sent him her best smile and hoped his heart had finally turned his brain her way.

"Look at you, up and about. How about an outing to the corral?" Crossing the room, she punched the disconnect, then placed the handset on the bedside table.

"Maddy, you can't leave." He grabbed her. As if to imprint her texture and shape on his hands, he slid them up and down her arms.

His mere touch, his heat tripped her pulse higher. But she wouldn't let herself hope only to be slammed down again. He had to spell it out.

She lifted her chin. "Why not?"

"I know I've given you hell these past days. I'm sorry. I needed time to work it out."

"You've done your best to drive me away. Why should I stay?" Her heart hammered so loudly she was sure he could hear its frantic beat.

"I have to say this right," he said. "Eight years ago, I wanted you, too, in spades. I denied my feelings, for Rob's sake. I've fought myself ever since."

"I know." That was a start, but she wanted— needed—more. She wrapped her arms around his waist. She felt his hard body go rigid, his muscles bulge with tension.

"I don't want to fight it any more. I know you're not that flighty girl I thought you were then. I do trust you."

"When I arrived more than a month ago, that would have been enough. Today it's not even close." She had to swallow down the tears choking her. "I'll ask you one more time. Why should I stay?"

His eyes held her with laser intensity. His restraint fell away, and the naked emotion in the blue depths made her breath catch. "God, Maddy. You were right. I love you. I need you, and not just for Bobby. *I* need you. Don't leave me. Stay and be my wife."

Tears blurred her eyes, but she couldn't look away from his face. Warmth suffused her as her love for him expanded. She stood on tiptoes to kiss him. "Oh, Holt, I knew you needed time. You're deliberate and cautious, not hasty like me."

"Then why were you going away? You have another contract. I heard you."

"I do, but it's only at the Circle-S." When he merely gaped at her, she forged ahead, praying he'd catch on. "Will wants me to take pictures for a website. And Faith and I have been talking about a bachelor cowboy calendar to raise money for a therapy riding program. Now that Bronc's getting married, do you suppose I could use the bunkhouse for an office and a photo lab?"

Like a pin deflating a balloon, her words seemed to expel the pressure within him. His breath came out in a whoosh. "Then...you're not leaving." He nearly stumbled on his bad leg, but she held him upright.

"I'm leaving, but only for the afternoon."

He rested his forehead on hers. He smelled of healing and hope. "I've been so hard on you but it's because I love you. Damn, that makes no sense."

Her laugh caught on a happy sob. "It makes a crazy kind of sense. You were afraid to love me."

"Maddy, I don't want to tie you to this valley. You have too much talent to fence in. If you want to do a shoot in Mexico or Honolulu or somewhere, I won't hold you back."

The glow of contentment began in her heart and rippled through her soul. "I'll always come back to you."

He cleared his throat, smiled. "Maybe sometime, when the ranch is on its feet, I could go with you."

"I'd love that. Bobby too."

The heat of passion shined in his eyes. "Bobby's napping, and Espie's doing laundry." He crutch-hopped to the door and pushed it shut. "How are your ribs?"

"Still sore but better." As he cupped her breast, comprehension struck her brain, and heat swept through her. "Your leg—"

He kissed away her objection. "We'll have to be inventive and make love like the porcupines."

Her smile widened as her eyes closed beneath his kisses. Her knees could be spread on warm toast. "Very, very carefully."

He laid her back on the bed, and they undressed each other slowly, lips lingering where skin was bared, sighs quickening as need built.

She felt her whole body dissolving under his hands and mouth. "Love me."

With the barrier of clothing removed, he tossed away the last emotional barrier he'd kept between them. He mated his mouth with hers, caressing her with thoroughness, with promise, with his soul.

Tenderness welled as he helped her to straddle him. "I love you. I trust you with my heart."

Her hands framed his face as she sank onto him. She glowed with pleasure and love. They gazed into each other's eyes as they moved together. The tension and excitement in his powerful body thrilled her. Her soul expanded with each stroke, with each sigh. He took her hands, kissed them, and linked his fingers with hers. She moved with him and over him, and pleasure swirled within her. Time lost meaning in the murmurs of need and giving in a long, liquid race that galloped away with them to a molten release.

Awhile later, Holt opened one eye. "Maddy, I forgot to use protection."

He felt her chuckle against his chest. "Maybe we made a little brother or sister for Bobby."

Sweet warmth spread through him at the thought of her carrying his baby. "I wouldn't mind. You wanna try again?"

She laughed, the lilting sound he loved. "So Mr. Control lost control? That's one for me." She sketched an invisible tally in the air. "I guess you do love me."

"You knew that before I did, sweetheart." Inspiration struck. "And you'll trust your husband's word I trust you?"

Her answer came in a kiss. "Holt, now you've said it, I believe you. I'm your wife. I love you." She laid her head on his chest. "Always."

"Always."

A word about the author...

Occasional bouts of insomnia led to Susan Vaughan's writing career. When she couldn't sleep, she made up stories to fill the long dark nights. Her stories throw the hero and heroine together under extraordinary circumstances and pit them against a clever villain. Besides curling up with a good mystery or romance, Susan enjoys walking her dog, boating, traveling, and gardening. A former teacher, she is a West Virginia native, but she and her husband have lived in Maine for many years. She is the author of 16 novels and two children's books. Find her at www.susanvaughan.com, where you can contact her, or at

www.facebook.com/susanvaughanbooks.

Thank you for purchasing
this publication of The Wild Rose Press, Inc.

For questions or more information
contact us at
info@thewildrosepress.com.

The Wild Rose Press, Inc.
www.thewildrosepress.com